BLADES OF HAVOC *book three*

skid SPIRAL

EVA CHANCE & HARLOW KING

Skid Spiral

Book 3 in the Blades of Havoc series

First Digital Edition, 2023

Cover design: The Pretty Little Design Co.

Ebook ISBN: 978-1-998752-40-9

Paperback ISBN: 978-1-998752-41-6

ONE

Luciana

THIS COULDN'T BE HAPPENING.

But it was, with sickening clarity. My mother was standing in front of me in the thin early morning light, just below the windows of the Boston apartment I'd called my own for the last several weeks.

Her eyebrows arched expectantly beneath the carefully sculpted waves of her dark brown hair—the same shade as my own, though mine was rumpled from sleep. I'd only given it a hasty finger-combing before I'd come down.

Her slender yet muscular body exuded the same aura of cool control it always had. She'd ordered me to come with her, and she expected me to obey without argument.

Knowing my mother, I was lucky she wasn't making the demand at gunpoint. No doubt she had a pistol concealed in her sleek pantsuit somewhere in case I forced the issue that far.

Her voice was equally cool. "Let's get going. The jet is waiting."

My legs stiffened with automatic resistance. "I don't want to go, Mom. I'm making a new life here."

Mom's eyebrows lifted higher. "What kind of life could you have running around this mundane city, living in a dreary building like this?" She flicked her hand toward the apartments behind me.

My heart lurched at the thought of her aiming her attention in that direction. I had no idea how much she knew about my exact living situation—or who I'd been living with. I had no idea how she'd found me in the first place, although I could make a few guesses.

Had Sheeran—the leader of the local gang that ran this territory for one of Mom's colleagues in the Devil's Dozen—complained to his boss after all, and the Harvester had brought my presence up with my mother? Or maybe Haggard, the lunatic who'd been stalking me for months, had tipped her off just in case our final confrontation hadn't gone his way?

I wasn't really the bloodlust-y type, but I wished I could drag that bastard out of whatever grave Rafael had dumped him in and kill him all over again.

As I searched for the right response to give Mom, apprehension prickled down my back. The three men I cared about more than anyone else in the world were sleeping two floors above us.

Rafael could hold his own in a fight, but Mom must have assumed he was with me. It'd have been too much of a coincidence for my bodyguard to have disappeared at the same time as I had unless we'd left together. She wouldn't have come unprepared to deal with him.

And if Niko and Jasper caught wind that something

had gone wrong and raced in to try to help me… My skater men weren't remotely ready to face off against the Deadly Rose.

She could cut them down as easily as blinking.

I kept my voice low, afraid to make too much of a scene on the quiet street. This early in the morning, only the occasional car rumbled by.

"I can move up to better things than this. I'm just getting started. I'm making a real career for myself with my figure skating, and this is what I want to be doing. It's not like you need me back home."

Mom let out a light scoffing sound. "You're my heir. Of course I need you. I have significant plans in the works, and you're a key part of them. Be glad that I tracked you down before your absence became too noticeable, or I'd be *much* angrier than I am. The skating was always a silly dream."

I swallowed thickly. I hadn't really thought my argument would work, but I'd had to try. I still couldn't give up.

My hands dug into the pockets of my hoodie, one of them curling around the knife I'd recently held to Quentin Wolfe's chest. It was because of Jasper's rival that I was down here way too early in the morning at all—although maybe I should thank him for that. He might have saved us a confrontation right at the apartment, where I couldn't have kept my mother away from my men.

"It isn't a 'silly dream,'" I insisted. "I'm doing well enough that I've qualified for the biggest competition in the entire country. If I can score well there, I'll be brought onto the national team to compete overseas."

Mom tsked her tongue. "Whirling around on the ice like some kind of circus performer. You've even dyed your hair like a clown." She wrinkled her nose as she took in the reddish coloring I'd used in the hopes of disguising my identity. "You're meant for more than that ridiculousness, Luciana. Please don't keep me waiting any longer."

I stared at her, anger flaring up inside me. A dangerous emotion, but for the moment it held me steady.

"I told you, I don't want to go. Why should I? I know you had Coach Balakin murdered to try to get me to stop skating. He didn't deserve that, and it didn't stop me anyway. I'm an adult—it's my life."

My mother leveled her coldest glare at me, her eyes like fathomless pits. "It has never been only *your* life from the moment you were born. You belong to the legacy of the Deadly Rose, and you will return and take your proper place. And if you don't come along right now, your new skater friends will meet similar unfortunate fates to Balakin's."

Nausea unfurled in my gut. She wasn't denying what she'd done—hell, she was doubling down, threatening to do it again.

And I knew she wasn't bluffing.

Images flashed behind my eyes: the memories of my old coach's bloody body, slumped on the rink in Austin—then Jasper, then Niko, chests slashed open, gore spilling out of them…

A sweat broke out on the back of my neck. My gaze flicked toward the apartment above us, terrified that I might see one of their faces in the window right now, about to force my mother's hand.

The panes were empty, but Mom caught my glance. She shook her head. "That turncoat bodyguard of yours won't be able to keep you here either. Rafael had better stay out of my way if he wants to even keep his head attached to his neck."

She maintained the same even tone, but I knew her well enough to recognize the fury simmering beneath. Oh, she was pissed off with him, all right.

"Don't do this," I said, fighting to keep my voice from shaking. Every nerve in my body jangled with alarm. I couldn't protect my men from my mother and however many of her people she had on call here, not on my own, not even with Rafael backing me up. And then she'd kill him too. "None of this was their idea. It was all me."

"That's the only reason they aren't already in their graves." My mom swiveled toward her car, the sedan parked on the other side of the street, and snapped her fingers. "And they'll remain living as long as you come along without any more of a fight."

That was probably the only reason she hadn't immediately killed them as punishment. She realized they were more valuable to her as leverage than dead. If she tore the three men I'd fallen for away from me, she had no way to force my hand. I'd have nothing left to lose.

But I *really* didn't want things to get to that point. What was the point in winning my freedom if the people I cherished most in my new life were gone?

I didn't know what I wouldn't do just to keep even one of my men alive.

I hesitated just for an instant, and Mom moved as if to stride to the apartment lobby instead. My pulse stuttered, and I pushed myself toward the car. "Fine, fine, I'm coming."

What other choice did I have?

I had to go with her for now, figure out what she was planning, and hopefully put together a plan of my own that would let me find a way back to my guys while keeping them safe. I could play along if it stopped her from dealing out vengeance.

As I walked up to the car, my fingernails dug into my palms. The driver, an ugly brute with a crooked nose and heavy-knuckled hands, got out to open the back door for me.

I sat down and slid over on the smooth leather seat with a reluctant jerk of my body. The motion woke up the ache in my side where Sheeran's men had done a number on my ribs before I'd brokered a sort of peace with him.

I'd pushed my body awfully hard since then, relying on a cortisone shot to dampen the pain. I'd meant to spend the next few days resting and letting myself heal.

So much for that.

So much for any of my goals. The National Championships were happening in just two months. Was there *any* way I could sort this mess out in time?

I didn't just need to get out from under Mom's thumb before the championships—I'd need practice time too. We weren't going to impress anyone if I showed up two months out of shape.

And it wouldn't be only *my* skating debut ruined. Jasper's comeback would fall apart too.

A smothering weight filled my chest. I gritted my teeth against the prick of tears at the back of my eyes.

They were going to be so worried—all three of them. Rafael would go absolutely apeshit. They wouldn't even know I was still alive.

But telling them what had happened could draw them right into the danger I was trying to spare them.

Fuck, fuck, *fuck.*

Mom lowered herself into the seat next to me, all

menacing grace. A shiver rippled over my skin as I watched her.

I hadn't seen her since the conversation when I'd realized that she'd had Coach Balakin murdered. Since it'd sunk in just how brutally ruthless she could be.

I hated her. Did she have the slightest clue how much acid ran through my veins when I looked at her?

Maybe, but she didn't give a shit as long as she got what she wanted.

She brushed her hands together and motioned to the driver. "Take us straight to the airfield. I want to get back to Austin as quickly as possible."

"Yes, ma'am."

Mom's gaze slid to me. I could feel her sizing me up, seething over the time I'd already cost her with this mission. But in front of her employee, she didn't harp on it.

I could probably look forward to plenty of harping later, when we were really alone.

I sagged into the seat and wet my lips, mentally scrambling for something to hold on to. I had to start strengthening my position as quickly as possible too. That was what Mom would have done in a situation like this.

To beat her, I'd have to think like her.

"You said you have plans that you need me for," I said with forced nonchalance. "Are you going to fill me in on what I'm getting into?"

Mom lifted her shoulders in an effortless shrug. "Oh, you don't have to worry about that yet."

"I'm not *worried*. I'd just like to start preparing myself. You want me to do a good job with whatever it is, don't you?"

I'd thought that appeal had a chance of hitting the mark, but Mom didn't look remotely swayed.

"Patience, mija," she said calmly. "I'll bring you up to speed step by step, as you need to know."

She added a firm note to the last few words—a hint of finality. She expected me to leave the subject alone now.

The ache of my ribs spread all through my torso, most of it not physical pain anymore. I tugged my gaze away, tuning out the growing sense of hopelessness as well as I could, and watched the last remnants of my new life drift by beyond the car window.

TWO

Niko

THE SUN WAS HITTING my eyelids from the wrong angle. Normally it didn't pierce right into them like this.

I knit my brow, trying to orient myself in my half-asleep daze, and rolled onto my side to put my back to the source of the light. My hand brushed a warm arm next to me.

My eyes popped open, and I found myself staring bleary-eyed at Jasper.

Oh. *Oh.* After last night…

After our very enjoyable time with Lou last night, sharing her between the three of us, we'd somehow all tucked ourselves around her on her bed and fallen asleep. That's why the window was in the wrong place. I was in the wrong room.

It was also why the man I found just as appealing as

our shared lover was lying just a foot away from me.

It was only the two of us in the bed now. The covers were rumpled, pooled around our waists. Lou and Rafael must have used their criminal stealth skills to sneak out of bed without waking us and go get breakfast.

Which meant I alone got this fantastic view of Jasper St. Pierre's sculpted torso. Of his wild auburn waves tumbling across his pale forehead.

I resisted the urge to brush them away from his closed eyes. Asleep, he looked more at peace than I'd ever seen him.

Adorably so. Not that I thought Jasper would appreciate being called "adorable," so I'd keep that thought to myself.

Last night had really been something. I'd taken part in a couple of threesomes during my wilder days in my early twenties, but a four-some was a totally different level of passion. And acrobatics. Somehow we'd managed to all find our satisfaction while pleasing Lou together.

She was some woman, no doubt about it. I'd have to remind her of that the next time I saw her.

For now, I could enjoy watching my adorable grump of a boyfriend—if I was allowed to call him that. We'd never actually talked about labels.

Jasper stirred, and his eyes opened to reveal the gray-green irises. For once, they looked more curious than stormy. He gazed back at me, and his lips curved up to form the tender expression he'd been giving me more and more lately. An expression that made me giddy.

"Huh," he said. "Good morning."

I couldn't hold back a grin. "What if we make it an even better one?"

His smile grew. "I could possibly be persuaded. Give it

your best shot."

How could I resist an invitation like that?

I scooted closer, tipping my head to seek out his lips, and he raised his chin to meet my kiss. The moment our mouths collided, heat rushed through my body.

This… This was fantastic too.

Jasper tucked one hand under my head, his thumb stroking over my cheek as he deepened the kiss. My pulse fluttered at the affection of the gesture.

Fondness and desire wound together in my chest. I trailed my fingers over the planes of muscle I'd been admiring moments ago, treasuring his hum of approval.

As I circled one of Jasper's pert nipples with my thumb, he flicked his tongue into my mouth. Then he withdrew it to test the edges of his teeth against my lower lip with an eager nip.

Pleasure jolted through my body. I teased my fingers down to his waist and back up again, and Jasper responded by grasping my hip through the sheets. In a gesture I suspected was more instinctive than conscious, he yanked our groins together.

The second our bodies aligned, it was obvious we were both already hard. My erection pressed into his with a spike of deeper arousal—and Jasper froze.

His lips lingered against mine, but the rest of his frame had gone still. His breath stuttered over my skin.

We'd never done more than kiss when Lou wasn't part of the equation. I was the first man Jasper had ever gotten intimate with. It wasn't surprising he'd have moments of hesitation and awkwardness.

His mouth moved against mine again, more cautiously than before. I could still feel the tension that had tightened his muscles.

Did he think he had to push himself farther than he was comfortable with to please me? Had I *made* him believe that, nudged him to experiment more than he was really comfortable with?

It wouldn't be the first time I'd overstepped with someone I cared about, too caught up in my own ideas of how our relationship should be to recognize their needs in time.

My stomach dropped. I returned Jasper's kiss carefully and then eased back with a smile so he wouldn't take my ending the make-out session as a rejection. I tugged my hips backward at the same time so I wasn't imposing so much down below either.

Apparently I hadn't been subtle enough in my withdrawal. Jasper blinked at me with obvious confusion. "Is something wrong?"

I could almost hear my sister calling me "Baka!" and making a rude gesture in my direction. Now I'd messed up in a totally different way.

I steadied my smile with all the genuine appreciation I could compel into it. "Of course not. I'm just starving. All that stomach grumbling can really ruin the mood."

Jasper's forehead furrowed, maybe because my stomach hadn't actually grumbled. His gaze held me in place with its penetrating power. "You just want to get breakfast? Are you sure that—"

Before he could finish a question I'd have fumbled to answer, the bedroom door burst open. Rafael stood on the threshold, his massive form filling the doorway, his dark brown eyes unnervingly wild.

"Have either of you seen Lou?" he demanded. "Do you know where she went?"

As I took in his frantic state, my throat constricted.

"No. She was already gone when I woke up. I thought she was with you."

Jasper nodded, sitting upright. "Same. She isn't in the apartment?"

Somehow Rafael's expression managed to darken even more. I half-expected lightning to start crackling over his head.

"She was already gone when *I* woke up," he said. "I thought she was getting takeout for breakfast to surprise us. But she's been gone for a while—too long. I tried texting her five minutes ago, and it's still showing as unread."

My pulse stuttered. "It's not like her to ignore you, is it?"

"No." Rafael turned on his heel and stalked down the hall. "She wouldn't have just *left*. There's no sign of anyone breaking in. How could they have without me noticing? Fuck!"

His obvious agitation set my own nerves on edge. I scrambled out of the bed and hastily tugged on my track pants.

Jasper followed, his eyes gone wide with worry. "This is her room. She left all her stuff—her suitcase." He opened the closet, where several outfits including her skating costumes hung. "The clothes she's unpacked."

Rafael's voice carried down the hall. "Her equipment bag is over here by the door. Skates are still in there and everything."

Jasper hustled to the living room, and I followed at his heels. Rafael was just picking up the purse Lou had tucked into her duffel bag.

He pulled out her wallet and clicked it open. "She didn't even take her cash or her ID."

My gut knotted. I had no idea just how bad this situation could be. I'd still been wrapping my head around the idea of Lou as a mafia heir who could be targeted by stalkers and gangs. How much worse could things get?

"What *is* gone?" I asked. "Did she take anything with her, or is it like she was grabbed out of the blue?"

Rafael spun toward me with a glower. "No one could have kidnapped her right from under my nose. She'd have put up a fight."

Jasper held up his hands. "We know. We're just trying to figure this out."

Rafael dragged in a deep breath. It was unsettling, seeing the man who was normally so intense and focused falling apart in a panic.

He seemed to gather himself and marched in another circuit of the apartment, taking stock. "I haven't been able to find her phone, and I didn't hear the alert when I texted her. So she went somewhere with that. I haven't found her keys either."

I forced my mind to think through the logic of the scenario. "Then she must have left the apartment on purpose. She stepped out but didn't expect to be gone for long enough to need anything else."

And then… someone had grabbed her beyond these walls? Had the Boston gang come after her again despite our truce with Sheeran—or was it some new enemy we hadn't been prepared for?

My hands opened and closed at my sides. I'd never felt so useless in my life.

Jasper picked up his own phone off the coffee table and flicked the screen on. He inhaled sharply. "She texted me."

"What?" Rafael was at his side in an instant. I hurried

over to peer over Jasper's shoulder.

Jasper frowned. "It must have come in while I was still asleep. It was sent around six thirty. But—this doesn't make any sense."

I could read the message for myself. *I'm so sorry. I can't do this anymore.*

That was it. No explanation, no indication of what "this" even was.

Rafael rubbed his mouth. "No. She wouldn't have ended things this way. Even if she decided it was too dangerous for her to keep skating, which I can't picture happening in the first place, she wouldn't have left *me*."

I wanted to protest, but I knew he had a point. Lou had tried to protect Jasper and me from the darker side of her past again and again. There was a slight possibility that she might have decided she couldn't risk dragging us into more danger.

But Rafael had been with her for most of her past. She knew he could handle it. It didn't make sense for her to run off on him without a word.

Rafael raked his hand through the short black coils of his hair. "It isn't her. Not really. She wouldn't have left on purpose, and she wouldn't have sent you that text as the only sign of it. Someone has her—someone who made her write that message hoping it'd convince you that she's okay, just gone."

We stared at each other, a sense of doom descending over the room. I could barely breathe.

"Who?" I forced myself to ask. "Who would have taken her?"

Rafael let out a growl of frustration. "I don't have a fucking clue—and I have no idea how we're going to find out."

THREE

Luciana

WITH OTHER COMPANY, I might have enjoyed the flight. Mom's private jet boasted buttery leather seats with ample leg room and a wide variety of refreshments served by one of her employees. The small craft soared smoothly through the air with just a faint rumble of the engine.

All the turbulence was going on inside me.

Mom lounged in the seat across from me, sipping a Cosmo from the glass she periodically set on the burnished imitation-wood table between us. She gave every appearance of being relaxed, but I knew her too well to believe it.

Every time she gripped the glass's stem, her knuckles paled with unspoken tension. The perfect ovals of her maroon fingernails tapped an intermittent rhythm on the tabletop.

I yanked my gaze away from her, but the view outside the window didn't comfort me at all. With every passing minute, we left the gritty streets of Boston behind.

I'd liked living in Austin, even if I hadn't enjoyed the overall lifestyle I'd been forced into under my mother's roof. It was a vibrant city with a quirky atmosphere I'd have been able to enjoy even more if I hadn't needed to worry about keeping up appearances for Mom's crew.

But now it was the last place I wanted to be. Every mile closer we got was a mile farther from my dreams of the National Championships. From the men who'd helped me reach for that dream.

What would they have made of my disappearance? They must have noticed by now.

Would they believe the stupid text Mom had insisted I write before she'd confiscated my phone? I didn't know whether I should hope that they did so they'd stay out of the danger or that they'd have more faith in me… and be even more worried about my safety.

Mom set her glass down again with a firm clink. "That expression doesn't suit you. A good leader doesn't show her emotions on her face. Anything you give away, our enemies can use to exploit you."

That was rich, considering that my greatest enemy right now was the woman giving me advice. I bit my tongue against pointing that fact out to her and drew my posture up a little straighter before she could criticize it too, willing the tension out of my face.

Play along, figure out what she was up to, and then untangle myself from the mess ASAP. That was the plan. I could follow it.

Mom continued to appraise me for a moment that felt like an eternity, her attention making my skin prickle with discomfort. She let out a soft sigh. "I've dealt with our underlings who helped you in your little bid for adventure. You won't be counting on them again."

Despite her admonishment to hide my emotions, my forehead furrowed before I could stop it. Which was probably a good thing, because she should see my genuine confusion.

"What are you talking about? No one at the house helped me. Even—"

I snapped my mouth shut before I could mention that Rafael hadn't either—he'd simply followed me and insisted on coming along. I could have taken off all on my own if I'd wanted to.

Mom hummed to herself as if my answer had given something away. I wasn't sure there was anything to be gained by arguing with her.

Instead, I gave her a little prodding of my own. "How did you know where to find me? I wouldn't think you'd listen to random tips."

She let out a chuckle, but there was acid in the sound. "Oh, I wouldn't call it 'random' when it came with video evidence attached. You should have known that with my connections, you couldn't expect to stay in hiding. But I suppose I should be glad you've gotten your restlessness out of your system."

Her tone carried a threat. I'd *better* have gotten it out of my system, she was saying, or I'd regret it.

I forced a slightly wider smile. "Yeah, I guess you could see it that way. Just, really—relying on a former employee you kicked out for being too much of a psycho… That had to sting."

I was taking a stab in the dark, but it landed. A muscle

twitched in Mom's jaw before she shook her head without answering.

It had been Haggard, then. That fucking asshole, screwing me over from beyond the grave.

At least I knew my truce with the Harvester's people had theoretically held. I couldn't imagine Mom would have collected me this peacefully if I'd brought her empire to the brink of war.

She took another sip from her Cosmo and kept the glass in her hand as a faint vibration rippled through the plane. "Let's leave your mistakes behind us, Luciana. We have a lot of future to look forward to—and prepare for."

My heart thumped a little faster. "Are you going to tell me what those preparations involve?"

Mom glanced around, confirming that the small crew on the jet was tucked away at the front where the thrum of the engine would make it difficult for them to eavesdrop. "Now that we're on our way, we may as well go over our initial steps—and my expectations of you."

Oh, joy. I kept my obedient smile plastered to my face while I seethed. I did need to find out what she wanted me to do. "Go ahead."

She grazed her fingernails over the table with a soft but unnerving hiss. "You should join the physical training regimen all of our core employees participate in. No one knows the exact reasons for your absence, but it would be wise to remind them of your strength and combat skills to help you re-integrate as an authority figure among them."

"I can do that." It'd also hone my skills for getting those employees off my back if I was going to make a break for it. And keep my body in decent physical shape.

"Yes, you can," Mom said with a dry edge to her voice. "I'm also going to have you accompany me during some of my social engagements with our more powerful supporters. I want them to see that you're present and ready to step up. No one should be getting any ideas about our chain of inheritance weakening."

I hated that word on her lips — *our*. It tied me to her in a sticky web, one I hadn't managed to wriggle free of despite my best efforts.

I could handle being paraded around in front of her friends. Nothing she'd mentioned told me why it was ever so vital that I came home, though.

"None of this sounds very urgent," I remarked, studying her.

Mom flicked her fingers dismissively. "We'll get to the important parts once we've established the groundwork. But I wasn't finished. I'll also be setting up meetings for you with a few other members of the Devil's Dozen. I'd like you to feel out their respect for the Deadly Rose and confirm that none of them have seen your disappearance as an opening to test us."

A trickle of cold ran through my chest to pool in my stomach. "You want me to talk to your direct associates? Would they even have heard about me leaving?"

Mom's knuckles paled again with her silent tension. "It's likely some of them have found out. We all keep a fairly close eye on each other's activities. But they don't know the reason, and we're going to keep it that way."

I could agree with that. Meeting with the other Devil's Dozen members was like walking into a lion's den. I'd rather not give them additional ammunition against me.

At least with Mom, I knew she wanted me alive and well so I could support her. With the jockeying for power that went on within the Devil's Dozen, the thirteen most powerful criminal kingpins in the world, any of them might be happy to see me fall.

I'd never met with any of the others before. I only knew them by name. Even with the Harvester, he'd never confronted me directly.

But Mom was determined that I was going to fill her shoes one day. Apparently she'd decided it was time to fast-track me up the ladder to a full second-in-command.

I wanted that role even less than I'd wanted to be a foot soldier. The invisible shackles that chained me to this life seemed to tighten around my wrists.

The weight of those bonds dragged at me. I couldn't help making one last-ditch attempt at changing her mind.

"Mom… You know I've never been enthusiastic about the work we do. I'm not sure how good I can be at it when it's not something I want. Are you sure it wouldn't be better for you to mentor someone you trust from outside the family, someone who does have a passion for it, to eventually pass the reins on to—"

She held up one finger to silence me. Her voice came out chillingly cool.

"You were born for this, Luciana. Our family is a pillar, and if a key piece falls aside, everyone will be watching for the whole building to collapse. You know better than to even ask that."

I did, but I hadn't been able to help it anyway. I swallowed thickly, groping for the right words to convince her, but nothing came to me.

And then she went on, her voice dropping ominously low. "If I hear any further talk about returning to your silly hobby and the company you found there, you can be sure you'll run to those men of yours and find them ready for their graves."

Panic shot through my veins. I clamped my mouth shut and shoved my protests deep into the back of my mind.

"Understood," I said, managing to keep my voice steady. "I won't let you down."

Mom let out a faint huff and sank back in her seat again. "I certainly hope you won't. But we'll shape you into the woman you were meant to be, one way or another."

I peered out the window at the tufts of white cloud and kept as much of a mask over my expression as I could. My spirits had sunk lower than I could ever remember, a dark cloud rolling over me.

There really was no way she'd ever *let* me revisit my skating career. Not even as a hobby. For now... I had to give it up, even though the thought made me want to scream and bawl at the same time.

All I could do was accept her demands in silence and thank my lucky stars for what I did still have. The three men I'd fallen for were alive and reasonably well. Mom wasn't asking me to do any tasks that were especially dangerous and violent... yet.

The only way that I was going to win my freedom was by appeasing her until I had a chance to escape. I just wished I could see a clearer way through to the ending— one that wasn't drenched in blood.

FOUR

Jasper

I WALKED through the kitchen and back to the living room with no idea what I was trying to accomplish but desperate to do something. No clues about Lou's disappearance offered themselves up.

Niko was pawing through the trash bin in case she'd thrown something away that would tip us off, a similar air of desperation rising off him. Rafael had folded his arms over his chest as he surveyed the apartment's common areas, but I could see the panic behind his air of stern authority.

My teeth gritted of their own accord. The frustration I'd been trying to hold in burst out of me.

"How the fuck could this have happened? Isn't keeping Lou safe your literal *job*?"

Rafael's gaze jerked to me. "Shut the hell up. If I knew how to find her, I'd be doing it."

"What, like you managed to protect her so well when you were lying in the same fucking bed as her?" My hands clenched at my sides. "What kind of bodyguard are you?"

He narrowed his eyes. "You were sleeping in that bed too, asshole."

Niko stepped between us, holding up his hands. "Whoa, whoa. Let's calm down. We won't get anywhere if we're attacking each other."

I knew he was right, but the tremor that ran through his pacifying voice only pricked at the tension inside me. With an inarticulate growl, I spun away from both of them and marched back to her bedroom.

The worst thing was not knowing if she was in danger… or if she'd decided sticking with us was too risky and left of her own accord. She'd snuck away without disturbing any of us.

I swiveled on my heel inside the room, scanning the bed with its rumpled covers, the suitcase she'd only half unpacked even though we'd been living here for several weeks. My gaze caught on a flash of bright orange half-buried under a hoodie.

Frowning, I marched over and snatched the object up. For a second, I just stared at it.

It was one of the cheap plastic sports bottles the owners of Hobb Creek's arena gave out as a promotional item. Lou must have nabbed one during our training there, months ago.

The arena's mascot peered back at me. I had no idea what the artist who'd designed it had been going for—the thing looked like a mix between a walrus and a penguin. Somehow I suspected the arena owners hadn't broken the bank commissioning that illustration.

An ache spread through my torso as I took it in. Lou

hadn't had any reason to hold on to this thing other than for the memories. Memories of the place where she'd first met Niko and me. Where she'd discovered that her dreams of making her mark on the ice could be more than just dreams.

I ran my fingers across the smooth plastic, my own memories playing like a film reel in my head: Lou, on the first day we'd met her, her eyes widening at the sight of us while she'd tried to play it cool. Lou, damp with sweat but still resolute during her training. Lou, grinning away, tears stinging her eyes during the announcement that we'd smashed the rest of the competition.

And now she was gone.

She'd cared enough to keep some tacky souvenir of our early training. She couldn't have cared *that* much and left anyway, without saying a word.

Right?

An impulse guided me to her equipment bag by the front door. I unzipped the side pocket she'd shown me once before, when we'd first been getting to know each other. The one that held the little scrap of fabric from her first childhood skates.

The fragile, grayed lace caught on my fingers. I lifted it up, rubbing the fabric gently between my fingers. My throat closed up.

"Guys!" I said, my voice coming out strained.

Whatever Rafael thought of my previous sniping, he hustled over in an instant, Niko beside him. My coach cocked his head. "What's that?"

"Her lucky lace." I tucked it back into the pocket for safe-keeping. When we got her back, it'd be right here waiting for her where she'd left it.

Straightening up, I turned toward the other two men.

"There's no way she'd have left purposefully without taking that with her. She's held on to that thing since she was five years old. Something *must* have happened to her—something that forced her to leave."

Rafael sighed. "That's what I already thought. I don't suppose you've found anything that would give us some idea what or where."

My head drooped. "No. There's nothing in here." I paused. "We don't know why she left the apartment, but that might not have had anything to do with how she got taken anyway. What if she *did* simply go out to get breakfast or something, and got caught up in trouble along the way? There might be evidence out there."

"This isn't a crime show," Rafael muttered, but he reached for the door. "I already did a brief sweep of the area, but it couldn't hurt to look again."

Somehow Rafael ended up taking the lead, even though checking outside had been my idea. Niko and I trailed behind him like stray dogs.

There wasn't a whole lot to inspect on our way out of the building. The lobby looked the same as always. So did the sidewalk beyond. I poked around in a hedge that lined a nearby parking lot and only spotted a few random pieces of litter.

Lou would have left a real message if she could have, wouldn't she?

What the hell were we going to do if she hadn't been able to? If all we had to go by was that final, vague text?

More irritation jittered through my veins. I couldn't help picturing how she'd looked after those assholes with Sheeran had pummeled her, how stormy black the bruises on her ribs had become.

Someone even worse might have her now. And we were doing shit-all about it. My hands curled into fists.

Then a figure stepped into view at the far end of the parking lot. A figure that was tall, blond, and guaranteed to piss me off even more in five seconds flat.

My stance tensed automatically. "What the hell are you doing here, Wolfe?"

Quentin had stiffened too. My rival studied me with the piercing blue eyes that always seemed to pick out the flaws I was most self-conscious of. But today his demeanor was unusually uncertain.

"I wasn't aware that you owned the city, St. Pierre," he retorted with only a trace of his usual snark. "A guy can go for a walk."

That might be true, but everything about his sudden appearance here—on this morning of all mornings—felt wrong.

I marched up to him. "Tell me why the fuck you're here or I'll give you a matching scar on the other side of that jaw."

Quentin's mouth tightened, making the pale line that cut through his lip stand out more starkly. "And of course you'd come at me like a goddamn caveman. It's amazing you can manage to stand up on the ice."

I restrained another growl. "You really don't want to fuck with me today."

"Because Lou's gone? Do you think you're going to find her in a hedge?"

If he hadn't caught me so off-guard, I might have grabbed him and slammed him into the concrete wall of the building behind him. Instead, I froze.

Rafael didn't have the same problem. He must have

come up behind me while we'd talked—he definitely caught that last remark.

The bodyguard barreled past me and snatched Quentin by the front of his white tee, jerking him within reach of his balled fist. "Tell us what you know—now, before I have to start breaking bones you'd rather keep whole."

Quentin flinched but kept his chin up. To my annoyance, I had to respect his composure in the face of Rafael's threat, just a little.

"All right, all right," he said tersely. "I was going to tell you about it anyway. I just wasn't sure— I came by to see Lou this morning. I wanted the chance to talk to her without the three of you hovering around her like vultures."

I rolled my eyes at the description, my own hands balling. "Talk to her about what?"

"That's none of your fucking business." Quentin's shoulders hunched slightly, but I couldn't tell whether it was the subject of their conversation that he was uncomfortable with or what he had to say next. "After we had our chat, I made to leave, but I wanted to see what she'd do. So I stuck around over here where she wouldn't notice me."

Niko had come over to join us too. He knit his brow. "You know you sound like a stalker, don't you?"

Quentin glowered at him. "It wasn't anything like *that*. And you should be glad I did, because I saw what happened next."

Rafael gave his shirt another menacing tug. "And what was that?"

"A car showed up right after. A woman got out and walked over to Lou." Quentin's mouth twisted. "Lou obviously wasn't happy to see her. It looked like they were arguing, but quietly. I couldn't hear them from over here. Finally, Lou went over to the car with her and they drove away. But I don't think she wanted to go. She didn't even go back to the apartment to get any of her things."

Rafael swore under his breath and relaxed his hold on Quentin. "Describe the woman. What did she look like?"

Quentin tilted his head as he thought back. "Middle-aged, thin, long dark hair. Stylish clothes. Like she was on her way to some high-class business meeting. It was weird."

I could tell from Rafael's expression that this was not good. He raked his fingers back over his black coils and sucked a breath through his teeth with a hiss. "God fucking damn it."

Quentin focused on him. "You know her? Lou seemed to—not in a good way."

"No, it's incredibly fucking bad." Rafael turned away from him to face me and Niko. "That's got to be Mireya—Lou's mom. You know everything Lou told you about her. And that's only a bit of it. If she's got her claws into Lou again, there's no way she's letting her go. She figures Lou *belongs* to her."

My heart skipped a beat. "Doesn't she care at all what Lou wants?"

Rafael shook his head. "What Mireya wants, she sees that she gets. And she wants an heir, not a figure-skating sensation. She's already killed to try to ensure she's got Lou under her thumb."

A chill sank into my skin, sharper than the late autumn air. "What the hell are we going to do?"

Niko shifted his weight from one foot to the other. "She'll have taken her back to Austin, then?"

"Most likely," Rafael said. "That's her base of operations."

I grimaced. "No point in sending a text or making a call, I guess. We know her mom's gotten control over her phone."

Quentin cleared his throat. "I don't know anything about this woman, but we're going to go to Austin and get Lou back, aren't we?"

I swung toward him. "*We?* How the hell do you figure you're any part of this situation, Wolfe?"

He glared back at me. "I figure I'm the person who told you how to find Lou in the first place. If she's in trouble, I want to help get her out of it."

A harsh laugh tore from my throat. I could barely believe what I was hearing. "Are you for real? After everything you've put Lou and me through? I have no idea what you're playing at now, but you can fuck off."

"If I'd done that to begin with, you'd have no idea what happened to her."

"Great. Now you've gotten to lord that over us. If you imagine you have *any* right to weasel your way into some rescue mission when I know you'd rather spit on us than—"

"I wouldn't," he broke in. "I came to make peace."

I fell silent, blinking at him. Neither Rafael nor Niko seemed to have any idea what to say next either.

Quentin stuffed his hands in the pockets of his jeans, looking uncertain again and even a little deflated. He dropped his gaze to the asphalt before meeting my eyes.

"You're right. I've been a prick to you all through the competition. You're lucky to have her, and I—I'm not such an asshole that I'd want to see her get shit on just to spite you. Okay?"

I scowled at him. "Okay. Sure. And I should care why?"

Quentin appeared to weigh his words. "I don't know exactly what Lou is mixed up in. But I really might be able to help if it's anything like it sounds. I know the shady side of, well, life better than you or Okabe here possibly could. I grew up on the wrong side of the tracks."

Rafael snorted. "There's nothing you could tell us that I wouldn't already know."

Quentin gave him an evaluating look. "Are you completely sure of that? You'd really throw away the possibility that I might contribute something useful?" His gaze slid back to me. "What's more important—saving Lou or holding on to our stupid rivalry?"

It was always your rivalry, I wanted to snap at him. *I never asked for it in the first place.*

But maybe that was all the more reason to let that animosity go. As much as it burned me up imagining having this jerk around while we tried to extricate Lou from her mother, I had to admit I was totally out of my depth.

It couldn't have been easy for him to make this overture. To approach us at all. He could have run off and taken what he'd seen to his grave.

But for whatever reason, Lou mattered enough to him that he'd stuck around to tell us. That he was debating with me now, practically begging me to let him pitch in.

I would be the real ass if I refused him over my grievances, which I could admit were a hell of a lot pettier than what Lou would be facing at her mother's hands.

I glanced at Rafael. His mouth had set in a flat line, but he inclined his head to me slightly as if saying it was my call. Wonderful.

He wasn't arguing any more either. Apparently he was willing to accept Quentin's intrusion.

And Niko's mouth had formed a tentative smile, as if he was almost *happy* about the chance to make an alliance.

Oh, for fuck's sake. It wasn't really a choice, was it? If there was any chance Quentin could get us closer to Lou and to freeing her from her awful family, how could I not take it?

We might need all the help we could get.

"Fine," I said. "You can come along, whatever we end up doing. But I don't want to hear any more insults about any of us, or you can get packing."

Quentin's lips twitched with a smile of his own. "I think I can control myself for a little while," he said, with a gleam in his eyes that had me praying I hadn't just made the worst mistake of my life.

FIVE

Luciana

I STARED at Austin's downtown skyscrapers across the water, wishing I was anywhere but here. I had to admit, the scenery was at least nice. My present company, not so much.

In the late morning, the lakeside boardwalk only held a few locals strolling around—enough for us to easily blend in as if we were only out for a casual jaunt too, but not so many we couldn't steer clear of them for privacy's sake. This was business, after all.

The lean man ambling along at Mom's other side, flicking his hooded eyes toward her as he smiled at her latest comment, was the leader of the largest gang in the state. His long-time alliance with the Deadly Rose had benefitted both of them. She sent opportunities his way and ensured no larger forces infringed on his territory, and he filled her in on any news his contacts picked up while keeping the smaller gangs from making any trouble for her.

It was obvious from the deference in his tone and his posture that he recognized how much more power she held than he did, but you didn't become a gang boss without plenty of ruthless violence. If this man had been an enemy, he could have made a lot of trouble himself.

Which is precisely why Mom had him on a leash.

I'd zoned out of the conversation after it'd turned to exchanges of compliments over how well the two of them had handled past business deals. Now, Mom rested her hand on my shoulder.

"I'm particularly pleased to see my daughter coming into her own as I've always known she would. Luciana will be stepping up in all kinds of ways now that she's old enough to start taking the reins."

The boss eyed me with a mix of wariness and uncertainty. He saw me as just as dangerous as my mother —and just as important to impress. Too bad for him, nothing about his criminal inclinations was going to appeal to me.

Too bad for me, I had to pretend they did anyway.

His mouth formed a crooked smile. "You must be looking forward to getting to take charge and show what you can do."

Take charge, while my mom had me on a leash of my own? Show what I could do, when I couldn't pursue the one thing I was actually good at?

I stifled a dark laugh and forced my mouth to form a warmer smile than his. Time to give another Oscar-worthy performance, after I'd already contributed a few thoughts on territory lines and underling discipline earlier in the conversation.

"It's been a long time coming. I know my mother's made sure I'm fully prepared. I'm looking forward to standing more prominently by her side."

Mom's eyes burned into me, silently evaluating my response. I hoped my clown-smile was enough to satisfy her. I was here; I was doing what she wanted. Wasn't that enough?

It turned out that it was. She gave my shoulder a graceful pat as if any kind of physical affection was normal between us.

"Luciana has been doing exceptionally well at every task," she said. "She's going to be a great leader someday. I couldn't ask for more than that."

Other than me actually *wanting* to be that leader, sure. But this was the third time this week that Mom had trotted me out for one of her major local allies. She was putting on a show of how cohesive our family was, how stable the line of inheritance.

I had no idea why, though. Was she afraid someone would challenge her authority? Surely showing me off wasn't going to make much of a difference.

The wind picked up, blowing a lock of my hair across my face—dark brown strands that I swiped away. Mom had sent me to a salon within a day of my return to restore my dyed red waves to their natural color.

Even on that small scale, she controlled *me* completely.

We meandered on into the parking lot and parted ways with the gang boss with respectful nods on both sides. Mom rested her hand on my back, guiding me back to the sedan we'd arrived in. I slid into the backseat, thankful that the tinted windows meant I could drop my false smile for just a moment.

Until Mom eased in after me.

As her driver started the engine, she shot me a triumphant glance. "You handled yourself well, as you did before. But of course, as a Cordova, you're a natural at this."

A natural at faking my devotion to her life of crime? Wonderful.

"I learned everything from you," I said honestly. "What are all these meetings leading up to, anyway?"

Mom leaned back in her seat, but I knew her too well to believe she was actually relaxed. "Not every action needs to be building toward an immediate goal. It's important that you build your relations with the people we rely on. Speaking of which, I have a more important meeting scheduled for you tomorrow."

I restrained a groan. "Another gang boss?"

"Not exactly." She aimed a narrow smile at me. "You'll be having lunch with a representative from the March Wind—one of my colleagues in the Devil's Dozen. On your own. I want you to feel her out without me present, see what she might reveal if she lets her guard down a little."

My heart sank. I'd had my fill of dealing with Devil's Dozen people after getting harassed by the Harvester's associates in Boston. "I'm supposed to just show up and chat?"

"Well, the meeting is technically to set up the terms for a possible business trade that the March Wind and I are discussing. That's all the excuse we needed. What I really want you to do is figure out how friendly the March Wind is towards the Deadly Rose in general."

My brow knit. "That's all?"

Mom clicked her tongue. "That's all?" she echoed. "I think you'll find, Luciana, that determining who our friends are is critical—sometimes even more than discovering our foes."

Sitting on the sleek chair in the high-end Houston restaurant, I fought the urge to squirm. Fidgeting definitely wouldn't fit the white-table-clothed, sparkling-chandelier atmosphere of the place.

My brief reprieve alone at the table didn't last long. I could tell who the March Wind's representative was the moment that she appeared at the host stand. A twenty-something woman in a posh business dress, her sleek black ponytail trailed between her slender shoulders. The hostess smiled at her and pointed in my direction. My stomach flipped over.

I let out a slow breath, girding myself. Now was not the time to be uncertain. I definitely didn't want to piss my mom off by screwing this meeting up out of nerves. To top that off, the March Wind was just as dangerous as the Deadly Rose.

I had to keep my balance on this tightrope walk; I had to do this right. It wasn't just my happiness at stake but my guys' lives if I screwed up and Mom decided to punish me for it.

The woman sank into the chair opposite me and offered her hand over the table. "You must be the Deadly Rose's heir. My name's Mara Reilly. It's a pleasure to finally meet you."

Finally? I guessed there must be some speculation among the other Devil's Dozen inner circles about each family's heirs.

I smiled back at her, trying to mimic that same

expression I'd seen Mom use on the gang boss yesterday. "It's good to meet you too. Thank you so much for agreeing to this meeting so we can see what we can work out."

She bobbed her head. "My employer is very interested in what we might accomplish together."

Mom had gone over the initial negotiations for the deal with me in detail before I'd come here. She wanted to expand our weapons trade into one of the March Wind's territories in northern California. In exchange, he wanted to take over the distribution of certain drugs in the southern part of that state, which was currently under our rule.

We couldn't discuss any of that outright, of course. After placing our orders and a little more bland small talk, Mara got down to business using vague language to hide her real purpose.

She brought up a map on a tablet and slid it across the table to me. "These are the areas where we'd like to increase our reach. We feel it's an equitable balance with the access you're requesting."

I scanned the map, comparing it to the instructions Mom had given me, and tapped one county. "This one we'd like to keep full control over. There are some delicate relations that need to be maintained there. But we could offer this region or this one instead."

Mara cocked her head, considering. "I believe the second of those would suit our purposes as an alternative. We'd like to keep the transition as seamless and simple as possible."

I pushed my mouth into another forced smile. "So would we. I'm glad that our interests align so well."

It was my first attempt at feeling out her and her boss's

attitude toward the Deadly Rose overall. Maybe a weak one, but I had no idea what exactly Mom wanted me to fish for. I couldn't exactly ask this woman if we could exchange friendship bracelets.

Mara returned my smile with the same blandly professional expression she'd kept up since she arrived. "It does appear that this arrangement will benefit both of us quite a bit. My employer appreciates your willingness to negotiate."

I didn't think I could read anything into that, warm or cold. The waitress saved me from having to figure out an immediate reply by arriving with our salads.

I couldn't have felt less hungry, but I jabbed my fork into the leafy green mix and chewed gingerly. Mara's gaze rested on me between bites of her own meal, and my skin prickled.

Was she studying me just as much as I was supposed to be evaluating her?

"Maybe there'll be other opportunities for us to collaborate with your employer in the future," I ventured in another tentative foray.

My probe was only met by a slight lift of Mara's thinly plucked eyebrows and a beat of hesitation. "If we see an opening for a satisfying exchange, we'll be sure to let you know," she said.

You couldn't get much more noncommittal than that. But then, I hadn't exactly poured on the enthusiasm either.

This whole conversation felt like an awkward dance— one where neither of us was willing to actually move close enough to touch the other person for fear of coming on too strong… or not being welcome at all.

I tried to earn a little more warmth from her by asking

a few questions about her home territory in California—nothing at all sensitive, of course. Mara answered readily enough but with a cool air that gave nothing away.

By the time we were getting up from our seats, I couldn't shake the sense that whatever Mom had hoped for from this meeting, I'd failed miserably.

Mara dipped her head to me. "I'll have my employer pass on his confirmation of the agreement by the end of the day."

I let her stride out ahead of me and gathered my nerves as I walked out to the car I'd driven here on my own. I wasn't enough of a leader to warrant a driver yet, apparently, but then, I was grateful for the time to myself without any of Mom's lackeys peering at me.

I'd appreciate the freedom more if it hadn't also felt like a slap in the face. It was a silent statement that she would find me regardless—that there was no hope of escaping again, so she didn't need to bother monitoring me that closely.

Not letting myself zone out in the driver's seat like I wanted to, I turned on the ignition and pulled out onto the road. In a matter of minutes, I was on the highway heading to what I had to call home for now.

I was halfway back to Austin when my phone rang. I already had it set out so I could quickly hit the speaker phone button.

Mom's voice carried from the tiny speaker. She didn't bother with a hello. "How was the meeting? Did you learn anything interesting?"

I winced, glad she couldn't see me right now. "I'm not sure. It sounds like the deal is a go, according to the terms you were okay with."

"No further overtures of alliance?"

"No," I said cautiously. "I tried to put out feelers and suggest that we'd be open to more without being too blatant about it, and the representative stayed very detached about the whole thing."

Mom hummed to herself. "Well, that's a little disappointing, but not totally surprising. I wouldn't worry about it."

She wasn't upset with me? That would be a first.

In the face of her good will, I pushed my possible advantage. "So, what's up next? More meetings, or do you have something else in mind?" What big plans did she have in the works?

"For now, I do have one more meeting for you to attend. Tomorrow you'll be seeing the young man who's essentially the Storm now to have brunch and get to know each other better." Mom paused. "You should take some care with your clothes and hair. Make yourself look… appealing."

My stomach knotted. "Is this a business thing, or are you setting me up on a date?"

Mom laughed lightly. "You can make whatever you want of the opportunity. But it wouldn't be such a bad thing if that option was on the table, would it?"

Fuck. Not only was she holding my fear for my guys' safety over my head, she thought she could set up a replacement for them too.

My jaw clenched, but even as every particle of my body balked at the thought of so much as pretending I cared what another man thought of me, I knew I had to agree.

"Sure. I'll look every bit the mafia princess, Mom."

"I'm glad to hear that, mija."

A term of endearment she rarely used. I didn't know how to take it now.

We ended the call, and I stared blankly at the highway ahead of me. This was my life now.

And if I wanted the men I'd fallen for to have any lives of their own, I had to stick with it until I could find a real way out.

SIX

Luciana

EVEN IN THE LATE MORNING, tourists were bustling in and out of the colorful entertainment complex in downtown New Orleans. A couple of street musicians played a jazz riff as I walked past them to the restaurant where I was meant to meet the Storm. Or the guy who was practically the Storm now, from the way Mom told it.

I stepped inside to subdued air conditioning and tasteful beiges and whites accentuated with a pop of gold. Another fancy-schmancy place for another wary encounter with one of my mother's peers.

At least it smelled like the food would be worthwhile. Scents of seafood laced with citrus and herbs tickled my nose and set my mouth watering.

The tables were packed, but the Storm had gotten us a reservation—and showed up very promptly. When I told the hostess there was a reservation under Storm, she flashed a smile and led me over to a table tucked away in a quieter corner, where a blond guy who didn't look like he could be out of his twenties yet sat waiting.

He stood up at our approach, and I studied him as surreptitiously as I could, re-evaluating my initial assessment of him as being one of Mom's peers. He was more like *my* peer—definitely closer to my age than hers.

He swept back his sandy blond hair and shot me a warm smile that held none of the reserve the March Wind's representative had shown me. I might not be hoping for an actual date, but I could appreciate the way his tailored dress shirt and slacks fit his toned body. As much as his age might have been surprising for someone already taking the helm of one of the Devil's Dozen empires, his stance exuded a cool confidence that suggested he'd earned the responsibility.

I couldn't let his seeming friendliness disarm me. He could still be an enemy. With the constant jockeying for power Mom had told me about over the years, all of the Devil's Dozen members were potential foes.

As I reached the table, the Storm swept around it to pull out my chair before I could tell him I didn't need that kind of politeness. "You must be the heir to the Deadly Rose," he said, still smiling. "It's a pleasure to meet you."

To my chagrin, my mouth took a moment to start working. I definitely wasn't a natural at this politicking stuff.

"Same," I said, which sounded suitably neutral, and sank into the chair. I had the sense that the guy's gaze skimmed over me before he returned to his own seat.

He was sizing me up too. That was what all of these meetings boiled down to in the end, wasn't it?

I folded my hands on the table in front of me, wishing

I had a menu to glance at and peek at him over. I still wasn't totally sure what Mom expected of me here. If she thought I was going to throw myself at this dude, she could forget it.

But this man, even if he was less than ten years older than me, held just as much power as my mother did. Controlled a criminal empire equally vast.

I had to tread even more carefully with him than I had with the March Wind's representative or with Sheeran back in Boston.

This was my first time meeting another Devil's Dozen member face to face. How had Mom even convinced him to go along with the meeting?

Maybe *he* was hoping he could score with me. A major notch in his bedpost, landing the heir to one of his colleagues.

The Storm signaled for a waiter, who appeared at his side in a blink. He had a couple of menus tucked under his arm, but my brunch partner didn't bother asking for them.

"We'll have the tasting menu," he said. "Water for me." He glanced across the table toward me. "What would you like to drink? The fresh-pressed juices here are excellent. But I won't be offended if you'd prefer something stronger."

Er, no, I thought I was much better off keeping as clear a head as possible for this conversation. "Orange juice sounds good," I said to the waiter.

As the man zipped off, I couldn't resist a dry remark. "I am capable of ordering for myself, you know, despite my feminine frailty."

The Storm chuckled. "I'm sorry—I wasn't trying to offend. I figured it was my duty to make sure you get the best possible impression of this place, considering my family owns the restaurant—and the rest of the complex as well. It's a matter of pride."

I picked up my fork and wagged it at him. "As long as you didn't steer me wrong."

"Oh, I think you'll be happy once the food starts arriving. And if you're not, you can smack me over the head with a menu and pick something else."

His gray eyes twinkled with amusement. I wondered if he would actually let me get away with dismissing his food choices—or with smacking him.

I wasn't going to let myself be charmed, but my posture had relaxed since I'd first sat down. This meeting was a far cry from yesterday's stilted conversation with Mara Reilly. It was hard not to admire the casual ease of this guy's banter.

Niko would have liked him. A pang shot through me as I thought of the men I'd left behind—the men I wished I was having brunch with instead, no matter how handsome or charming the Storm might be.

If he was planning on putting the moves on me, he'd be disappointed. My heart belonged to someone else. Three someones.

I just had to hope he'd take no for an answer without a fight.

Our drinks appeared in a flash, and I sipped my orange juice while I debated how to steer the conversation next. The burst of tangy sweetness over my tongue had my eyes widening.

Okay, this really was amazing stuff.

As I lowered the glass, the Storm aimed another smile at me, this one slyly knowing. Then his expression turned unexpectedly serious.

He cleared his throat. "You know, before we go any further, I should say—I'm not sure what your mother's told you, but I got the impression— Let's just put it as, if either of you were hoping that a more-than-friendly relationship would develop between us, you should know up front that I'm already taken."

A laugh of relief tumbled from my mouth. I found myself grinning back at him. "Oh, good. Thank you for clearing that up. Because I am too. But I'm not sure my mother cares about that."

I clamped my mouth shut, afraid I'd overshared with the honest remark, but the Storm's next smile was soft with understanding. "I bet she's putting a lot of pressure on you to meet her expectations, huh? Believe me, I know what that's like. I'm just glad we're on the same page."

I exhaled in a rush. "Yeah. Me too." I considered him more thoughtfully. Mom would still want to know where she stood with him—and for me to make a good impression. "I, ah, don't mean to make things with her sound bad. She's very good at what she does, and I know she mostly just wants me to follow in her footsteps just as well."

That much was true, even if I was leaving out how little I agreed with her about my calling.

"From what I know about the Deadly Rose, I don't have any trouble believing that," the Storm remarked cryptically. "But it's good to see she's also raised you to have a mind of your own."

Ha. That part wasn't so much Mom's doing as my one possible rebellion.

I shrugged, my smile going crooked. "I try."

The waiter reappeared with two small plates that contained a meticulously carved appetizer—some fruit I couldn't recognize in its current state, drizzled with spices. I dug my fork in and nearly swooned at the blend of flavors that laced my tongue.

My companion's mouth stretched into a full grin. "I can see we won't be needing the menu."

I mock-glowered at him. "Be grateful for your head."

Over the next few dishes, which were all equally delicious, it was easy to fall into a breezy back-and-forth as if we were acquaintances simply getting to know each other better. But I never completely let go of the tension coiled inside me, the constant awareness of how much influence the man across from me could wield.

It was still possible his charm was an act. That he was trying to lull me into complacency for some unpleasant goal.

Even if I wanted nothing to do with the criminal world, I had to keep up my role while I was here. And that meant I couldn't show any cracks, any weaknesses.

The Storm took a bite of cheddar grits that had proved to be as soft and fluffy as a cloud and swallowed. "I hope I've made a good impression. It's not often you get the heir to the Deadly Rose in your restaurant. What do you think?"

"It's wonderful, er, Storm. Really."

I could have face-palmed. *'Storm', Lou? Really?*

He brushed a lock of sandy hair away from his eyes. "These titles drive me nuts sometimes. They can be such a pain. You can just call me Beckett."

He was giving me his real name? I didn't think that was very common between the Devil's Dozen members, although I supposed it wouldn't be too hard for any of them to figure them out with a little digging.

But handing it over without a challenge felt like a peace offering.

I couldn't help relaxing a little more. I could offer him the same in return. "I'm Luciana, but everyone calls me Lou."

He tried it out. "Lou. Short and sweet, right to the point. I like it."

"Pretty fond of it myself."

He poked at a crawfish on his plate with seeming idleness, but his next question was anything but careless. "I have to admit, I'm curious why your mother wanted us to meet up right now. I'm assuming it wasn't just an attempt at playing Cupid, but she was vague in her request."

I hesitated. "And you agreed anyway?"

He shrugged with another glimmer of amusement in his eyes. "I was curious. I like to know what's going on with my counterparts."

"Well, I—I'm not totally sure myself." Maybe I could get more of an answer by acting ignorant than trying to play it cool like I had with Mara. "I haven't been very involved in the Devil's Dozen side of things before now. Have the Deadly Rose and the Storm families typically gotten along?"

How were relations between us now, in his perspective?

Beckett cocked his head, his gaze going pensive. "As far as I'm aware, we have. I don't think we've associated much at all outside of the monthly meetings and occasional communication around the places where our territories border each other."

I took a gamble. "I think maybe my mother would

like to build more of an association. If you're open to it. I could tell her that, if you are."

The corners of Beckett's eyes crinkled with another smile. "I guess that would depend on what the association involved. I have been glad to see her at the table, giving us a little break from the monotony of old white guys who think they run everything."

I had to stifle a snort. "You're a white guy too."

Beckett laughed. "Sure, but hopefully you don't think I'm *old*. I'd like to think my ideas about good business practices are at least a little different from the others. My dad and I have argued about that subject often enough."

He was willing to challenge his father's views? Was that why he was seen as the Storm now, even though from what Mom had said, his dad was still alive?

I didn't know how to ask that without sounding way too nosy, but I filed the fact away for later and simply ventured, "It can be difficult getting the older generation to see things differently."

"No kidding. But I believe in following my conscience and carving my own path if I need to." His eyebrows lifted. "Just have to make sure I don't piss off anyone quite so much that they decide it's time to carve *me* up."

"Yeah." My heart beat a little faster, but it felt right to admit, "I don't always see eye to eye with my mother either. I'm… not sure I want to be in the whole business of running the Deadly Rose empire the way it is now."

That was much safer than saying I had no interest in anything to do with it no matter how you sliced it.

Beckett nodded without any sign of shock. "You'll get your chances to adjust course if you look for them. Once you start proving yourself, it's harder for anyone to squash you down."

"Right." Despite my best efforts, my answering smile felt stiff.

Beckett took a sip of water with a thoughtful air. Then he dug into his pocket. "Look, I don't know what your situation is exactly or how you're dealing with it. But I have been there. If you think there's anything I can do that might help, don't hesitate to reach out. I mean that."

He passed a business card over to me, a phone number and email address printed on it in bold lettering. I stared at it, my stomach flipping over, and quickly stuffed it into my purse.

"Thanks," I said, willing down a flush of embarrassment. Had I sounded like I *needed* help?

I did, didn't I? I was in over my head, and I had no idea how to swim to shore. Or where a safe shoreline even was.

But could I ever trust another member of the Devil's Dozen, even one who seemed as kind as Beckett did?

I tossed out a smart aleck remark I barely thought about and dug into my food again. All the while in the back of my head, my thoughts were spinning.

Even if things got really bad in Austin… would I be willing to take the help this guy had just offered me?

Rafael

A NEON SIGN in the shape of a beer bottle buzzed in the bar's front window, flickering for a second as it cast its red glow across my eyes. I scanned the sidewalk around me and the view through the glass before heading inside.

There was no sign of any of the Deadly Rose lackeys I could recognize. This place wasn't a typical hang-out of theirs, but I'd known a few people from my earlier life who'd frequented the place. Which was why I'd made it my first stop since arriving in Austin.

I stepped through the doorway into the reek of alcohol and surreptitious joints. The place was crowded with most of the seats around the table and the bar taken, raucous voices bouncing off the low ceiling. On the tiny stage at the far end of the main room, three dudes with scraggly beards were fiddling around with some instruments, squinting at their equipment as they tested the cords.

Maybe I could be done here before I needed to endure their musical stylings.

I didn't want to leave the loft for very long anyway. I *thought* the figure skaters had taken my warnings to heart about sticking to the quiet neighborhood on the fringes of the city where gang activity should be nearly nil. But the prick who'd insisted on joining the three of us in our search for Lou struck me as both restless and not in the habit of following orders.

Hopefully Jasper and Niko could keep him in line. I really didn't need another problem.

Lou would never forgive me if I got either of her other boyfriends too mixed up in the danger that waited for us here.

I moved over to the bar, ordered a beer since I didn't want anything that'd give me a real buzz while I needed to stay alert, and continued my survey of the bar-goers. My gaze caught on a slim middle-aged man in an untucked pin-striped dress shirt and jeans, sauntering from the restrooms over to the curve of the counter.

"'Nother Johnnie Walker on the rocks," he called to the bartender loud enough for me to make out his voice over the din, with a rap of his hand against the polished wooden surface.

The bartender fixed the drink without a word, and I moseyed around the counter to where I could lean against the empty seat next to my target.

"Hey, Albie. It's been a while."

The man swiveled toward me, and his eyebrows arched. "Rafael! It has been. Where've you been hiding yourself these days?"

I smiled grimly, knowing he wouldn't really expect an answer I wasn't going to give him. You had to be careful with Albert Thimbal. The small-time scam artist didn't pledge his loyalty to any particular gang, preferring to keep his ear to the ground and make use of any advantage he could get.

If anything major was going on within the criminal world of Austin, he'd know. And he wouldn't tattle on me to any of my former associates unless it seemed particularly worth his while—which was more guarantee than I'd get from most of my old contacts.

"Here and there," I said nonchalantly, and motioned to the bartender that I was covering Albert's drink. "Been out of the loop. Got a little time to shoot the breeze?"

He shot me a grin full of teeth that wished they'd seen braces in his teens. "If you're paying, I can talk."

He picked up his drink and we drifted over to a booth in the corner, as secluded as any seating in this venue got. Albert took a tentative sip and eyed me with obvious curiosity. "What's eating at you?"

I shrugged as if it was no big deal. "Oh, nothing urgent. I'm just trying to get the lay of the land now that I'm back. Any big news in the last couple of months?"

"I guess that depends on what you call big."

I narrowed my eyes at him and decided I'd better stop beating around the bush. "Have the Cordovas been up to anything interesting?"

Albert swirled his glass, the ice clinking against the sides. "Heard a lot of guys came out of the head lady's house worse for wear not that long ago. She was upset about something." His focus on me turned even more speculative.

I kept my expression vague. "I caught a few murmurs about that. Got the impression it had something to do with her daughter."

"Oh, yes, the heir. Whatever happened with her, Mireya Cordova is showing her off all over the place now."

I had to will the tension that gripped my body not to stiffen my stance. "Really? Showing her off how?"

Albert took another gulp. "Trotting her out in front of this boss and that one, lots of little meetings she's not being as secretive about it as you'd expect."

My stomach sank. "Any idea what all those meetings are leading up to?"

He shook his head and drained the rest of his glass. When he lifted an eyebrow at me in question, I nodded, and he made a grabby gesture toward a passing waiter to ask for another.

"Beats me," he said as I passed a couple of bills over to the waiter when he brought the drink. "She hasn't been *that* open about it. But I've got to say, there's something I don't like about the… the vibe in the city right now. It's got a feeling like there is something big on the horizon, and maybe not anything good."

An uneasy prickle ran down my back. I thought of the phone call I'd gotten from one of my former colleagues under the Deadly Rose not that long ago, warning me that Mireya wanted Lou back for some major plan. "You figure it's something the Cordovas are going to push forward?"

Albert sighed. "I don't know. It's just a feeling. But my hunches are usually pretty good." He pulled his drink closer and took on a tone that told me he was done with the conversation. "Thanks for your generosity, Rafael. Stop by for a chat anytime."

I stood up and made my way toward the door. I doubted anyone else I'd want to reveal myself to could tell me more, so there was nothing left for me here. At least I knew Lou *was* in town, and that her mother hadn't been so angry with her that she'd hurt her in any way that prevented public appearances.

I'd mostly been worrying about the slim chance of running into any of the Deadly Rose's goons. A moment later, I realized that could be the least of my problems.

I was five feet from the door when a burly man with distinctive patterns shaved in his close-cropped coils pushed through the doorway. My pulse stuttered. I would have turned and made for the back entrance if the guy's gaze hadn't already fixed on me.

He strode forward and clapped me on the shoulder. "Torres! Never thought I'd run into you around here. Seemed like you have better things to do now that you've moved on and up, huh?"

"I don't forget where I came from, Salvador," I said in a voice I forced to stay even. "I guess our paths just haven't crossed before." Too bad I hadn't kept up that streak.

Salvador looked me over with the air he always had as if he were an uncle sizing up his least favorite nephew. The asshole only had about five years on me, but he'd always enjoyed talking down to me as if he held so much more seniority.

He crossed his arms over his broad chest. "Oh, yeah? So you haven't forgotten Edmundo then, cabrón?"

My teeth set on edge. This was the last thing I needed while I was trying to run a stealthy rescue mission. "Never have, never will."

But getting into a fight in the middle of this bar wasn't going to help me or Lou.

Salvador shook his head chidingly. "That's funny, because I could have sworn we were supposed to hear about some big explosion, but it never came…"

A deeper chill rippled through me. I forced a mild

smile onto my face. "Some things take time. Speaking of which, I've got a job to take care of."

"Oh, do you?" Salvador's voice carried after me as I sidestepped him on my way to the door. "Jumping to that rich bitch's tune now. Fucking sad."

I didn't bother responding, just pushed out into the evening hoping he wasn't invested enough to follow me.

I hurried down the street, wanting to get some distance from him before I hailed an Uber. My lungs were burning, and I realized I'd been holding my breath.

Fuck Salvador and whoever still stood with him. They had no fucking idea…

It'd been so much better when I'd been able to leave Austin behind. But I couldn't stay gone while Lou was trapped here.

I shoved my anger aside. When I'd left the bar well behind, I stopped by a dingy brick office building and pulled out my phone.

In the back of my mind, images were forming of Lou stuck in her old bedroom in the Cordova mansion, as trapped and alone as if her mom had shoved her into a prison cell. Without me, she'd have no one to count on there.

I had to get to her—soon. She needed to know she could turn to me. She'd have no idea I'd even tracked her this far.

I needed *her*. To see her sly smile, to hear her vibrant laugh, to wrap my arms around her. To know that I was protecting her every way I could, like that precious woman deserved.

I hadn't realized my heart could feel this empty until now.

As I ducked into the Uber, I kept my phone in my

hand. We knew Mireya had gotten control over Lou's phone. But she and I had planned alternate means of communication back when I was still acting like a proper bodyguard, when she'd faced much more immediate dangers on a daily basis as her mother's heir.

Like she would be again now.

From what I'd seen and heard, those avenues were likely to be my best options of reaching out to her. I couldn't count on catching her at any of these meetings Mireya was setting up.

Lou had better have remembered those old schemes. Better be checking up on things just in case.

Que Dios me ayude if she'd given up because I hadn't gotten here faster.

In the phone's web browser, I brought up a forum for missed connections. Typed out a message that she'd recognize if she saw it, but no one else would understand.

For the skating angel I met at the crossroads, I heard that there's a lot of cheap equipment at the outlet store on Pine Street. Looking forward to shopping with you there if you're up for it — how's 6 o'clock Thursday night sound?

I hit the post button and sagged back in the seat. Now all I could do was wait and see.

"You sure she's coming?" Quentin asked for what had to be the twelfth time that night. He shifted on his feet, glancing around the abandoned outlet store at the few empty racks that'd been left behind when the last tenants had vacated it. A few lonely shirts hung dejectedly from their hangers. "You're sure she'd ever think we're going to meet her *here?*"

My voice came out in a growl. "She and I know each other well enough to understand this kind of thing."

The bastard had been getting on my nerves all day. The worst part was that his impatient skepticism was starting to infect the two men who should have trusted me more.

Jasper paced a few steps across the worn linoleum before returning to us, raking his hand through his shaggy hair. "What if she *doesn't* come? What would our next option be?"

"We'll figure that out if we need to," I said. "It's still a couple of minutes before six. She isn't even late."

Niko swiped his hand across his mouth and pushed his lips into a smile I could see was tense. "There've got to be other ways to get in contact with her, right?"

I restrained a glower. "If she doesn't come tonight, then we try again tomorrow, and the next night. She might not see the message right away, but she'll give it a shot when she does."

And if it went on for more than a few days without Lou turning up... Yeah, then we'd have a problem. One I'd rather not think about.

Niko glanced at his phone and typed out a message that was quickly answered with a cheery ping. I suspected he was talking with his little sister again.

Jasper sighed and shoved his hands in his pockets. And Quentin started prowling through the back of the store, wrinkling his nose at the discarded clothing. His mouth twisted into a sour expression.

If he made one more snarky remark, I was going to—

Thankfully for both of us, I never needed to complete that thought. Because just then the door I'd picked the lock on and left ajar eased open, and Lou darted inside.

Her new bangs, redyed to her previous dark brown,

drooped across her face, and her shoulders were furtively hunched, but my heart leapt at the sight of her all the same. And when she raised her head and caught sight of the three of us in our cluster in the middle of the room, the smile that lit her face flooded me with the sweetest relief.

No, not just relief. Love. As I hurried to meet her, my chest swelled with the emotion I hadn't known I would ever feel. Hadn't known it was possible to feel this strongly.

But as I tucked my arms around her slender frame, a pang that was more bittersweet shot through my joy.

I loved this woman, sure—but even if she was with me now, I couldn't be there for her anywhere near as much as I wanted to. Not while she was still tangled in her mother's snare.

EIGHT

Luciana

I WASN'T NORMALLY the most emotionally expressive person in the world. Mom had taught me to hold my cards close and reveal my feelings cautiously.

But seeing my three men in front of me for the first time in over a week, I couldn't hold back the joyful tears that sprang into my eyes.

I threw myself at Rafael first, mainly because he was closest. As I wrapped him in the tightest hug I could offer, he chuckled, sounding just a tad choked up himself, and hugged me back with his chin tucking over my head.

"Glad you got the message."

"Glad you thought of using the forum," I replied. I'd cycled through our planned covert methods of communications a few times since Mom had dragged me back to Austin, but my hopes hadn't been high.

I forced myself to ease back from Rafael, but only so

that I could grab the guy next to him in an equally emphatic embrace.

Jasper's brawny arms encircled me, and he planted a lingering kiss on my forehead. "It's good to see you've survived so far, Punk," he said, the gruffness of his voice not quite hiding the rasp of emotion.

His words brought a prickle of fear into my gut, but I ignored it for the moment. "It's so good to see you too. Even if you're still a grouch."

As he laughed, I turned from him to Niko, who was smiling bright as the sun. He gathered me up against his slimmer frame and nuzzled the side of my face. "We were awfully worried about you, Angel. All of us."

I would have assumed he meant all three, but as I pulled away to match his smile with a beaming one of my own, a fourth figure who I hadn't noticed at the edge of the room took a step toward us.

My gaze jerked toward the unexpected member of the group, and my stance went rigid.

Quentin stopped where he was, still several feet away between the sparse clothing racks, and ran his fingers over his blond hair, which was slicked back as neatly as always. His sharp blue eyes held some of the same wildness I'd seen when he'd called me down from my apartment right before Mom had grabbed me.

When he'd told me how he couldn't stop thinking about me and then kissed me.

In my shock, my voice came out cold. "What are *you* doing here?"

His mouth slanted at a crooked angle. Before he could speak, Niko jumped in. "Quentin helped us figure out why you'd disappeared. He saw your mother take you away."

Rafael nodded, his impassive expression giving away nothing of his feelings on the third skater guy he was now shepherding around. "He insisted on coming along, and I figured he'd make more trouble than it was worth if I couldn't keep an eye on him. Claims he knows the wrong side of the tracks and that he wants to help if he can."

His voice took on a slightly dry tone with the second sentence. Jasper simply scowled. I couldn't imagine he'd been happy about his rival coming along for the trip.

I was silent for a moment, taking in what they'd said and studying Quentin. The twist of his mouth had shaped it into a tentative if crooked smile. His gaze burned into me with its usual intensity.

When he'd come by the apartment, I'd figured he'd been looking for more ways to mess with me and Jasper. Or to get his rocks off and then move on. But he'd been willing to trek all the way across the country to try to get me out of this mess?

That didn't fit with the coolly competitive guy I'd thought he was.

I shifted closer to Jasper automatically, taking his hand to sling his arm around my waist. I was both starving for contact with the men I'd had to leave behind and determined that Jasper didn't imagine for one second that my interest in him had faded.

"How much does he know?" I had to ask.

Rafael shrugged. "The basics. Enough to realize he's stepping into a shitload of danger."

"We *tried* to scare him off," Jasper muttered, but he held me with a tenderness totally at odds with his tone. It wasn't me he was annoyed with, that was for sure.

"Well, thank you," I said to Quentin. "Never thought

I'd see the day when you'd actually work *with* Jasper instead of trying to tear him down."

It was a purposeful jab—a test of his response.

Quentin simply bobbed his head in acknowledgement. "The least I could do if you're in trouble."

Which I was. The prickle that'd jabbed at me earlier spread into a larger ache.

And now my men were in trouble too.

I glanced up at Jasper, unable to resist rising on my toes to give him a quick kiss on the cheek. "*None* of you really should have come, though." I reached out to squeeze Niko's arm and then cast my gaze toward Rafael. "My mom… She might kill you if she finds out you're here. No hesitation, no questions asked."

Just saying it left me queasy.

Niko raised his chin. "We're not leaving you to deal with her on your own. There has to be a way to get you away from her."

"And we'll take whatever risks necessary to make it happen," Jasper added.

Rafael let out a light huff. "You know I'm not walking away from the danger."

I swallowed thickly and curled my fingers tighter around Jasper's hand. "But—there's Nationals too. You'll miss your chance—"

"Fuck that," my partner broke in emphatically. "I couldn't compete without you, and I sure as hell wouldn't want to anyway. If we get our way, you'll be right there beside me in time for us to skate together."

My heart sank. "It's not going to be easy. I can't just run away again. She'll know exactly where I went—and even if we laid low, now that she knows about you and Niko too, it'll be that much easier for her to track us down. And she's made it clear that if I go against her orders again, she's going to punish me by hurting all of you."

Rafael's lips formed a grim smile. "Then we have to make her believe that she's better off letting you leave."

"I wish." I exhaled in a ragged sigh.

"Is there anyone else in town you could join up with against her?" Quentin ventured. "Safety in numbers and all that. We could even put out feelers and—"

I shook my head with a jerk. "No. The four of you have to stay out of sight and not draw any attention—especially from the criminal underground. Anyone who's strong enough to even irritate my mom, she's got either under her thumb or too scared to even look at her funny. You have no idea how much power she can wield or how quick she is to use it."

Niko spread his hands. "We'll play it safe while we need to. But as soon as there's anything we can do to help, you've got to let us know."

"And fast," Rafael said with a hint of a growl.

I nodded, torn between reluctance to drag them any further into my problems and relief that I wasn't facing those problems alone after all. "I'll need more time to figure out a strategy that'll actually work. So far... I haven't seen any obvious way to get myself out of this. But I'm not giving up."

Rafael's subtle smile returned. "That's my girl." He cocked his head. "Do you have any idea why she was so determined to get you back right now? I've heard murmurs about big plans, but no one seems to know what they are."

I let out a rough chuckle. "Me neither. She isn't telling me any more than she has to—she knows I'm not committed to staying if I have any choice in the matter. But I am getting the impression that she's building up to something major."

I squeezed Jasper's arm one last time, leaned in to offer Niko a quick kiss, and then gave Rafael a final hug. An ache ran through my heart as I forced myself to pull away.

"Thank you for coming. Just don't make me wish you hadn't. I shouldn't stay any longer or she might get suspicious. We can pass messages back and forth through the forum to keep in touch."

"We'll be waiting for your call," Jasper said. "Whatever it takes."

I said my good-byes and hurried out before my eyes could overflow. My pulse thudded heavily through my veins as I walked back to my car, which I'd parked a couple of blocks away for caution.

But for all my fear and the sense of loss at leaving them again, my spirits felt lighter than they had in days. As I drove back to the Cordova mansion, my mind replayed those moments standing with my men, knowing they'd braved the wrath of the most dangerous woman in the country to come to my rescue. Even if they couldn't do any actual rescuing yet.

I strode through the deepening evening from the sprawling garage up to the broad front door. A few of Mom's lackeys were hanging around near the entrance, but all their smartass remarks had dried up since I'd gotten back.

Maybe seeing the furor Mom had gotten into when I was gone had given them a little more appreciation for my presence.

I headed past them up the sweeping staircase and along the hall to my bedroom. I wanted nothing more than to flop onto the bed and dream of running off with my men and leaving all this crap behind me.

But just as I reached for the door handle, a faint squeak of hinges sounded behind me.

"Luciana? I'd like a word."

Mom stood in her office doorway. Her expression was cool and impenetrable enough to set my nerves jangling.

Had she somehow figured out about my meeting with the guys? I hadn't seen her when I'd left the house, but I'd planted the idea that I was planning on going out for pierogies for dinner when I'd seen her earlier in the day.

If she'd seen through that lie, we were already screwed.

Avoiding her was hardly an option when she was staring right at me. I plastered an obedient smile on my face and ambled over at her beckoning. "Sure. What's up?"

Mom's nose wrinkled slightly at my casual tone, but she motioned me into the room without comment. "How was your Polish dinner?"

"Oh, you know," I said glibly, hoping she couldn't hear my heart about to thunder right out of my chest. "Not as fresh as when Zuzanna was here to make them, but it hit the spot well enough."

Mom hummed to herself and strolled over to her desk. She wasn't giving off an angry vibe, at least, so maybe I was safe after all.

I didn't think she'd asked me in here just to inquire about my meal, though.

She took her time getting to the point, a common tactic of hers designed to give her time to evaluate the other person's mood. As she straightened an already neat pile of papers on her desk, I held myself still and calm, waiting.

Brushing her hands together, she turned to face me

again. "It's time to discuss our next steps. Across the meetings you've been a part of and my own outreach, it's becoming clearer who will side with the Deadly Rose, who's brushing us off, and who is inclined to stay neutral." She shook her head with a disproving click of her tongue. "I was hoping that boy who sees himself as the Storm would be a little more intrigued, but I haven't heard a murmur from him since your brunch."

She figured Beckett was brushing her off? "I don't think he knew what you were looking for," I pointed out. I sure as hell hadn't to be able to tell him. "Apparently he's already got a girlfriend, so framing it as a date wasn't a draw."

Mom flicked her hand dismissively. "An obvious overture of any sort warrants a particular response if there's any thought to a deeper alliance. That's fine. He can snub us all he likes… for now."

A chill ran down my back. "And what happens later?"

Her sharp smile chilled me even more. "We'll get to that. Before we make any significant moves, there are a few outliers I'd like you to approach. The most important of those is the new Blood Hunter."

"Another heir who's just stepped up?" I asked, still trying to untangle her insinuations about the future.

"No, a usurper." Mom's smile widened slightly as if she liked the idea. Maybe she did, as long as it wasn't her throne being stolen. "She has only a little experience within the Devil's Dozen. And she's not much older than you, so I'd imagine you'll have more common ground than there'd be between her and me."

"And we want to find that common ground because…?"

Mom shot me a look as if thinking I should keep up.

"She's a wild card. But as a woman who's bringing new ideas to the table, I'm hopeful that she'll see the benefits that would come with adjusting the balance of power."

Adjusting the balance of power. And Mom was fussing over who wanted to ally with her and who wasn't taking the bait.

A horrible suspicion clawed its way up through my chest. "Are you… Are you trying to find allies so you can overthrow some of the other Devil's Dozen members?"

It wouldn't be a totally absurd move, would it? Banding together with a smaller group to shove out the others, dividing the losers' territory between the winners so there were fewer at the top, each with a bigger piece of the pie.

I could totally see Mom going for that. And becoming even more of a menace than she already was.

But if she failed… That kind of treason against her Devil's Dozen colleagues would warrant a death sentence.

Not a hint of agreement showed in Mom's expression —but she didn't look scandalized by my suggestion either. That convinced me I was right before she even gave her carefully bland response. "We're simply taking stock of where we stand—and what we might do from there. You should never leap into action until you're sure of your plan's success, Luciana."

Oh, yeah, that was as much of a yes as I could imagine Mom ever giving. Holy shit.

She intended to turn on some of those other top bosses—the kings and queens of the criminal underworld. How much territory was she hoping to gain? Did she figure she'd double her holdings? Triple them?

How many more people would be terrorized under her reign?

Did she really think it was worth risking everything we had on a crazy gamble like that? Or maybe she'd already found enough support that it didn't seem so crazy.

As those questions whirled in my head, a strange elation tickled up from my belly. I didn't like what I was hearing, but it also might be exactly the leverage I needed so much.

Mom was holding my men's lives over my head to get her way. If I could threaten something *she* cared about, it might balance out our own power struggle.

I tipped my head to the side as if I were thinking over Mom's words. "Then I guess we'd better make sure. When did you want me to talk to the Blood Hunter?"

NINE

Luciana

I RECOGNIZED the Blood Hunter the moment she stepped into the elegant coffee shop Mom had picked out for this meeting in downtown Atlanta, which apparently was neutral ground between their territories.

I'd never seen a picture of the woman before and only had Mom's brief description to go by. But I think even if I hadn't known to expect long black hair or dark eyes vivid against pale skin, I'd have identified her as a force to be reckoned with before she'd even crossed the room.

Despite her slim frame, the Blood Hunter's every movement emanated physical control and strength. Her steady gaze as she approached the table spoke of plenty of will power as well. I considered myself a skilled fighter when the situation called for it, but every inch of my skin prickled with the knowledge that this woman could have me pinned in a matter of seconds, no matter what I did.

Like Mom had said, she wasn't that much older than me, late twenties at most, but when she stood over the small table I'd chosen, I felt like a kid. A kid who had no business trying to play the kinds of games my mother wanted to involve me in.

I had to anyway, though, so I'd better put on a good show.

I started to stand up as a sign of respect, but the Blood Hunter lowered herself into the chair across from me before I could get to my feet. She didn't show any sign of caring about those sorts of niceties.

It was far from standard protocol for her to be speaking with me at all. In Beckett's case, his agreeing to meet with someone who didn't even have the authority to sit at the Devil's Dozen table yet could be explained by the fact that there was still some uncertainty about whether he or his father truly held the title.

The Blood Hunter had no heirs. From what Mom had told me, she'd ruled for the past few years after killing the man who'd claimed that name before her.

Why had she done that? What had she been after?

Questions I definitely couldn't ask someone who could not just kill *me* in a snap but was a total stranger on top of that.

"It's good to meet you," I said with a quick smile. "Thank you for taking the time."

The woman studied me intently enough that my pulse stuttered. "What is this about? The Deadly Rose indicated that you had a time-sensitive issue to discuss with me."

Augh, why had Mom phrased it that way? Of course, maybe the Blood Hunter wouldn't have shown up at all otherwise.

She sure got straight to the point. There was none of Beckett's friendly warmth here.

Who would have thought I'd find myself wishing for another brunch with the Storm instead?

"It isn't really one specific issue," I said quickly, summoning the talking points Mom had coached me on. "But we're on the cusp of making some major changes with some of our dealings. It's an ideal time to build on our existing alliances and form new ones."

The Blood Hunter continued to eye me with a slightly skeptical expression. I had to fight the urge to shrink inside my blouse.

I was the Deadly Rose's daughter. I could be a force to be reckoned with too.

Never mind that I didn't actually want to be forcing a conversation like this on Mom's behalf. What unholy terror would Mom unleash on the world if she got her way and transformed the whole structure of the Devil's Dozen?

After a long enough silence that I was itching to fidget, the Blood Hunter rested her hands on the table. "And she wants an alliance with me? Why didn't she meet with me herself?"

Thankfully, Mom had covered her expected approach to that subject in depth. Admitting the truth wouldn't have gotten her what she wanted.

I lifted my chin. "I'll be taking over more and more authority within the Deadly Rose empire in the coming years." *If I can't get myself the fuck out of this hell.* "Since we're both relatively new to this kind of work, she figured you and I might have more common ground. If you'd prefer to speak to her directly—"

The Blood Hunter shook her head with a jerk. "This is

fine. Is that your whole pitch? What would we be allying on?"

I motioned vaguely with my hands, hoping I didn't look as uneasy as I felt. "We could create more of a partnership between our empires. Combine some of our business interests. Work together against any threats. More people on your side can't be a bad thing, right?"

The woman across from me blinked slowly, pensively. "Depends on the friend. I've held the title of the Blood Hunter for years now, though. Is there something happening right now that's brought on this overture?"

"I've recently come of age to take on more responsibility," I said. "It's gotten my mother thinking about the ways our world could benefit from fresh ideas, a shift in the old habits and patterns. Reaching out to the colleagues she respects most is part of that."

I couldn't tell if the Blood Hunter appreciated or even believed that my mother might respect her. She flicked her thumb over her lips and then fixed me with an even more penetrating stare.

"Are any of the things you're saying *your* ideas, or are you just parroting what the Deadly Rose told you to say? She doesn't seem to have much respect for you if she's hanging around just a couple of blocks away, monitoring you."

A chill ran down my back. I'd known Mom was staked out in her car not far from the café, waiting for me to report back, but she'd been subtle about it. The Blood Hunter wasn't supposed to have noticed.

But she had, somehow or other. How could I explain that away when I was supposed to be claiming that Mom had put all this authority in my hands?

And if the Blood Hunter had picked up on that covert

fact, what else did she know that we hadn't expected her to?

I hesitated with my lips parted, my throat aching with the honest answer I couldn't give. I didn't want to pretend I was wholeheartedly behind Mom's deeper treachery either, especially if this woman already suspected something was up.

Before I could fumble out a response, the Blood Hunter stood up with a rasp of her chair's legs against the floor. "That's enough of an answer. I'm not interested in all the complicated internal politics of the Devil's Dozen. You can tell your mother I'd prefer to simply be left alone."

With that, she strode out of the café, not even sparing me a backward glance.

A waitress breezed by, giving me a puzzled glance, and my face flushed with embarrassment. Who knew what she'd made of my oddly brief meet-up?

I gulped the last of the coffee I'd ordered while I was waiting, left a ten on the table that was more than twice my actual bill, and slipped out of the café a few minutes after the Blood Hunter had left. There was no sign of her outside, but it was impossible to know how she might be keeping an eye on us still.

Well, there was nothing to do but trudge back to Mom and make my disappointing report.

I took a couple of turns and crossed a crowded parking lot to where Mom had told me the sedan would be waiting. The Blood Hunter hadn't even been wrong, had she? Here I was, dutifully trotting back to my mother whose plans I wanted nothing to do with, like I was a puppy being brought to heel.

But the Blood Hunter had no idea what I had at stake.

My nails dug into the meat of my palms hard enough to leave marks.

Mom had driven us this time, not wanting to talk with a driver who could overhear. I dropped into the passenger seat next to her. My heart thumped hard, but I dipped my hand into my purse as if I were making sure I hadn't forgotten anything back at the café.

I *wasn't* here just for her ends. Not that I could let her find out my private purpose.

Mom's gaze took me in assessingly. "That was a short meeting. What happened?"

I exhaled in a rush of frustration. "The Blood Hunter isn't interested. She seemed suspicious about the fact that we'd reached out at all, and after she heard my reasons, she told me she just wanted you to leave her alone and then walked out."

Her eyes narrowed. "That kind of a snub? I knew she was inexperienced, but..." She shook herself, but anger still simmered beneath her next words. "There are only three women in the Devil's Dozen. You'd think she could at least recognize the potential value in having each other's backs."

"According to her, she doesn't want anything to do with the politics in the Devil's Dozen." I knit my brow. Now I *really* wanted to know why that woman had claimed her spot at the table. She didn't seem to have any more interest in fulfilling her expected role than I did.

Mom scoffed. "She's taking that attitude, is she? No idea how much guidance she's losing out on that I could have offered." Her tone darkened. "Well, she'll regret throwing my generosity back in my face when she finds herself without any chair at the table at all."

A quiver ran through my veins. There. She'd just

openly admitted that her end goal was to displace at least one of her colleagues.

My mouth had gone dry, but triumph sparked in my chest all the same. Because in my purse, my phone was recording this entire conversation. I now had a concrete record of Mom's illicit plans.

"We don't need her," Mom went on as she started the engine. "The fewer who join us, the less we have to share. Someone like her doesn't deserve her piece of the pie."

"I'm sure you'll find other people who'll stand with you," I said, careful not to indicate any personal support of her plans.

"Oh, I already have." A cruel smile curved Mom's lips. "And when it's time, *all* of the others will regret their choices."

TEN

Quentin

GO FIGURE. The muscle head had picked what must be the most rundown rink in the state of Texas for the three of us to practice.

My nose wrinkled reflexively as I took in the dingy arena. Several of the fluorescent bulbs fixed to the ceiling were flickering; a couple were burned out. The boards around the ice were smudged and in a couple of places outright cracked.

The stands hadn't fared much better. We tramped past a section of benches that were cordoned off with caution tape because the seats had slanted right off their bases with massive dents.

The smell of stale sweat and grease from fast food wrappers left in the stands made my stomach turn. As we reached the boards, I couldn't hold back a complaint.

"This is it—seriously? This is the best arena you could find in all of Austin?"

The massive man who was apparently Lou's gang bodyguard or something like that swung around to fix me with his intimidating glower. My stance tensed, but I stared right back at him.

"The point isn't to skate in luxury," he said in his dark rumble of a voice. "The point is to keep a low enough profile that you all don't get *killed*."

Jasper let out a huff and hunkered down on a bench to pull on his skates. "I'm fine with those priorities."

My lips pulled into a grimace. "There wasn't anything even a *little* better maintained? Who knows if this ice is even—"

Rafael cut me off. "It's this or nothing. Up to you whether you skate."

He swiveled and marched back up to the door where he was going to keep watch.

I watched him go and let my gaze sweep over the dank space again. My stomach knotted.

The vibe of this place wasn't exactly unfamiliar. If anything, it reminded me way too much of the rink where I'd first trained as a kid. The crappy place near home that mostly got used for low-rent birthday parties and community center lessons.

My skin itched uncomfortably with the sense of having been sucked back into the past. I'd moved on to better digs than this in the years since then.

But I couldn't see that continuing to argue with Rafael was going to change my situation—other than it'd make him and the other two guys who'd grudgingly agreed to loop me in on this mission even less friendly.

I hadn't had the opportunity to do anything to

actually prove my worth since I'd told them what I'd seen happen to Lou back in Boston. No doubt Jasper was chomping at the bit for any excuse good enough to send me packing.

Not that I really wanted to hang around him this much, but I knew there wasn't a hope in hell of me doing anything for Lou on my own. I wouldn't even know how to get in touch with her.

Squaring my shoulders, I dropped my bag on one of the benches and retrieved my skates. The ice looked decently smooth, at least. If there was anything that could make me feel better, it was honing my performance.

It'd be nice to get lost in the practice zone just for a little while. And I was going to need that practice to get up to speed with my routines.

By the time I'd laced up, Jasper and Niko had already moved onto the ice. Niko was saying something in a low voice and motioning to one end of the rink.

I wasn't sure how Jasper was going to get much done without Lou here, but I guessed he could work on his spins and jumps, if not the synchronization piece. It wasn't any of my business. They hadn't said a word directly to me since we'd come in—obviously they planned to have their own little practice session separate from me, like I wasn't even here.

Restraining a sigh, I pushed off across the ice. With each flex of my muscles, I felt how many days it'd been since I'd gotten a proper workout. Strength exercises and cardio routines in the apartment just didn't cut it.

I closed my eyes, playing the song from my short routine in my head from memory. Niko said something that I ignored until I caught my name.

I blinked and looked over at him. He shot me a wary

smile. "How much practice do you expect to do without your partner?"

Jasper muttered something I couldn't totally make out but might have been along the lines of that I'd better not think I was stealing his. My teeth set on edge, but I answered with cool evenness.

"I didn't rank high enough to qualify for Nationals in pairs anyway. I'm going back to singles—I can compete based on last year's ranking."

Niko's narrow eyebrows arched slightly. "That could be tricky when you haven't been practicing your singles routines for most of the season."

I shrugged. "I'll manage."

He had no idea what I was capable of. I'd pulled off plenty of trickier tasks in my life—like getting to this point in my career at all.

The two of them wouldn't know anything about the kind of struggles that'd taken. Especially Jasper born with that silver spoon up his ass.

I cast off into a brief series of warm-up moves, getting a feel for the ice. Niko went back to ignoring me while Jasper started his own warm-up.

I was just considering where to start my real practice when the door next to Rafael swung open.

A petite but curvy figure appeared with a swish of a familiar dark ponytail. Lou bobbed up to give Rafael a quick kiss and then hustled down the steps to the rink, where Jasper and Niko were already skating over to the boards to greet her.

The sight of her gorgeous face, lit up with the bright smile that stretched wider as she took them in, made my heart skip a beat. And the athletic slopes of her body in her tight long-sleeved tee and leggings… God, that woman was something.

Something that wanted nothing to do with me. She grabbed Jasper and then Niko in an embrace before yanking on her skates, the flush in her cheeks somehow making her even prettier. But as far as I could tell, she didn't so much as glance my way.

"I don't think Mom suspected anything," she told them in a breathless tone that made me want to capture even more of her breath from her lips. "But I can't stay more than an hour."

"I'm just glad you could make it at all," Jasper said in a tone I could have gagged at, especially because Lou responded by giving him an emphatic kiss.

It wasn't really disgust roiling inside me. Jealousy seared through my chest.

But what had I expected? I'd been a total prick to her and her partner for months, even if her partner at least partly deserved it.

It was going to take time before she realized I could offer something good too.

I turned away and narrowed my thoughts back to my routine. I knew the moves by heart. It shouldn't be that hard to trigger the muscle memory.

My mind drifted into the comfortable zone of calculation. I knew exactly how many inches I needed to lift my leg with this spin, or to get off the ice in that jump —and how many *more* inches would take me from acceptable to applause-worthy.

As much as I wanted to be at the latter stage immediately, it was better for my body to aim a little lower to start. A strained muscle or tendon could end the whole competition for me.

Piece by piece, I'd build what I could achieve back up.

I pushed off the ice, picturing the exact angle that my body would need to tilt to perfect the first move. My eyes narrowed as I sped forward.

Another powerful push, this time upward. I twisted my body in a perfect pre-rotation, and smiled when I came down under two thirds of a second later. A textbook triple Axel, from my airtime to the position of my body.

Maybe I'd even be able to push it to a quad before Nationals.

I probably should have stuck with my singles routines to begin with. But it'd been too infuriating that Jasper had found a loophole to avoid going head-to-head right when I was sure I could beat him.

Whatever. Competing one way or another was more important than showing him up. I could admit that much.

And he'd maybe even earned his victory over me and Jess at Finals. I could also admit that their epic free-skate performance hadn't relied only on Lou's skills.

At the other end of the rink, her laugh pealed out. I resisted the urge to glance over and try to guess what had provoked her amusement.

Going through the motions of the routine, I kept my attention on the precise angles and the amount of power I would need to make sure that each move was faultless. But every now and then, I couldn't stop my gaze from snagging on Lou. Her grace as she soared across the ice was close to hypnotizing.

When I was concentrating on my own run-throughs of both of my routines, I summoned a reasonable sense of satisfaction. I had them memorized—many of the spins and jumps were the same as I'd performed with Jess, just in a different order.

I didn't have that far to go before I could bring them up to scratch. And Niko had been worried about me.

I might have rolled my eyes, except right then I noticed Lou loping up the steps to the door, her skates slung over her shoulder.

Fuck! I'd gotten lost enough in my concentration that I hadn't noticed her hasty preparations to leave. Had it already been an hour?

Niko and Jasper were still on the ice, Jasper raising his hand in a farewell wave that Lou returned as she reached the door. My heart lurched.

I couldn't let her just leave—not when we hadn't exchanged a single word.

Ignoring whatever stares the other guys might be aiming my way, I flung myself toward the bench where I'd left my skate guards, tugged them on, and bolted up the stairs. Rafael didn't say a word as I barged past him, but I heard the rasp of his footsteps as he followed me into the hall.

Like he thought I might be a threat to Lou. For fuck's sake.

She was already halfway through the desolate reception area, just steps from the outer doors. My voice caught in my throat for a second before I forced it out.

"Lou, wait!"

Lou paused. I could see how she tensed in the instant before she turned to face me with wariness in her deep brown eyes. "Yeah?"

"Yeah?" I repeated. "Is that all you've got to say? I came all this way to help you—aren't you even a little glad to see me?"

Even as the words tumbled out, a flash of shame washed over me. Could I have sounded more pathetic?

But Lou's expression did soften a little, so maybe the sappiness was worth it.

She heaved a breath. "Look, I appreciate what you did —working with the other guys to find me. Thank you. But how much do you expect to change just like that?"

"Just like what?" I demanded.

She crossed her arms. "You *know* you acted like an asshole from the moment I met you—and even more so to Jasper, who you also know I care about a heck of a lot. Just because you admitted it the other day doesn't erase all those weeks. What, did you think all you had to do was lay on a little flattery, and suddenly I'd fall in love with you instead?"

My face heated, but I raised my chin. "I wasn't looking for 'I love you's. I just—I want to get to know you better. In all sorts of ways. You're not a one-guy kind of woman, and that's totally fine. I'd be willing to share you if it means you give me a chance to show you that I can be *more* than just an asshole."

Lou's gaze held me pinned in place. Her lips twisted in a wry smile. "It's not that easy, you know. I'm not sure if I want anything at all to do with you after the way you treated us. How long are you even going to be able to keep the peace with the three of them?"

"As long as it takes," I insisted. "You're more important than all that crap."

She let out a soft huff. "We'll see, I guess. It's going to take time before I can figure out how to feel about you, even if you mean that."

She spun on her heel, and this time I let her go without trying to call her back. How could I demand more from her right now when everything she'd said was true?

When she needed to get out of here to make sure her mom didn't come down even harder on her.

But as I watched her vanish beyond the double doors, my stomach sank. How the hell was I going to convince her to look beyond the past?

I strode back to the rink, gathering all my resolve. I'd just keep demonstrating my intentions until she believed me. That was all there was to it.

I'd never met a woman who awed me half as much as Lou did. I'd proven a lot of people wrong about me and what I could do, and I could prove to her that her first impressions had been wrong too.

When I returned to the rink, Niko was standing by the boards watching Jasper complete a jump, neither of them showing any sign of concern about my whereabouts. I didn't know whether I should be relieved or annoyed.

Well, they probably figured Lou could look after herself, which was fair enough.

I was just yanking my skate guards back off when my phone buzzed in my bag. In my distraction, I picked it up on autopilot and raised it to my ear before I'd glanced at the call display. "Hello?"

My mother's voice crackled from the speaker. "Oh, good, you finally picked up. It's about time."

My shoulders stiffened. Shit. I'd been dodging her calls ever since we left Boston, just texting an excuse she obviously hadn't bought for a second.

My conversation with Lou had left my emotions frayed. I spoke more tersely than I meant to—more than I'd usually have let myself, knowing how easy it was to set the woman off. "What do you want? I'm trying to practice —which is what you *should* want me to be doing."

Mom sucked in a sharp breath. "Don't you take that

tone with me, Quentin. Don't make it sound like I'm the bad guy here. When were you planning on having a real discussion with me? You up and disappear without a word, ignoring my calls, and all that after you fucked yourself over at Finals with your stupid idea to skate pairs."

My vision blurred with a toxic mix of emotion I couldn't afford to let out. "I've been busy."

"Busy? Busy ruining the career I worked so hard to make sure you could build. You can't even spare ten fucking minutes to talk to your mother? What did I do to deserve such a shitty excuse for a son? Where the hell are you?"

I'd gritted my teeth through the tirade, knowing there was little chance I'd get a word in even if she'd have cared about how I defended myself. At the final question, I rasped out, "You don't need to worry about that."

"Of course I'm fucking worried! My lord. Who knows what other braindead decisions you'll make without me watching over you? Now get your act together and start giving me the respect I'm owed—and I expect to see you skating your goddamn heart out at Nationals in singles, or you'd better believe—"

The tension inside me overflowed. "Don't worry," I interrupted. "I'm not going to throw a whole competition just to piss you off."

Then I tapped the button to end the call, bracing myself as if she could slap me across the head all the way from home. The way she no doubt would have if she'd been in front of me.

The way she had more times than I could count when I was growing up. Even left me with a pretty little scar on my face to remind me why I shouldn't cross her.

But I wasn't a kid anymore. I was twenty-one—in the

eyes of everyone else in this fucking country, I was an adult by every possible measure.

So why the hell could she still make me feel like a cringing elementary schooler with a few well-placed insults?

I turned off my phone before Mom could launch into a barrage of texts or calls and slid it back into the pocket on my bag, only registering then how clammy my hand had gotten. My gut had tied itself in at least a dozen knots.

Fuck. How was I going to focus on practice like this?

I looked up, and my stomach sank all the way to my feet. Niko and Jasper had drifted closer while I was talking to Mom. They were both studying me now, Niko looking concerned, Jasper mostly just awkward.

He was the one who spoke first though, after a rough clearing of his throat. "What was that about? We couldn't help hearing—it sounded like a pretty intense conversation."

My face burned. Like I hadn't faced enough humiliation for one day. But telling Jasper off would only make it sound more like a big deal rather than less.

Instead, I shrugged, shoving all my uncomfortable emotions deeper inside. "It was nothing, really. My mom just doesn't know when to shut up. She has a lot of shitty opinions about my career, but I'm used to that."

A glimmer of startled recognition lit in my rival's eyes, one that horrified me even more as I realized what it meant. When I'd first gotten into the professional circuit as a junior competitor, there'd been a couple of public incidents after disappointing competitions... One where Mom had berated me outside an arena loud enough that a news crew had noticed and recorded some of it, and then the time when she'd smacked me hard enough that I'd banged my face against a railing and cut open my lip and chin.

No one had really tried to *help*, not that I could think of much anyone could have offered that would have been useful. They'd just reveled in the drama of it all until some other news story took over.

That'd been a long time ago. I'd gotten better at managing her moods and expectations over the years.

Jasper wasn't going to start pitying me now, was he? He'd probably assumed the tirades had stopped once I'd gotten older or forgotten about it entirely until now.

Something softened in the other guy's face, but instead of nauseating platitudes, his lips quirked into a wry smile. He rubbed the back of his neck before saying in an equally wry tone, "Well, I think I've had enough of the ice for today anyway. Anyone else up for waffles for dinner? That always puts me in a better mood."

I blinked at him. "Waffles?"

"Sure. Breakfast for dinner is totally a thing." He jerked his head toward his bag. "I even brought a bottle of maple syrup from where we were training in Ontario so we've got the proper Canadian stuff. I could spare you a dollop or two. If you ask nicely."

The glint in his eyes was more teasing than anything now, but in a way that felt almost... friendly rather than heckling. I didn't know how to respond.

Niko slung his arm casually around Jasper's waist and grinned at me too. "I know, the man is insane. But I have to admit the maple syrup is pretty nice."

I wasn't sure I'd ever had anything other than regular table syrup. I mentally flicked through my charts of calorie counts and protein quotas, and then shook myself.

The two of them weren't being weird about my whole

mom situation. And they were volunteering to spend more time with me.

I wasn't going to get anywhere with Lou unless I was getting along with the guys she'd already chosen for herself too.

I aimed for the same dry but not hostile tone. "Jasper St. Pierre is trying to give me early diabetes—I guess it's my lucky day."

Niko laughed. "That sounds like a yes to me." He waved at my skates. "Get changed and let's head out. I'm sure we can manage to drag Rafael along too."

I sat down on the bench with a half-hearted grumble and snuck a sideways peek at Jasper as he wiped down his own skates. Watching for any sign that he was regretting his invitation.

Weirdly enough, he hadn't lost his smile.

Huh. I wasn't going to admit it out loud, but… maybe they weren't such bad guys after all. I might actually enjoy this dinner.

ELEVEN

Luciana

STANDING off to the side of my bedroom window, I watched as Mom got into the back of the waiting car. The sleek sedan pulled out of the mansion's driveway and headed down the main road beyond.

I'd overheard her telling one of her underlings that she had "errands to run." No telling exactly what those were, but I figured it'd give me at least an hour before she returned. And in the middle of the morning, barely anyone else in the house was roaming around.

Which made it the perfect opportunity to carry out a little "errand" of my own.

I slunk down the hall to her office door, twirling a lock pick between my fingers. When I caught no hint of anyone stirring in the rooms nearby, I knelt down, retrieved the second pick from my pocket, and went to work on the lock.

Mom had seen that I was well-trained. The lock was a good one as standard deadbolts went, but that only meant it took me ten seconds rather than five to disengage it.

Stuffing the picks back in my jeans, I turned the knob carefully. Not that anyone other than Mom hung out in this room, and I knew she was gone.

Voices traveled up the stairs from the foyer. I froze and then leapt the rest of the way into the office. Holding my breath, I eased the door shut as quickly as I could while keeping the click of its closing quiet.

No footsteps mounted the stairs. I stood there with ears pricked through several nervous thuds of my heart and then exhaled in relief.

I turned toward the rest of the room, my gaze skimming over the antique furnishings and their neatly arranged contents. Mom was a big believer in "everything in its place."

Her laptop sat in the middle of the elegant desk. She'd even left it open.

With a giddy skip of my pulse, I hurried over and rested my hands on the keyboard. My tap to wake up the screen brought with it a password window.

Shit.

I grimaced at the screen and made a couple of attempts—her birthdate, my name. But Mom was smarter than that. And also not particularly sentimental, as I was well aware.

The chances of me guessing her password before I got locked out and revealed my treachery were pretty much nil. With a sigh, I moved away from the computer.

The desk offered plenty of other opportunities to dig up some kind of evidence of Mom's plans that I might be able to use for additional leverage. I peeked through the few papers she'd left in a tidy stack at one corner and then tugged open each of the drawers in turn.

I found business receipts and contracts, financial statements and random notes, but nothing that looked like it related to her intended attack on some of her Devil's Dozen colleagues. But then, anything to do with that she'd presumably want to keep extra hidden.

I tapped on the back of the drawers in turn and couldn't suppress a grin when one wobbled a little. When I curled my fingertips over the edge, I was able to tug open a narrow hidden compartment that held a few more pieces of paper.

The first thing I pulled out was a piece of printer paper, folded once, with a list of names of what appeared to be companies: *East Marling Electronics. Fletcher and Co. Pawn Shop. Terry's Boutique.*

Next to each company name, Mom had added brief notes in red ink. *Weak security system. Manager gambles.* That sort of thing.

A list of vulnerabilities. She could be evaluating our own business ventures, but I didn't recognize any of the names.

I pulled out my phone and snapped a picture of the list so I could search for those companies later and see if I could figure out why they mattered to her.

As I fished behind the hidden compartment again, my fingers snagged on a more tightly folded paper. Easing it out, I discovered it was a map of the United States.

Sections of various states were circled in a few different colors. I wasn't sure what most of them represented, but I couldn't help noticing that a significant portion of Massachusetts including Boston had been marked off.

That territory belonged to the Harvester. Was she

visualizing which pieces of the country she hoped to gain in her takeover, or was it just a coincidence?

I wasn't taking any chances. I snapped several photos of the map as well, a couple of the whole thing and then more closer up on different areas.

I was so intent on my documentation that the sound of footsteps didn't filter through my concentration until they were right outside the office door. My head jerked up with a jolt of panic.

My mother's voice carried to my ears, making my panic spike even higher. "You'd better tell Damien that I expect him to come to *me* next time, or he isn't going to have any fingers left to keep doing his work."

She must have been talking to one of her underlings. She'd come back early—someone she'd meant to meet had stood her up?

I didn't have time to wonder. As I shoved my findings back in the drawer as quickly as I could manage, keys clinked on the other side of the door. Fuck, fuck, fuck.

One of those keys rasped into the hole. I nudged the drawer closed and flung myself across the room toward the nearest viable shelter: a big potted fern spaced just far enough from the window that I could crouch down and squeeze between the wide clay pot and the ledge.

I'd only just ducked into place when the door swung open.

"Stupid prick making me wait around for nothing," Mom muttered as she came in. "He won't be doing *that* again."

I could only imagine what horrible punishments she was devising in her head. My stomach knotted.

Please let her only be coming in to grab something before she took off again. If she stuck around and got down to work... Every passing second would mean another moment when she could unleash that anger on me.

Mom sank into her chair behind the desk. To my relief, I heard no sign that she'd noticed anything awry so far.

With a rustle, she withdrew her phone from her purse. She sighed and leaned back in her chair, making the wheels squeak faintly.

Whoever she'd called must have answered quickly. The tension smoothed from her voice, leaving it coolly nonchalant.

"Hello. I thought it was about time we touched base. I've narrowed down the list, and we shouldn't wait too long to get the ball rolling."

The list? Rolling the ball?

My pulse hitched. Was she talking to one of her co-conspirators? If she was going to say something incriminating, I needed proof.

Ever so carefully, I slid out my own phone and tapped the screen to start it recording.

Another squeak told me Mom had stood up. As she listened to the person on the other end, she paced behind her desk, her stilettos clicking on the polished hardwood.

Then, to my horror, she came around the desk and strolled across the rug toward the window.

"Oh, don't worry about that," she said languidly. "My people know how to keep their heads down when necessary. I'm sure yours can be circumspect as well."

Her scarlet fingernails dug into the curtain close enough to my hiding place that I spotted them through the fern's fronds. I held my body even more rigid as she yanked the fabric aside.

Starker sunlight streaked into the room. My mouth went dry. If she took even one more step and glanced down—

She stood, staring out the window, for a few seconds longer, and then turned on her heel to face the desk again.

"Oh, the others are smart, but they're not as sharp as they think they are. They've gotten complacent. It'll never occur to them to suspect anything like this until it's too late."

With every comment she added, I was increasingly sure this conversation was about her backstabbing scheme. I tipped my phone in her direction in the hopes that it would pick up her voice better, wishing I could hear the other side of the conversation too. Which of the other Devil's Dozen members was she talking to?

"Yes, I think that could be good to begin with, as we discussed before. The south end, around the square. What time do you think would give us the best balance of crowd cover and minimal witnesses?"

As she paused to take in the answer, I rubbed my free hand over the muscles in my thigh, which were starting to burn. I had plenty of muscle power and endurance, but this crouch wasn't a position I'd ever needed to hold in my figure skating practice.

The floorboards gave a soft creak under Mom's pacing feet. "Yes, and the water is a good option too. We'll put something in it—that'll do the trick. But not right in the Rosewood. We're better off going for a more discreet route."

Papers crinkled on her desk. Then she ambled back toward me. A cold sweat broke out down my back.

"That'll be fine. Let's get this done as quickly and quietly as possible. You know what your part is."

She whisked past me. If she'd glanced sideways, I'd have been a goner, but before I could do more than clench my jaw, she'd swung toward the door again.

Mom tucked away her phone and headed out of the office.

The second the door thumped shut in her wake, my shoulders sagged. I exhaled in a long but still cautiously quiet rush and stopped recording.

I wasn't home free yet. For all I knew, she'd just gone to grab a snack or convey a few orders and then she'd be back. I couldn't risk emerging until I was sure she wouldn't be close enough to see me.

I waited one minute, and another, straining my ears for her voice. When I heard it again, it was through the windowpane.

She was out front, giving orders to a couple of the sentries. Nowhere near the second-floor hallway. I had to get the fuck out of here before that changed again.

I had no idea what any of the things I'd overheard meant, but I could worry about that when my head wasn't on the line.

I squirmed out from behind the pot and dashed for the door. With my hand on the knob, I pressed my ear close and listened to make sure the coast was clear before yanking it open.

But, just my luck, as I eased it closed behind me, a voice traveled from the far end of the hall.

"What are you up to, señorita?"

I spun around to see one of Mom's higher-level lackeys leaning in a doorway several feet away. Shit.

Octavio pushed himself straighter and prowled closer, arching his pierced eyebrow at me. The twin gold spikes glinted against his darker brown skin. His dark hair fell raggedly to his chin, adding to his general air of menace. "You're not supposed to be in there."

I put on my best don't-fuck-with-me face, my eyes narrowing and my lips pursing. For the first time in my life, I hoped I resembled Mom.

"I think that's up to my mother, don't you?" I retorted. "I was grabbing something she asked me to get for a job she wants me to do, not that it's any of your business."

He made a scoffing sound. "Oh, yeah. And what is this thing you needed so badly, huh?"

I raised my chin at a haughty angle. "Did you miss the part where it's none of your business? If she wanted you in on it, I'm sure she'd have told you."

A spark of anger lit in Octavio's eyes. I was rubbing my higher position thanks to my familial ties in his face, and he didn't like that at all. The guy had been working for Mom for as long as I could remember, so I supposed I couldn't blame him for seeing me as a bit of an upstart.

But all he needed to believe was that he'd better not question his boss about how she handled her own daughter. Not when he couldn't be sure whether I was lying.

"She tells me plenty, pequeña rosa," he growled. "Pretty soon you're going to find out that you can't just bounce in and out of here whenever you want. It takes commitment to keep an operation like this running, and as far as I've seen, you've got nada."

I gave him a hard look in response. "As long as my mother's happy with my 'commitment,' somehow I don't care what you think. Unless you'd like me to mention your concerns to her?"

His mouth tightened, but he took a wary step back. "Just keep it in mind."

With one last glower, he stalked away.

I hurried back to my bedroom, my stomach twisted painfully tight. As long as he didn't call my bluff, I'd be fine.

He hated me because he wished he was in my place. Dios mío, I wished he was too. Let my mom pass on the torch to him instead of me, and we'd all be happier.

Somehow I didn't think he'd ever believe that. And that made him my enemy.

TWELVE

Niko

THERE WAS nothing I enjoyed more than seeing my two skaters whirl across the rink, hitting their marks with the same precision they had at Finals even though they'd been short on practice in the last few weeks. It was pretty amazing that I even *had* two skaters I could consider "mine."

But as I watched them from my spot near the boards, two worries nagged at me, dampening my spirits.

One was the unanswerable question of whether Jasper and Lou would be able to compete at the National Championships at all. We still had more than a month to go, but we hadn't made any definite progress in dragging Lou out from under her mother's thumb yet.

That didn't matter, of course. Whatever practice time she could make it out to this rundown rink for, we had to use as if we were sure we needed the preparation.

The other worry had to do with what I was seeing in front of me. Yes, my skaters were going through the motions, but something was missing. The soul-stirring emotion they'd provoked with this routine wasn't hitting me the same way, and I didn't think it was only because I was familiar with it. I'd seen it plenty of times before Finals too, and it'd brought tears to my eyes then.

No, Jasper and Lou weren't totally connecting with the material the way they had before. Which was probably understandable, given the tensions hanging over them as well.

It was my job to bring them back into harmony with the music and the movements.

After they'd struck the ending pose for the free skate program, I went over to join them. "Your rhythm and positioning is excellent, both of you. But I can tell you're a little distracted. Not your fault, obviously, but there's a little trick I'd like you to try out."

Jasper lifted his eyebrows in a typical skeptical expression, softened by his crooked smile. "A trick?"

I grinned back at him. "Just a little something that I've found helps me—how would you say it? Get into the groove?"

Lou rubbed her hands together in anticipation, always ready for a challenge. "Lay it on us!"

I tipped my head toward the speakers I'd set up on the boards. "When you go through the routine again, I'd like you to sing along with the lyrics, as much as you can."

Jasper's eyebrows shot even higher. "You want us to *sing*? We're figure skaters, not a band. Shouldn't we be saving our breath for the moves?"

I shrugged, still smiling. "I don't mind if you take it a little easy and adjust to fewer rotations. And you don't even need to use the right words, just make some kind of sound that matches the melody. The point is to get yourself fully in sync with the music and the emotion it's trying to convey."

Lou rolled her shoulders. "I've never been much of a singer, but I'll give it a shot." She elbowed Jasper. "Come on, it could be fun."

Jasper gave her a teasing glower. "You have strange ideas of fun, Punk."

Lou laughed and tugged him over to their starting position. I could tell from the loosening of his stance that he was going to give my suggestion a fair try too.

After I'd started their song playing again, my gaze wandered briefly to the other end of the rink. Quentin had claimed about a quarter of it for his own use. The last time I'd checked in on him, he'd been attempting a swift donut spin. It appeared he was still at it, his leg wobbling a bit before he managed to get it into its arcing position.

When he straightened up again, a dark scowl clouded his expression. I couldn't suppress a twinge of sympathy. It had to be hard for him, coming out here to Austin to help Lou while leaving his coach back in Boston, trying to train without professional guidance.

I'd have stepped in as well as I could, but he'd brushed off most of my overtures—and I had to admit that I wasn't sure I'd really do him more good than harm. I was new to this whole coaching thing, and I'd never really studied his skills on the ice before. I could advise Jasper and Lou from a position of familiarity. I didn't have anything close to that with Quentin, and he didn't have time for me to learn everything I'd need to in order to be really useful.

He shot a puzzled stare at Lou and Jasper when they took off across the ice, their voices wavering alongside the vocalist in the song. Their singing might not be the most in-tune I'd ever heard, but the eager gleam that was lighting in their eyes and the passion flowing through their limbs was all that mattered.

Partway through the routine, they ran out of breath and their voices fell away. But they swept into their final lift with the same vivid emotion that had captivated the audience at Finals. My cheeks ached with the stretch of my smile.

We weren't beaten yet, no matter what Lou's mother had to say about it.

Lou glided over to me, her whole face lit up. "That felt amazing!"

Jasper trailed behind her, rubbing the back of his neck, but I could tell from the pleased flush in his cheeks that he'd felt the difference too. "As long as we aren't doing that when we have an audience," he muttered.

Quentin took the opportunity to skate closer to the center of the rink where he could take a longer lead-up. He pushed himself into the spin again, whipping his leg up and around while curving his back.

It looked perfect to me this time, but clearly something about the attempt still failed to meet his exacting standards. With a curse, he jerked himself out of the pose. Without a word to us, he marched off the ice, yanked off his skates, and stomped off to the locker rooms.

Jasper frowned, watching him go. "Not so cool and cocky now."

His tone was wry but not really critical. I still felt the need to say, "He is kind of on his own here."

Lou let out a huff. "It's his own fault. I didn't ask him to make this big sacrifice in his career to follow me out here." She paused. "I mean, I'm not hoping he fails, but I wouldn't want him thinking that I owe him something when it was his decision."

I gave her shoulder a reassuring squeeze. "And he shouldn't think that. His past behavior hasn't exactly made it easy for you to, ah, appreciate his presence." My smile returned. "Speaking of appreciation, how about that singing technique? You two looked like you really got into it—it definitely showed in your performance."

Lou grinned. "Really? It did feel pretty good even if it was kind of embarrassing at the same time."

"You've still got the right spark," I said, directing the words at both her and Jasper. "I can see everything in you that made your performance at Finals amazing. Hold on to that, and you'll be golden at Nationals."

Jasper made a dismissive sound, but his eyes glinted playfully. "I guess eventually I'm going to have to learn to stop questioning your ridiculous advice, huh?"

I wagged a finger at him. "Because it's not ridiculous at all."

He laughed. "Only you could make stuff like this sound like a reasonable technique."

Shifting forward, he leaned in with his head lowering toward mine. I felt the kiss coming, and my pulse hiccupped—but not just in anticipation.

Before I had a chance to think about what I was doing, I pulled back a step. Jasper froze, his fond expression fading into uncertainty.

My stomach twisted, but I didn't know what to say. We'd just been talking about the sacrifices Quentin had made—what about all the opportunities Jasper had given up and was setting himself up to lose? Some of them were for Lou… but some were because of me.

I'd shoved myself into his life without really worrying

about the consequences, hadn't I? And look where we'd ended up. The dreariness of the dim arena weighed down on me.

Jasper ducked his head and then looked up at me again, his forehead furrowed and his jaw tight. He looked so much like the frustrated guy he'd been during our first weeks of training that my gut twisted.

"What's going on?" he said, his voice gone rough. "You keep avoiding getting much into anything… physical. If you've decided you don't actually want that kind of relationship with me—"

My stomach lurched. "No, it's nothing like that. I do." More than I felt comfortable saying.

Jasper eyed me warily. "Then what is it? Because something's obviously wrong."

I fumbled for the words. "I just—I've been thinking about how we got started. I came all the way from Japan and badgered you into letting me coach you. But that—all of this—should be your choice."

Confusion still darkened Jasper's eyes. "It is. I thought I made that pretty clear. Why would you be worrying about it?"

Lou was watching me too. An ache expanded inside my chest at the thought of my deepest reasons. Reasons I'd rather not have admitted to with two people I'd come to care about so much.

But the feelings and trust we shared were exactly why I had to be honest with them.

My gaze darted away for a second before I wrenched it back to Jasper. "I've made… mistakes in the past. When it comes to my relationships."

Lou knit her brow. "What do you mean?" she asked softly.

Guilt soured my mouth. "A few years ago, I was dating a man I met in Japan. He wasn't a skater—not in the public eye at all. We'd gotten along really well, and I thought it could lead somewhere… But I've been out since I was a teenager, dealing with the judgments and the prejudice. I was so used to brushing it off like it didn't matter."

I paused, cringing inwardly at the memory, and forced myself to keep going. "*He* wasn't out, not even to his family. And during an interview on live TV, one of the hosts asked me about my romantic life, and I just said his name, automatically. Only good things, obviously, but there was no taking it back. His relatives, his friends, his employer and colleagues—I don't know how many of them ended up finding out, but they all could have, and he was horrified. And furious with me. To say the relationship ended badly is putting it mildly."

Thinking back to the flippant way I'd tossed out his name—with the arrogant assumption that if I could handle living this long in the spotlight with people knowing, it couldn't be that big a deal—left me queasy.

"Oh, shit," Jasper murmured.

My voice faltered. "His parents heard. They disowned him, shut him completely out of their lives. I screwed up his life with one stupid comment… He said I was selfish, that I only thought about myself, about looking progressive for my fans and making controversy—not caring how it affected anyone around me. And I can't say he was wrong."

Lou grasped my arm, her eyes wide. "It was an accident. Of course you wouldn't have done it on purpose."

I smiled wanly. "I didn't mean to hurt him, but I did it

anyway because I wasn't thinking outside of my own perspective. I didn't consider the fact that he had a life beyond me with consequences I wasn't used to."

I shifted my gaze back to Jasper. "So it's really important to me that I don't get too caught up in my interests ahead of someone else's again. The last thing I'd want is for you to have felt pressured to go along with… any of this. The coaching, our relationship…"

For a moment, Jasper simply stared at me. Then a chuckle I wasn't expecting at all tumbled from his mouth.

"I get why you'd be worried after what happened before. But come on, Niko. Have I *ever* had a problem telling you when your approach was getting on my nerves?"

My lips twitched with the start of a warmer smile. "No, I guess you did let that inner grump out pretty often."

Jasper shook his head in amusement. "It was opening up about the fact that I did want to pursue something more with you that I had trouble with. I wouldn't have let myself admit it if I wasn't *one hundred percent* sure I want this, totally of my own accord, because it makes me happy."

I rolled that thought around in my mind. "I suppose you might have a point. But once the press finds out about our relationship—it's bound to happen eventually when we're together so much—"

He snorted and slung his arm around me, tugging me close. I couldn't help melting a little into the warmth of his solid frame.

"Fuck the press," he said with a hint of a growl that sent a shiver of electricity over my skin. "They can think what they want, and so can my family and anyone else who decides to have an opinion about it. The two of us—or, well, the four of us I should probably say—have something good, don't we? That's all that matters."

"Hear, hear," Lou put in, raising her hand as if offering a glass in a toast and beaming at us.

I found myself grinning back at the two of them, my spirits abruptly lightened. "That is what matters the most. And we do have something good—something *very* good. I'd imagine even Rafael would have to agree with that."

I hugged Jasper tight with one arm and drew Lou in with the other, tugging them together into a joint embrace. As Lou pecked my cheek and Jasper leaned his head against mine with a pleased hum, my heart swelled with joy.

This time, it seemed I'd done something right. Now if only I could free Lou from the shadows of her past, we could really get somewhere.

THIRTEEN

Luciana

THE PRACTICES I snuck away to were the only bright spots in my days. When I drove down the street toward the Cordova mansion after my latest skating session, my spirits still felt light from soaring across the ice with my men around me.

But as I pulled through the gate, all my remaining peace dissolved at the sight of a small army of Deadly Rose goons filing into a row of matte black SUVs.

Heart sinking, I parked in my usual spot in the garage and hustled back out to where Mom was standing by the front steps, overseeing the crowd. "What's going on?"

Mom motioned a few more men into one of the vehicles. In the wan light of the security lamps cutting through the dusk, her face looked tight. She smiled when she saw me, but there wasn't a particle of warmth in the expression.

"Oh, good, just who I was waiting for. You have work to do."

That was news to me. I searched my mind briefly for any memory of Mom telling me she had a task for me tonight and came up with nada. But telling her that wasn't a wise idea.

I crossed my arms over my chest in the sort of resolute pose she'd have encouraged me to take in front of our underlings. "What do you want me to do?"

It was an awful lot of underlings for the sort of jobs she'd sent me on before. I didn't think we needed two dozen guys to guard me at a meeting. Although I guessed that depended on who I was meeting.

Mom's smile only sharpened. "It's time I confirmed that you can handle yourself in action as well as in conversation. The Deadly Rose needs to crack down hard —one of our subordinate gangs tried to double-cross our people in a deal."

A chill flooded my chest. "And you want me to go with the guys?"

Mom's gaze pinned me in place. "I expect you to *lead* them. Take charge, direct the battle, make sure we come out on top. With an enemy this pathetic, it shouldn't be much trouble for you. A good starting place for building respect."

Without another word, she pushed a gun into my hand. I closed my fingers around it reluctantly, my throat constricting.

I knew nothing good could come from arguing with her, but charging off into a gang fight was the last thing I wanted to do. The violence and bloodshed was the part of the criminal life I'd always hated the most.

How could I say no? The second I defied her, especially in front of her underlings, she'd be sending a bunch of them to track *my* men down and deal out her sick brand of justice.

And they were even nearer at hand than she realized. It was a good thing my men had been holding on to my equipment bag and training clothes for me, so there was no hint of where I'd been to tip her off. God, if she found out that I'd been meeting up with them behind her back…

The fresh wave of icy fear propelled me into action. "Of course. I'll get the job done."

It was only criminals I'd be ordering our people to mow down, not innocents.

It could be worse.

Mom looked me up and down with penetrating eyes and then waved me toward the SUV at the head of the line. "Octavio will fill you in on the details and act as your second in command. I want to hear all about your victory when you get back."

Well, now it was definitely worse. I forced myself to stride over to the vehicle, where the man who'd hassled me after I'd searched Mom's office was watching me with a glower. He ducked into the back seat as I reached him and only let his lip curl into a hint of a sneer when he was out of my mom's sight.

"The *pequeña rosa* is in charge tonight, huh?" he said as I climbed in after him. "You got your brilliant plans all worked out?"

I narrowed my eyes at him. "I believe in hearing what we're up against *before* I start planning, if that's okay with you, *hombrecito*."

The dig did its duty. His full lips pinched together, the glint of his piercing flashing as his eyebrows dipped down. But he could say nothing. I was right, and he knew it.

The driver up front turned the key, and the engine roared to life. My heart thumped with a sickly erratic beat as the SUV headed onto the road.

Octavio swiped his hands together impatiently. "Listen up then. We're laying down the law with the Anacondas. They run things out of an old low-rise apartment building that was condemned a few years back but never torn down. The thing has four stories with a fire escape along the left side, leading to hall windows on each floor. There are three regular entrances on the ground: front, back, and right."

I nodded, picturing the layout as well as I could in my head. "Got it."

"Good. Most of those pendejos will probably be hanging out inside. The Anacondas don't do a whole lot of business, which I guess is why they got grabby and stupid. We can expect they'll have three or four people hanging around outside the building keeping watch, maybe a few more since they probably realize we're pissed. But we left it a couple of days so they'd start to get complacent. Now it's time to carve a message for the rest of the city in their blood."

I tuned out the churning of my stomach. "Got to make an example of them." My fingers tightened around the grip of the pistol.

Chances were I was going to have to fire the weapon tonight. I might very well need to kill someone myself. Why had these idiots decided to try and screw over Mom *now* of all times?

Octavio was studying me. "So you got a plan or

what?"

If I faltered, he'd report it back to Mom. Hell, he'd probably give as scathing account as he could get away with no matter what I did. I couldn't leave any openings for him to criticize me.

This part of life under the Deadly Rose might make me nauseous, but Mom had roped me into enough discussions and past assaults for me to have a decent idea of how she'd have handled the assault. What I needed to consider. How to maximize their casualties while minimizing ours.

I could at least make sure as few of the men I was leading died as possible.

Not letting Octavio rush me into a careless decision, I spoke firmly and steadily. "We want to give the enemy as little time to prepare as possible. All the cars race in around the building at once—shoot the guards on sight. We enter through every available entrance including several guys going up the fire escape and smashing through the windows. All our force, all at once, before they even realize what's happening."

"The fire escape?" Octavio said with undisguised skepticism. "It's not like they'll have the ladder lowered for us."

I shot him a sideways glance. "I know. Park one of the vans right under it. Not that hard to hop from the hood to the roof and up, right?"

Octavio's silent scowl suggested he was pissed off that he couldn't find more to complain about in my suggestions. He shook his head with a sigh. "I hope you know what you're doing here."

"My mother seems to think I do," I retorted with an edge in my voice, reminding him of who had set this whole situation in motion. "Now are you going to relay the plan to the others or am I?"

He muttered something under his breath, but he got out his phone. In alternating English and Spanish, he conveyed my instructions to people in all of the cars.

I sank back in the leather seat, keeping my face composed in a mask of disinterest. Just another night, just another gang shootout.

Just another urge to vomit.

I wished I could close my eyes and completely shut out the horrible scenario I'd found myself in for a minute, but Octavio would take that as weakness. So I trained my gaze straight ahead and clamped down on my queasiness and flickers of panic as well as I could.

If this is what it took to protect those I loved, then I had to follow through. I wasn't letting down the men who'd done so much for me over a weak stomach.

I just hoped Mom would be happy with only one test and this wasn't the first of many.

Before that thought could fill me with even more horror, the driver jerked the wheel. "Coming up on the building," he said. "Just a few blocks away."

Octavio looked at me. "We hit them all at once?" Like he was giving me the chance to reconsider.

I stared right back at him. "The plan hasn't changed. Let's do this."

The driver pressed on the gas, and the SUV hurtled forward. The engines of the other vehicles roared behind us. Octavio pulled out his gun and rested it on his thigh before pressing the button to roll down the window.

The next several seconds passed in a frenetic blur. The driver whipped the SUV up onto the sidewalk and parked it with a jerk. Octavio was already firing through the window, other shots blaring as the rest of our army targeted the outside guards.

Through the open window, I watched two men near the brick building's front door jerk and crumple, bloody splotches dappling their shirts. The Deadly Rose force was already pouring out of the vehicles and charging toward the building.

Octavio heaved open the door, and all I could do was follow him. I wouldn't earn the respect Mom wanted by huddling in the backseat like a coward.

I was sending these men into the fight to their possible deaths. I'd damn well better have the guts to stand with them.

As I dashed across the sidewalk, a man ahead of me rammed his shoulder into the door. It burst open, and he headed inside, more shots ringing out. I lifted my pistol instinctively, grimacing at how familiar the gesture felt, how easy it was to fall in line with my mother's expectations. With the past I'd wanted so badly to shed.

I sprang through the doorway after the handful of men who'd taken that entrance. Shouts and footsteps were thundering from all around as the rest carried out my strategy to surround and overwhelm the building's inhabitants.

A man in a sweat-stained tee lunged out of a doorway with a knife. My hand jerked around; I blew a hole in his forehead before he could stab the blade at my chest.

As he toppled over, a shudder ran through me. I blanked my mind against the revulsion and pushed myself onward.

My ears rang with the booming of the gunshots. I moved from room to room, checking that any Anacondas in the place had been taken down.

Several other bodies lay sprawled across the floor. I didn't recognize any of them, and they were dressed shabbier than Mom would have tolerated. It looked like my army had cleared at least the first floor of opposition without any of our own falling.

I was just coming up on a kitchen at the back of the building when a skinny woman sprang at me, her fingers clawing at my face. My finger squeezed the trigger before I'd even processed that she wasn't holding a weapon.

Her head snapped backward with the close-range shot. Blood splattered the walls—and my face and shirt.

"Fuck. *Fuck.*" Bile rose up my throat, and I just barely swallowed it down.

Her body slumped lifeless on the floor. Had she been part of the gang or just a sort of groupie? Or even a customer partaking of whatever goods they sold?

Too late for that to matter now.

But Dios mío, this was not where I wanted to be. Not *who* I wanted to be. Who the fuck was I to decide who lived or died—to blast their lives away over petty squabbles?

I was supposed to be on the ice, conveying beauty and emotion for an audience, making them dream of things they hadn't imagined possible. Instead I'd been dragged into hell.

And now I was an instrument of that hell, this sick system that revolved around the most violent competition, all over again.

The kitchen beyond my latest attacker was empty. Nothing after it but the back door the Deadly Rose men had bashed down.

"First floor's clear!" I hollered out, my voice sounding distant to my ears.

A waft of cool night air washed over me from the open doorway. The shots were already slowing above me. They didn't need my leadership to finish this massacre, did they?

I drifted outside, taking a few steps into the shadows of the parking lot there. My head spun. I gulped a deep breath of the fresh air, wincing at the sticky patches of blood cooling on my skin—and two figures solidified on either side of me.

"What do we have here?" a hostile voice snarled.

They must have been Anaconda members who'd just arrived from someplace else. I whipped around, yanking my hand up, but I couldn't shoot both of them when they were in opposite directions.

I moved too slow in my uncertainty. One of my attackers hurled a fist at me. I dodged, but his knuckles caught my wrist, making me lose my grip on the gun.

I ducked and snatched after it—and a sudden thump sounded just a few feet away. Massive arms whipped forward to snatch one guy's head and shatter his spine with a wrench of his neck.

My fingers caught on the pistol. I jerked it up in time to put a bullet in the second guy's chest, just as the new arrival jabbed a knife into his throat.

I swung around to face off with this new figure, and the bottom of my stomach dropped out. The massive man's face was shadowed by the hood of his sweatshirt, but I'd have known him anywhere regardless.

"Rafael!" I hissed. "What the hell are you doing here?"

He frowned, pitching his own voice low. "I've been keeping an eye on you, like always. You think I'm going to let your mother just send you wherever? I couldn't let those pricks get the upper hand."

I wanted to protest that I could have handled myself,

but I wasn't totally sure that was true, not when I felt so out of sorts. This slaughter was nothing like the operations I'd carried out of my own accord for my own purposes.

What would Niko and Jasper have thought if they'd seen this? Oh, God…

I yanked my mind back to the present and the one thing I did know. "You shouldn't have risked it! If any of Mom's people see you, if she finds out you followed me here and you're trying to help me, it's a death sentence."

Rafael's gaze seared into mine. Then, before I could react, he dragged me into a tight embrace.

"It's worth the risk," he murmured, insistent but strained. "It's always going to be fucking worth it to make sure you're safe. Lou… I love you. You know that, don't you?"

I shouldn't have been capable of the glow of happiness that lit in my chest. He'd never said that before, not in the actual words.

My throat choked up, and my legs wobbled beneath me. I'd never said it to him either.

I pushed myself back so I could meet his eyes. "Good. Because I love you too. And that's why you need to get out of here before anyone else sees you."

Rafael gave a curt nod with obvious reluctance. He hurried off into the darkness. With an ache in my heart, I let myself watch him go for just a second before I turned back to the site of the battle.

The guns had fallen completely silent. I'd only made it halfway down the first-floor hall when most of our men trooped down the stairs to join me.

A few of them held up bulging bags. "Got some loot to bring back too. Might as well take what we can, right?"

"Yeah," I said. "Waste not, want not." It wasn't as if

stealing was worse than what we'd already done to these people. None of the corpses around us would have any use for their stash now.

Octavio appeared among the others, blood streaked across his cheek but otherwise the same as he'd looked in the car. "Every Anaconda in the place is down. I think we've made a clear statement about betraying the Deadly Rose."

I forced a stiff smile. "Then we're done here. Let's clear out before we have to deal with cops too."

The drive home felt like it took a million years. When the SUV parked outside the mansion, I peeled myself out of the back seat to find Mom waiting on the front walk, her eyes gleaming. Octavio had already called her to let her know how the raid had gone down.

She patted my shoulder with a smile that might have actually been genuine. "Good work, Luciana. I knew I could count on you. You really made a statement, both for our people and our enemies."

"I did my best," I managed to say, and motioned vaguely to my bloody shirt. "I think I'd better go get cleaned up."

"By all means. Then we'll have to enjoy a victory drink."

I trudged upstairs and swayed for a second before I managed to direct my body into my en-suite bathroom. The sight of myself in the mirror, hair mussed and face dappled crimson, brought back a surge of disgust and shame.

I looked like I'd orchestrated a bloodbath… because I had.

I couldn't squirm out of my clothes fast enough. After

turning the shower as hot as I could stand, I stepped into the scalding spray and let it stream over me.

No matter how much I scrubbed my skin, I couldn't wash away the dirty sensation. I was soiled all the way down to my soul.

Mom was happy with my performance today. She said this was the *start* of proving myself.

What the hell was she going to ask me to do next?

I closed my eyes and leaned against the tiled wall, suppressing a sob. I couldn't keep doing this—I couldn't be what she wanted. Trying to meet her demands was killing *me*.

Finally, I shut off the water and pulled a towel around me. Back in my bedroom, I stared blankly at my closet without any ability to care about what clothes I put on.

My gaze fell on the purse I'd brought to my brunch with the Storm. The one I'd tucked Beckett's card into after he'd told me I should let him know if I could use his help.

Was there anything he *could* do for me? I couldn't be sure. But it was possible… and he might know how to reach out to the Blood Hunter too.

I knew that Mom saw them both as her opponents. The enemies of my greatest enemy should be my friends, right? At the very least, they might be able to help me gather more evidence so I'd have enough leverage to break out of her hold for good.

Even if it was a small chance, it was better than no chance at all.

I crossed the room to the chair where I'd left the purse and groped inside it for the card. Then I sat down on my bed with the burner phone I'd picked up to communicate with my men, staring at the number printed on the smooth cardstock.

Taking a deep breath, I punched in the digits and brought the phone to my ear.

FOURTEEN

Luciana

BY THE END OF PRACTICE, my muscles were burning in that familiar way I loved, but the sensation wasn't quite enough to wipe away the anxious tension that'd gripped me all day. I sat down on the bench and tugged my laces loose, unable to contain a sigh.

Jasper dropped down next to me, his forehead furrowed with obvious concern. "Are you doing okay? You've seemed a little out of it. I mean, your skating was great, but whenever we took a breather…"

I knew what he meant. It'd taken all my will power to stay focused when we launched into the moves of our routines. Any moment when I hadn't had that immediate goal in front of me, my thoughts had scattered.

I grimaced. "It's just getting to me, being back in that house. Being around my mom. I never know what she's going to ask of me next."

I couldn't tell him everything. I didn't want him to think of me blasting away desperate attackers in some rundown apartment building. As far as I could tell, Rafael hadn't mentioned anything to the other guys about the raid I'd led, and I'd rather they never knew.

I'd rather *I* never had to think about it again. In the back of my head, the memories of the jerking figures, the splatters of crimson, and the feel of the blood drying on my skin kept playing, flaring up behind my eyes at random moments.

Next time, Mom might ask me to do something even worse. And I had no idea what, when, or where.

My skin crawled just thinking about it.

Niko leaned against the boards across from us, his mouth slanting into a sympathetic smile. "It's understandable that you'd be distracted. I can't even imagine what it's like for you being trapped in this situation."

I squared my shoulders. "I'll get through it. It helps a lot that I can escape out here to the arena and see all of you. Gives me something to look forward to."

My gaze flicked toward the one guy I wasn't totally counting in my "all"—Quentin, still gliding around the far end of the rink as he perfected one of his step sequences. Since confronting me and demanding recognition for his efforts in tracking me down, he'd given me plenty of space. I hadn't heard him heckle Jasper once. In fact, this morning I'd come in to see them exchanging comments that had left Jasper *chuckling*.

Maybe Quentin really was doing his best to shape up not just his skills but his attitude too. And he was letting me decide how I felt about his efforts rather than getting pushy about it.

As I watched, he finished the final bit of footwork and paused to swipe a few strands of his pale hair back from his forehead. His gaze caught mine. His lips twitched with a hint of a smile, like he wasn't quite sure it'd be welcome but wanted to offer it anyway.

I wasn't going to be a total bitch. I shot him a quick smile in return and then looked away.

Why the hell had my love life needed to get even more complicated at a time like this?

Jasper slung his arm around my shoulders in a brief but emphatic hug. "You should just focus on what you need to get through this mess. We understand that you can't be one hundred percent on the ball with everything that's going on."

His supportiveness brought a lump into my throat. I yanked off my skates and reached for the rag to wipe off the blades.

A ping pealed out of my bag—the text alert sound for my burner phone, not my regular one. My pulse hiccupped, and I snatched at the pocket.

There was only one person who had that number who wasn't here in the arena with me. What did the acting Storm have to say to me today?

I tapped through to see the full text he'd sent. *It looks like one of the Deadly Rose's people tried to gain unauthorized access to a property of mine. I'll be dealing with the immediate response on my end, but I thought the surveillance footage might be useful to you.*

Then there was a link. I clicked on it and found myself staring at a list of image and video files.

Proof. Solid proof of my mom messing with one of her Devil's Dozen colleagues. The corners of my mouth lifted along with my spirits.

"What's up?" Niko asked, coming into the stands. "Good news?"

"I think so. A little more leverage to add to the stash I'm building."

I couldn't use it against Mom until I was sure I had enough to stop her in her tracks and shield me and the guys for the rest of our lives, but every little bit got me closer to that goal.

As I tapped hastily at the touch screen, transferring the files to a cloud server I'd set up to save all my recordings and other evidence, Rafael strode down the stairs from the rink's doorway.

"Everything's been quiet outside," he reported. "No sign of anyone having followed you or sniffing around."

I stuffed my phone back into my bag and let out my breath with a sensation of relief I knew wouldn't last—but that I'd treasure while I could. "Good. The one upside to Mom being busy planning a massive takeover is she doesn't have a huge amount of time to notice every time I leave the house."

Jasper glanced at the other two guys and then at me, a smile that looked a little sheepish crossing his face. "Speaking of that... Do you think you could get away with staying gone a little longer? I was thinking we could just go out and grab a coffee or something."

I blinked at him. "A coffee?"

His gray-green gaze held mine, so hopeful despite the careful way he was phrasing the question that it tugged at my heart. "I know you have to play it safe and there isn't much time for anything other than practice. But it'd be great to even have an almost-date, just the four of us hanging out like we used to..."

The lump that'd formed in my throat before expanded

enough to momentarily choke off my words. I swallowed hard, wrenched by the recognition of how much I missed being surrounded by my men all the time. Sharing meals with them, watching TV with them, cuddling up on the sofa or in bed…

All the little pieces a relationship was made up of—the pieces we'd lost the moment my mom had dragged me back to Austin.

And she was ruining even this. Because I had to say, my voice gone rough, "I don't know if that would be a good idea. Risking being seen together anywhere at all public…"

But I needed him to know how much I missed him. How much I still wanted him.

Rather than trying to continue in words, I scooted closer on the bench and pulled Jasper into a kiss.

God, I'd missed all of this so much. I'd kissed him since we'd reunited in Austin—I had earlier today when I'd arrived for practice. But this time I threw myself whole-heartedly into the embrace as if there were no other demands weighing on me.

Jasper twined his fingers in my ponytail, tugging me even closer. As we both gave ourselves over to the kiss, his heat enveloped me. I wanted to melt right into him and never come up for air.

Except there were two other men I craved just as much. I let my lips linger against Jasper's for a few seconds longer, and then I pushed to my feet and grasped the front of Niko's shirt.

Niko beamed at me in the moment before our mouths collided. There was a sunny quality to his heat that was nothing like Jasper's but equally appealing. His deft fingers traced over my cheek while he tucked his other hand around to the small of my back.

I'd almost forgotten how well I fit against his slim but toned frame.

At a gruff clearing of a throat, I eased away from Niko to grin up at Rafael. "I'm not going to leave you out."

My bodyguard's eyes smoldered with a promise that left my skin tingling. "You'd better not, brat."

The low lilt he added to the teasing nickname had me drenching my panties. I hopped up on the bench above mine so we were practically the same height and threw my arms around his broad shoulders.

As he claimed my mouth, Rafael scooped me right off the bench. Enclosed in his brawny embrace, I felt invincible, untouchable. He couldn't really protect me from all of my mother's power, but I reveled in the impression anyway.

When he splayed his fingers across my ass, my pussy clenched. I kissed him with even more hunger, but every nerve in my body quivered with the knowledge that this wasn't enough.

I was going to take in everything my three men could give me. I'd had to deny myself too long as it was.

At the shift of my body, Rafael lowered me so I could stand. I teased my fingers down his solid chest and peeked at him through my eyelashes. "Secure the door and then come right back?"

His burgundy eyes outright blazed. He charged up the stairs two at a time, and I reached for the other two men.

Jasper and Niko watched me intently as I guided them back onto the rink rather than remain in the cramped stands. I tugged the down jacket Niko had been wearing off his shoulders, enjoying the quickening of his breath, and spread it out on the ice.

"Come here," I said, gripping their arms as I sank down on the makeshift cushion.

As he knelt next to me, Jasper drew me into another kiss. Niko settled at my other side and slipped his fingers up my back under my shirt. I hummed eagerly at their combined attentions, but the shape of another man drew my attention.

Quentin came to a stop several feet away from us, his posture rigid, his starkly blue eyes both scorching and uncertain. "I guess this is my cue to go?"

I paused, willing down the longing searing through my veins long enough to really consider the question.

I wasn't ready to invite Quentin *into* our little interlude. I didn't know if I'd even want to be kissing him again onc-on-one, let alone adding him to the hard-won cooperative understanding that'd formed between the three men I'd already fallen for... one of whom he'd been a total asshole to up until a few weeks ago.

But a flicker of a memory rose up—seeing him at the locker room door while I took Niko and Jasper, all of us drenched by the shower. How hot it'd been knowing he was watching us.

He'd insisted that he could handle sharing me. Why not find out just how much he'd actually meant that?

I arched an eyebrow at him. "That's up to you. You got off on watching before. Maybe you could learn something about what sharing really means."

His pale face flushed. He drifted over to the boards, and I thought he was going to storm off. But he stayed there, his gaze burning into me, as Rafael strode onto the ice to join us.

I shifted my attention back to the three men I intended to fully enjoy this stolen time with. None of them looked remotely concerned about our spectator—if anything, I caught a competitive gleam in Jasper's gaze.

Oh, he'd like to show Quentin just how much the other guy was missing, no doubt.

As our mouths crashed together again, I slid my hands beneath my partner's shirt over his sculpted abs. At the same moment, Niko unclasped my bra with typical deftness. He reached around to fondle my breasts. The swipe of his thumbs over my stiffening nipples had me gasping into Jasper's mouth.

Rafael shed his own jacket to add to our padding against the icy chill. He stroked his hands up my legs to my thighs, chuckling when I arched into his touch, urging him farther.

"You've gotta practice that patience, brat."

I grunted dismissively and leaned forward to capture his mouth. Behind me, I caught a hitch of breath as Jasper turned to Niko for a kiss of their own. Despite the cool air, heat wafted around us, leaving me burning for more.

I yanked at Rafael's shirt and took a moment to run my hands and my eyes over the expanse of muscle I'd uncovered. As he smirked and gripped the waistband of my leggings, I twisted to free my other two men from their clothes as well, unwrapping them like they were Christmas presents.

Niko laughed as garments went flying, skimming his fingers over my bare skin and Jasper's at the same time. Jasper couldn't seem to decide whether he wanted to be branding Niko's lips or the side of my neck more, so he switched back and forth between the two.

I had no complaints.

As I wriggled fully out of my leggings, Rafael leaned in to press a kiss to my naked belly. At my encouraging murmur, he dipped his head lower to lap his tongue over my cunt.

I moaned, bucking toward him, and my gaze veered across the rink. Somewhere in the middle of our making out, Quentin had vanished.

I guessed it'd been a little too much for him after all. Or maybe the thrill hadn't been quite the same when he'd gotten permission, and he'd only felt awkward about gawking.

I wasn't sure if I should be disappointed, but the swipe of Rafael's tongue over my clit sent a rush of pleasure through me that washed any thoughts of the man *not* with us right out of my head.

A cry broke from my throat, but my hands felt too empty. I groped out and found the rigid length of Jasper's erection straining against his boxers.

When I dragged the fabric down and wrapped my fingers around his scorching skin, my partner groaned. He rocked into my grasp, pinching my breast and then tipping his head back to welcome another kiss from Niko.

Niko was still playing with my other breast. I swayed between the three of them, lost in the bliss they were conjuring in my body, wishing this moment could last forever.

Rafael sucked hard on my clit, and more pleasure spiked inside me. I could feel myself teetering on the verge of my climax, but this wasn't how I wanted to come, not just yet.

I dragged myself over onto my knees and nudged Rafael backward. "Payback time," I murmured, and lowered my head over his rigid cock.

It was hard to fit my lips around his thick girth, but I took him as far as I could go. Rafael cursed under his breath and wound his fingers into my hair, pulling it free from the ponytail.

As I slicked my tongue around him, my other men didn't neglect me. Jasper followed, leaving a trail of kisses down my back as he fondled my breast. His hand delved between my legs to mimic the motions Rafael had been performing moments before with his mouth.

Then I heard the tear of foil, and Niko's lithe hands grasped my hips. He positioned himself behind me and slid right between my slick folds until my pussy was perfectly full.

I moaned over Rafael's cock and began to rock more emphatically between the two men. The clench of Rafael's hand in my hair and the playful smack Niko gave my ass urged me onward.

Jasper was still working over my clit, his fingertips brushing the spot where Niko had joined me. Niko let out a ragged breath and turned partly toward the other man.

"Straighten up on your knees."

As Jasper adjusted his position beside me, I curled my fingers around Rafael's erection in place of my mouth so I could glance over and see what our mischievous coach was up to.

The gleam in Niko's brown eyes was all desire. He kept up his same eager rhythm inside me, pushing deeper at just the right angle to make me gasp, and lowered his head to suck Jasper's cock into his mouth.

"Oh, fuck," Jasper mumbled. He braced his hand against my back, stroking his fingers back and forth, and clutched Niko's hair with his other hand.

Seeing the two of them enjoying each other as well as

me gave me the giddiest thrill I could have imagined. I bowed over Rafael again, determined to channel as much of the pleasure radiating through my body into him as I could.

Rafael's chest hitched, and his fingers tightened in my hair. He pulled on it with increasingly forceful tugs, spreading that blissful sort of pain through my scalp just the way he knew I liked it.

Niko thrust into me faster, hitting me at the perfect spot inside. I slammed back to meet him and drank in the panting of Jasper's breath beside us, the pleased sounds emanating from Niko's throat, the groan that reverberated from Rafael's chest.

Niko gave my ass another light slap that nearly tipped me over the edge. Then, still working over Jasper's cock with his mouth and pounding into my pussy with his cock, he delved one finger into the cleft between my ass cheeks. It circled my back opening and then eased inside.

Bliss flooded my body at the extra stimulation, and I moaned so hard Rafael jerked at the sensation from my mouth. With the movements of our bodies, the clothes beneath me shifted so one knee pressed into the frigid ice, but I didn't give a fuck. I was floating away on all this heady delight.

With one more press of Niko's finger, I came apart. My cry echoed off the high arena ceiling. Ecstasy swept through my nerves from every direction, casting me up and over like a tidal wave.

Even as I continued to shake with the pleasure of it, I clamped my mouth back around Rafael's cock. My hand slipped between his legs to cup his balls. Rafael shuddered.

"Lou," he growled in warning, but I didn't need it.

I sucked even harder, and his cum exploded into my mouth.

I drank it down greedily as if I'd been starving for it. Behind me, Niko bucked to his own release. His groan vibrated across Jasper's cock, and Jasper sputtered a curse as he followed us all over the edge.

With our limbs wobbly from the exertion and the impact of our orgasms, we collapsed together in a sweaty jumble on the pile of discarded clothes.

Niko stroked my hair and Jasper's simultaneously, his smile bright. "As much as I like working with both of you, I like playing even better."

Jasper let out a buoyant laugh. "And aren't we lucky that you're so good at both."

Rafael pressed a kiss to the top of my head. "*We're* lucky we had this stubborn woman to force us to get along."

I had to laugh too. "And here I was thinking I'm the lucky one."

Niko's hand drifted lower to trace the winged tattoo stretching across my shoulder blades. "We're here for you, Angel. Because of you. Because you're something special."

Jasper raised himself up on one elbow, catching my gaze. "Yeah. And don't you dare let your mom convince you of anything else."

My throat closed up again with a swell of emotion that was pure joy… and love.

This was where I wanted to be. Who I wanted to be with—always.

I'd told Rafael I loved him the other night without hesitation. It struck me now that I could have said it honestly to both of my skater men too.

The words itched in the base of my throat, but it didn't

feel like the right time. I didn't want there to be any chance that they'd think I was babbling in the haze of fantastic sex rather than meaning it with all my heart.

I couldn't let anything stop me from returning to them again so I'd have the chance to tell them just how much they meant to me.

FIFTEEN

Luciana

I ARRIVED BACK at the mansion in a better mood than usual, the thrill of my interlude with all three of my men still humming through my nerves. The muted sound of music and voices filtered through the windows as I pulled through the gate. A bunch of Mom's underlings were taking a little recreational time in the backyard, their laughter carrying on the breeze.

The night, for once, felt welcoming.

I parked the car in my usual spot and got out. A quick glance over my street clothes confirmed that I'd brought no trace of my extracurricular activities with me. My skating stuff was safely stashed at the men's apartment. No reason for anyone to suspect I'd been doing more than grabbing dinner or taking in the city's sights.

Then I stepped past the front door and found Mom waiting at the base of the broad staircase.

She took me in with a cool expression, her arms crossed over her pale business suit that contrasted sharply with her tan skin and dark hair. My stomach plummeted with the immediate awareness that she was pissed.

"Luciana, come to my office, now," she said in a clipped tone, and spun with the expectation that I'd hurry after her.

Octavio's scornful expression flashed in my mind. Had he told her that he'd caught me slipping out of her office the other day? Shit. I'd been banking on his ego not wanting to risk mistakenly accusing me, but he had been acting pretty hostile toward me. He might have decided it was worth the potential consequences to try to screw me over.

That fucking prick. As if I even *wanted* any authority over him.

I had to play it cool regardless. My heart thudding, I strode up the stairs after Mom. "What's this about? Has something urgent come up?"

Mom didn't say a word as she stalked ahead of me. All I could do was trot along behind her like the little dog she'd trained me to be.

My teeth gritted, but I forced myself to keep walking. Defying her before I even knew what was up was a surefire route to disaster.

She stepped to the side of the office doorway to let me walk in and jerked the door shut in my wake. I stood awkwardly in the middle of the room while she marched over to her desk.

Then she whirled to face me. "How long did you think you could keep this up before I caught on? You don't really think I'm an idiot, do you?"

I bristled even as my nerves jolted with a deeper panic. What the hell was she talking about?

"Of course not," I said quickly, reining in the urge to babble. "I don't even know what you—"

Mom cut me off with a scoffing sound. "Don't give me that mierda. I know you're still skating."

I stared at her, my voice dying in my throat. She didn't know that I'd been gathering evidence against her, looking to undermine her schemes. That would have been good if she hadn't instead stumbled on the one secret that could destroy not just me but the men I loved too.

My mouth opened and closed a few times before I found my words. By then, it was probably too late to put on a believable show, but I gave it my best bewildered tone anyway. "Skating? I only went out to—"

"No," she said sharply. "Enough lies. I know how you look after you've been at practice, that head-in-the-clouds expression you get. Nothing else ever affected you the same way. I noticed it a couple of days ago, so I put a tracking device on your car. And where did that tracking device point to after you left today? It stopped just a few blocks away from a skating arena and stayed there for three hours."

Dread wrapped icy fingers around my gut. I couldn't deny her accusations when she had that much proof. It wasn't like I could convince her I'd been doing something else in the drab neighborhood around the rink.

Had she already sent someone to find out whether I'd been skating *with* anyone else? To hurt the guys as my punishment?

Oh, hell, no.

There was nothing I could do to fix this. Now that she'd caught on, she'd never let me leave the house without tracing my movements. I'd be lucky if I even got a chance to warn Rafael and the skaters.

There was nothing I could do… except play the hand I'd already been building.

A flicker of starker fear shot through my chest at the thought. I'd hoped that I'd have more leverage before I revealed my cards.

I'd gathered quite a bit of proof, though. It was probably enough.

It'd better be, because there'd be no coming back from this gamble.

I lifted my chin and drew on all the anger and frustration that'd burned inside me since I'd watched her step out of her car in Boston. "All right. I've been skating. So what?"

It was Mom's turn to stare. Her eyes narrowed. "So what? I told you that you're done with skating. You don't have time for that ridiculous hobby. Your attention needs to be here."

"It's my life," I said firmly. "I love skating, and I wouldn't *want* to live if I couldn't do it anymore. So I don't see why you should get to decide that for me. I've done everything you've asked of me even while fitting my practices in—you wouldn't even have realized if it wasn't for me being *happy*. What do you have to complain about?"

Mom's lips pursed so tightly it was a wonder they hadn't turned white. I'd talked back to her now and then in the past, but only brief throwaway remarks. Never such blatant, insistent defiance.

It was like I'd blown a fuse in her brain. There was no telling how viciously she'd retaliate when she got over the shock, but I couldn't back down now. I held her gaze unflinchingly.

When Mom spoke next, her voice was laced with venom. "I want you totally focused on the business. We're in the middle of something big, something that requires all your energy and attention. If you can't manage that in your current situation, then I'll simply have to rearrange your priorities *for* you."

There was no doubt what she meant by that. She hadn't tracked down my men yet, but she could be seconds away from doing so.

But then, she quite possibly would eliminate them no matter what I said next. So I'd better make this good.

I honed my own voice into a blade, even cooler than hers. "You're right, we are in the middle of something big. Huge, even. And wouldn't it be a horrible shame if the other Devil's Dozen members found out that one of their own is plotting against some of them?"

Mom's stance stiffened with twice as much shock as when I'd simply argued back. I didn't think it'd ever occurred to her that I might not just defy her but outright stab her in the back.

But I'd learned my methods directly from her. To get what you want from someone, hit them where it hurts.

Before she could snap out of her stunned silence, I snatched my phone from my purse and flicked through my recordings to one of the most recent ones. Then I slammed my thumb down on the track.

Mom's voice warbled through the speaker, distant but clearly audible. "My people know how to keep their heads down when necessary. I'm sure yours can be circumspect as well."

In the pause that followed, Mom lunged at me. Her arced fingernails snatched at the phone in my hands.

I yanked it out of reach, dodging backward at the same moment with years of trained combat instincts. My free hand came up in a fist, my feet falling into a defensive stance even as my pulse thundered in my ears.

Check. Mate.

"There's no point," I spat out before she could launch herself at me again. "Break this phone and nothing changes. Do you think *I'm* an idiot? Of course I've backed up the files—somewhere you could never reach them."

Mom's lips drew back in a snarl. "You little bitch—"

I glared right back at her. "I'm exactly the bitch you made me into, Mom. I learned from the best. And if anything happens to me, all the proof I've gathered will be sent out to the people you'd least want getting their hands on it. So don't think that taking me out will solve your problems either."

She didn't know how much I had. It could have been just that one conversation—but even that conversation had contained plenty of hints about her plans.

And for all she knew, I had a hundred times more.

Mom studied me for a minute, marinating in her rage. A shadow crossed her expression, and she drew herself back a step with a twist of her mouth.

"My own daughter, threatening everything I've worked for. Everything I've built *for* you. I can't believe it's come to this."

Beneath her obvious anger, she sounded almost sad.

I couldn't bring myself to feel sorry for her loss. I'd been telling her I wasn't the daughter she expected me to be for years. It wasn't my fault she'd never listened.

I squared my shoulders. "I don't want to destroy your

empire. I simply don't want to be a part of it. You just won't accept that."

"Luciana—"

"I know, I know. It's my inheritance and all that. But skating is the most important thing to me in the world. I'm *good* at it."

Mom snorted. "Skating, *important*? Do you even hear yourself? Dancing around on the ice is a pastime for little kids. It should have stayed that way for you too. You're never going to be respected the way a Cordova woman should when you're prancing around in sparkly outfits begging for attention. What we do is in the real world, where the consequences actually matter."

I reined in my irritation at her dismissal. It wasn't as if I hadn't heard her talk that way about my dreams before. "Agree to disagree. It matters to me, and it's my life. It's about time I started fighting for what *I* want that life to be."

"Not a very good start," Mom said in an acid tone. "Throwing all your family loyalty out the window."

I shook my head. "I'm not, though. That part is up to you." I also wasn't such an idiot that I figured I could simply walk away with this threat hanging over us and trust that my men and I would be safe.

"I'll stick around and go along with your schemes," I went on. "I'll keep my mouth shut about the people *you're* betraying. On two conditions: You let me keep skating like I have been since I got to Austin, and you leave my men alone. You try to get in my way or hurt them, and you'll be the one ruining your plans. It's up to you."

Mom's gaze seared into me. "This is a dangerous game you're playing, mija."

I shrugged. "Like the work you have me doing isn't already incredibly dangerous?"

She exhaled in a rough sigh. "Fine. Have your ice time. Dally with these men you find appealing for some strange reason." Then she pointed a rigid forefinger at me. "But you'd better not slip up even slightly when it comes to carrying out my orders and fulfilling your side of the deal, or you'll be the one regretting it."

Even though I'd won this round, a chill prickled down my back, dulling my sense of victory. "I won't," I said.

But I had no doubt that from here on, Mom would be looking for any possible way to turn the tables on me and regain the power I'd stolen from her.

And if she managed to, there'd be no takebacks. My men and I were screwed.

SIXTEEN

Luciana

JASPER SWEPT me up into the air, and I glided along over him with my arms stretched wide. The chilly rink air washed over me, but I took nothing but enjoyment from it.

Especially since my recent confrontation with my mother had come with one upside. Now that she knew I was skating and grudgingly accepting the fact, we didn't have to hide anymore. Rafael had hooked us up with training times at a subdued but brighter and cleaner rink on the opposite side of town from our earlier digs.

Unfortunately, I couldn't take total enjoyment from the lift itself. A pang of strain ran through my legs and up my back, and my balance wobbled.

Jasper sensed my wavering and caught me in his arms before I could outright fall. As he lowered me to the ice, I grimaced.

When we eased to a halt, I swiped at the sweat on my brow. "Sorry. I should have had that."

Jasper waved off my apology. "Hey, none of us is perfect. You've been doing great."

Niko drifted over to join us. "It's understandable that you're getting tired. This is the longest you've been able to stay at practice since you got to Austin. You're going to need to rebuild your stamina now that you don't have to be quite as careful about your time."

I sighed, but I knew he was right. Even standing still, my legs still felt a bit shaky. The muscles in my calves ached. The physical workouts I'd done with the lackeys back at the mansion didn't compare to getting out on the ice properly.

I let out a growl of frustration. "I hate that I've lost so much time. How am I going to catch up for Nationals even with the longer practices now?"

Jasper squeezed my shoulder. "You'll get there, Punk. We've got a month to get totally into shape."

Niko flashed a smile at both of us. "I've seen you accomplish more amazing things than that already."

A hiss of skate blades announced Quentin's approach. He circled us with a teasing glint in his pale eyes. "You'd better not give up after you forced me back into singles and all."

I rolled my eyes at his gentle heckling. "You wouldn't have qualified for pairs even if we hadn't been in the running."

He laughed. "I don't know. Maybe seeing your skills scared the shit out of my partner and threw her off. I, of course, was totally unaffected."

"Of course," I repeated dryly. "Well, you don't have to worry about it. There's no way in hell I'm backing down."

Quentin's mouth stretched into a grin. "Just what I wanted to hear."

A twinge of affection rippled through the sense of defiant resolve he'd provoked in my chest. He hadn't actually been laying into me—he'd been trying to raise my spirits in his own way.

I was probably never going to receive gentle reassurance from Quentin Wolfe, no matter how badly he wanted to get into my pants.

I rolled my shoulders, revving myself up to take one last stab at the routine, but a text alert pinged out from my equipment bag. The sound I'd assigned only to my mom.

My pulse hiccupped. "I'd better see what that's about," I said, swallowing a lump of trepidation, and skated over to the stands. "It's my mother. Probably nothing important, just her finding whatever way she can to still mess with my skating time, but if I leave her waiting, she'll—"

My voice faltered as I took in the message that had popped up on the screen at the tap of my finger.

You're going to need to continue gaining the respect of our employees if you expect to retain any of my good will. I've set up a meeting Thursday night with the Hellborn for an exchange of our steel merchandise. I want you to lead the hand-off. Make sure you're properly prepared.

My stomach sank. Had she really not been able to wait to deliver her instructions in person, or was she so angry with me that she preferred to keep me at a distance for the moment? Or maybe she'd simply wanted to distract me from my practice like I'd initially figured.

But the real reason for my dismay was the job itself.

Jasper had joined me, peering at the screen over my

shoulder. "The Hellborn? Somehow I'm guessing they're not a boy band."

I made a face. "They're a local gang in Dallas—a lot less powerful than my mom's organization but a significant ally in their territory. She said 'steel,' so it'll be a shipment of stolen cars we're handing off."

Niko studied my expression from where he was leaning on the boards. "Is this outside your usual responsibilities?"

"Not really." I shook off my nerves as much as I could. "It's just that the guy who usually handles the exchanges for the Hellborn hates me. I met him a few years ago on a job with my mom, and he kept taking jabs at me. So I had a few choice things to say in return… which a bunch of his colleagues overheard. He was obviously pissed off that I'd made him lose face, but he couldn't really retaliate against me with my mom right there."

The memories swam up through my mind of that prick Maverick and his sneering insinuations. Mocking me when I hadn't identified the exact make of a particular car, implying that I was just tagging along like a little kid, not contributing anything useful.

When he'd gotten a little bolder and suggested a few ways I could *make* myself useful, complete with crude gestures, I'd known I couldn't let it stand. So I'd informed him in vivid detail of just how pathetic I imagined his skills in that department were and how small a dick he had to work with.

The image of his glowering face, flushed with humiliation but also a crapload of anger, made every muscle in my body tense up.

Jasper scowled. "It sounds like he deserved the backlash."

I smoothed back my ponytail. "Oh, he absolutely did. And he's probably been waiting to pay me back ever since. This time I won't have my mom there to make him nervous about disrespecting her… She'll want me to prove I can handle him and the rest of those goons without relying on her."

Which meant this meeting was going to be a hell of a lot more dangerous for me than a simple exchange of merchandise. But I didn't want to spell that out for the men around me.

My fingers hovered over the screen. I had the momentary urge to tap out a message asking Mom if she was sure this was a good idea, but I reined the impulse in.

I was supposed to be showing how strong I was to keep *Mom's* desire for vengeance against me in check. This was the first big ask she'd made since I forced her into our own deal—I couldn't chicken out already.

No doubt she remembered that incident from three years back. I'd bet she was counting on Maverick giving me a hard time.

Well, if I could stand up to her, facing this asshole should be no problem at all.

Sounds good, I wrote back, as if there was nothing I'd rather do with my Thursday night. *I'll keep everyone in line.*

Then I stuffed my phone back into the duffel bag, pretending my gut hadn't turned into a ball of queasiness. My arrangement with Mom wasn't going anywhere near as smoothly as I'd hoped.

Even if I took care of the Hellborn no problem, what was she going to get me into next? Was she even still trying to groom me as her heir, or was she hoping someone else would take me out of commission to diffuse my threat against her?

No, she had no idea how I'd set up the evidence I'd stored. For all she knew, even me getting injured would prompt an email to her fellow Devil's Dozen members. She wouldn't take that chance.

But she'd tread as close to the line as she could if it meant making me regret crossing her.

Jasper gave me a tentative nudge of his elbow. "Do you want to go another round?"

I dragged in a breath, and all at once I felt more than ever how exhausted I was. I'd already gone two hours longer than I'd been able to any time since we'd reunited in Austin. My ribs, still a bit tender after getting badly bruised in Boston, were aching a little too.

Maybe I could use a break. If I pushed myself too hard all at once, I'd ruin my chances of competing that way instead.

"You know," I said reluctantly, "I think I'd better call it a day."

Niko's eyes twinkled. "Let's go grab some dinner, then. You two…" He paused and glanced toward Quentin. "You *three* could all use some fuel after all that exercise. And I'm sure Rafael would appreciate a change of pace from standing guard over the rink entrance."

I managed a genuine if tight smile. "Yeah. Dinner sounds good. Let's live a little."

And hope that I'd still be alive and well after Thursday night to live some more.

SEVENTEEN

Jasper

"PIZZA?" Quentin muttered from the passenger seat beside me. "Don't any of you count your carbs? Protein's what'll keep your muscle mass up."

My hands clenched around the steering wheel, but Lou swatted him from behind, saving me the need to respond. "Last time I checked, there's protein in cheese and pepperoni. And no one said you *had* to join us for dinner."

Quentin tensed up for a second before the playfulness of her tone must have sunk in. It was weird seeing him this on edge, eager to please someone other than himself.

Remembering how Lou had thrown my own emotions for a loop when I'd first met her, I could almost feel a little sympathetic.

Almost.

Quentin sighed, but his own tone lightened to match

hers. "I suppose one slice won't hurt anything. I'll see what else they've got on the menu."

I restrained a groan of frustration and drew my focus back to the traffic around me. Quentin *had* been on better behavior since we'd come to Austin. I knew it was mostly for Lou's benefit even when she wasn't with us, but I could give him a little credit for self-control—and do my best to rein in my own irritation.

The right lane was packed with parked cars. I eyeballed them for my chance to veer over to make the turn I needed to. One started flashing its turn signal to pull out into traffic, so I switched to the brake to give it a chance to enter ahead of me.

Quentin let out a huff. "Jesus, St. Pierre, who taught you how to drive? We could have been halfway across town by now."

The jab raised my hackles in an instant. "Some of us learned to be courteous to other drivers on the road."

He snorted derisively. There was a familiar quality to the sound that cut right to the quick of my nerves. "There's polite and then there's being a total wimp about it. You know, if you want to get anywhere in life, you've got to—"

"Maybe I don't fucking care what you have to say about it," I burst out. "Let me drive however the hell I want to drive!"

The car jerked to a stop at a red light, and uncomfortable silence clogged the car. A burn of embarrassment spread up the back of my neck.

He'd only been casually hassling me. I hadn't needed to start yelling and swearing at him. So much for keeping my temper in check.

After a blip of shock, Quentin simply shook his head

at me. His nonchalant reaction abruptly reminded me of what he'd said about his mother. How many times had he needed to deal with *her* snapping at him out of the blue like I'd just done?

Fucking hell.

As I sucked in a deep breath, trying to steady myself, Quentin clicked his tongue chidingly. "And there's another thing. You're going to keep getting distracted from your performances if you let people rile you up at the drop of a hat."

I managed to keep my voice at a normal volume, though it still came out sharper than I'd have liked. "Thanks for the tip. It'd be easier if you didn't have a knack for sounding just like my asshole dad."

Quentin let out a scoffing sound. "He couldn't have been that bad when he funded all your training with his posh job."

My anger flared back to the surface and crackled through my retort. "He didn't spend a goddamn penny on my skating. It was all my mom—until he made *her* stop when I was eleven and after that it was all on me and whatever sponsorships I could scrounge up. He *hated* me training."

Quentin's mouth opened and then closed again. I'd managed to stun him into silence. I guessed it wasn't totally surprising—given the kind of money my dad brought in from his job in corporate law and the trappings of privilege that I'd grown up with, people tended to assume that I'd never struggled to fund my pursuits.

Was that what Quentin had figured all this time? That I'd had everything I'd worked so hard for just handed to me?

The awkward silence lingered for a minute, and I

cursed myself inwardly. It was the first night we'd been able to go out and do something with Lou, an actual date, and I'd ruined the evening before it'd even really begun with my stupid temper.

Then Niko's buoyant voice carried from behind me. "You know the only problem with a pizza place? They probably don't serve Calpis."

The remark was so out of the blue and yet so Niko that a laugh sputtered out of me. "I'm not sure *anywhere* in Austin serves Calpis. It's a good thing you seem to be able to survive without your fizzy milk."

"Just you wait until I get my hands on some and make you try it," Niko said. I could practically see the mischief dancing in his eyes. "You won't believe you ever doubted its deliciousness."

"I'd give it a try," Lou piped up.

I gave a brief grunt. "Now you're making me look bad."

Rafael backed me up with a low chuckle. "Don't worry —I'm with you. Milk and carbonation should not mix."

Niko gasped in mock-dismay. "Just for that, I'm force-feeding *you* the first bottle."

A smile tugged at the corners of my lips. "Shouldn't you save it all for yourself if you finally find some?"

"Hmm. You might have a point there. I'll have to reconsider my plans."

We all laughed, even Quentin, and the tension in the air seemed to fade. But as I parked outside the pizza place and stepped out into the cool early-winter air, apprehension still niggled at me. Niko reached over to give my arm a reassuring squeeze before we headed into the restaurant, and I couldn't miss the concerned glances Lou was shooting my way, as if she were evaluating whether I might be on the verge of melting down.

I grimaced inwardly. Why had I gone and said all that stuff about Dad? I'd mentioned my family issues to Lou before, but not quite how far he'd gone in his refusal to support my career. She'd probably assumed it'd been limited to criticizing *how* I was spending his money, not refusing to offer any cash whatsoever.

And it was humiliating to have lost my temper at all.

I placed my order half-heartedly and mostly listened as easygoing banter flowed around the table.

Rafael eyeballed the massive milkshake Lou had requested. "It's bigger than your head. You're really going to drink all of that?"

"I'm capable of incredible things," Lou informed him with a cheeky grin.

"I'm not sure you'll be capable of fitting any pizza in your stomach after that."

Quentin flashed a smirk. "I could always take it off your hands and save you from yourself."

Lou arched her eyebrows at him. "No rescuing necessary here."

Niko leaned toward Quentin with a sly glint in his eyes. "So you'll go for dessert, then? It's only pizza you object to?"

Quentin straightened up with an authoritative air. "The most important factor in an ideal athletic diet is balance. My body is the machinery I use to perform my routines. I'm screwing myself over if I load it up with too many useless calories."

Lou tapped the side of her glass. "Protein. Fat. Calcium. All necessary in a balanced diet."

He smiled at her. "That's why I'd take a milkshake off your hands but not a slab of chocolate cake."

Niko knit his brow in a show of bewilderment. "Your priorities seem very sad for your taste buds."

Quentin just shrugged with an amused expression, and it occurred to me that he was starting to feel like a normal part of our group rather than an unwelcome intruder. Somehow he was fitting in with us as if he actually... added something to the dynamic. Something not entirely horrible.

The thought sent a twinge of warmth through me at the same time as it made me want to throw the guy through the restaurant window. Okay, so my feelings about his presence definitely hadn't untangled themselves yet.

As I gulped down my last bite of my third slice of pizza, Niko got up and tugged on my shoulder. "I saw a dessert display case near the door. Come on, let's see what they've got. I know *you* have a sweet tooth."

I couldn't argue with that, especially when I took in the momentarily pensive light in his bright eyes. His request wasn't just about indulging in sweets.

Lou leapt to her feet and grabbed my hand. "You're not picking for all of us! I've got to have a say too."

I let myself be basically dragged over to the glass case just past the cash register. I couldn't really regret the trip once I took in the offerings. Choosing between tiramisu, cannoli, and sfogliatelle was not going to be easy.

As he studied the array next to me, Niko looped his arm around mine. "Is everything all right? The conversation in the car obviously brought up some bad memories, and you've been quiet since then."

Lou   nudged   her   shoulder   against   mine companionably. "Yeah. If you want to talk about it, you know we're here."

In the face of their gentle support and the fact that they'd thought to pull me away from the two guys I wasn't as comfortable opening up in front of, my chest ached with affection. "You brought me over here to corner me, huh?" I said, but I didn't put any rancor into the words.

Lou pecked my cheek. "Just making sure you know we've got your back."

Yes, they did. I exhaled a little raggedly and forced a tight smile. "I've already told you some of it, Lou. My dad was a jerk, criticizing everything I did, but especially the skating. He and my mom argued about it a lot."

Niko frowned. "I didn't realize they withdrew their financial support so early."

"It is what it is." I rubbed the back of my neck. "I guess I should be grateful he never brought out the insults when we were in public like Quentin's mom did. Although on the other hand, at least she *wanted* him to skate. My mom had some money of her own from an inheritance that she put toward my skating, but Dad got more and more pissed off about my 'sissy pursuit' as I got older, and finally he threatened divorce if she didn't stop."

Lou released a sound like a growl. "And she bowed to the pressure, huh?"

"It's hard to blame her. She was choosing between her entire marriage and something that was just one part of her kid's life. She couldn't have known back then that I'd manage to make a career out of it."

Niko slipped his arm right around my waist and gave me a sideways hug. "But you did, even without their money. You paid your own way."

I dipped my head. "Yep. It was a struggle sometimes,

especially getting that first sponsorship—nothing big, just enough to keep me in ice time and basic equipment. It's hard to know what to say sometimes. Everyone always figured I had tons of support—financial and emotional— but I was teetering on the edge of having to quit more than once."

"He's a total prick to freeze you out like that," Lou said tartly, but with a vehemence that made me think it was a good thing she'd never encountered my father. Things would probably not go well for him, especially if she happened to be armed.

She flexed her hands before shaking off a little of the tension that had come over her. "You don't see him anymore, do you? You shouldn't let what he thought get to you. He was obviously wrong to dismiss your talent."

"Yeah." My head drooped. "I don't know. It's hard to set all of that history aside. My mom is great, really—she's always been there for me in every way she can without totally blowing up her marriage. I know how much it hurt her, fighting with him over me. Thinking she might lose him completely. When they weren't dealing with my skating interest, they were really happy together."

I paused and then admitted the doubt that'd weighed on me for so long. "Sometimes I wonder if it was really worth it. I was so set on pursuing skating that it messed up both of their lives, hers especially, and after all that, it's not as if I've accomplished anything so incredibly great so far."

Niko scoffed lightly and gave me a little shake. "What are you talking about? You're great already, and soon you'll be proving that to even more people than you already have. I wouldn't have chased you halfway around the world otherwise."

Lou poked me in the arm. "Yeah, you're a superstar who just needed a bit of a break for understandable reasons. Really, the two of us should start an Unsupportive Parents Club. It sucks, but we're not letting them win."

I couldn't help smiling at her enthusiasm. "I probably shouldn't complain when I know what *you're* dealing with. You're right. No one gets to win but us."

"That's the spirit!" Niko leaned closer to the display case. "Now about that dessert…"

In the end, we ordered five portions of tiramisu for the table, figuring that if Quentin turned his nose up at the treat, the rest of us could easily find a way to make his portion disappear. As we returned to the table, the waitress was already bringing the dessert plates over.

Quentin eyed his like he was scanning it for its calorie count, but he kept any snarky observations he might have had to himself. As I settled into my seat, he glanced at me, hesitated, and leaned closer so he could pitch his voice for just my ears.

"Hey, I—I'm sorry about before. About stirring up shitty memories. It's hard not to fall into the habit of getting on your case, but I really didn't mean to poke a sore spot like that."

I could tell from his awkward stance and the faint flush that'd come over his face that he meant it, as embarrassed as he was to be apologizing. Well, I guessed he would know what it was like having the baggage of harsh parents.

I offered a small, crooked smile in return. "I appreciate the apology."

Quentin paused again. Then he said in a halting tone, "It's actually pretty impressive that you got that far all on your own dime."

Somehow the acknowledgment did more to smooth over the animosity between us than his apology had. I had to answer, "Considering the challenges we've all had to deal with, it's pretty impressive any of us are here."

Quentin's eyes glittered with eager determination. "And not going anywhere."

He deigned to take a bite of his dessert and seemed to contemplate its flavors for several seconds while he chewed. When Lou tried to steal a chunk off his plate, he tugged it closer with a waggle of his fork.

Watching him, my urge to throw him out a window—or send him back to Boston on his own—faded away. He had been an ass, but I'd never have expected the old Quentin to admit he'd done anything wrong, let alone apologize for it.

If even Quentin Wolfe could adjust his attitude for the greater good, then there wasn't any reason I couldn't too.

EIGHTEEN

Luciana

THURSDAY NIGHT FOUND me in the last place I'd have wanted to be: the back seat of one of Mom's cars, being driven by a Deadly Rose lackey to a hand-off with a man who probably wanted to dance on my corpse.

And lucky me, I had *another* man shooting daggers at me with his dark eyes from the seat beside me.

"I hope you're ready for this, pequeña rosa," Octavio said in a disdainful tone, rubbing his forehead just above his spiky eyebrow piercing. "Maverick has been chafing in the Deadly Rose yoke lately, getting big ideas about who should really be in charge. I'd be surprised if he *doesn't* try to screw us over today to show off for the rest of his stupid outfit."

Oh, great. So not only did Maverick have personal reasons to want to stick it to me, he'd become even more of an aggressive asshole in general.

"Thanks for the heads up," I said, keeping my own voice even.

Octavio narrowed his eyes at me. "Your mom will expect you to put him in his place. Permanently." He drew his finger across his throat in a gesture that couldn't have been more unambiguous. "Make a clear statement to the rest of the gang."

My stomach twisted with a jab of queasiness. More blood on my hands to appease Mom? Not that I thought Maverick deserved to keep living his life of violence and assholery so very much, but every death I dealt out myself felt like another boulder weighing on my conscience.

Was that even what Mom would want? She hadn't given me any orders to that effect when we'd talked directly earlier this evening, only that she expected me to keep the Hellborn in line. If she had a specific opinion about how I did that, normally she'd have said it outright.

I kept my answer noncommittal. "We'll see how it goes."

Octavio shrugged and slouched back in his seat. "Your funeral if you disappoint her."

I studied him from the corner of my eye. He was laying it on pretty thick.

I already knew *this* asshole didn't have my best interests at heart. Was he promoting some agenda of his own under the guise of it being Mom's? Or simply hoping to trip me up by pointing me down a path Mom wouldn't have wanted at all?

No doubt he'd be oh so happy if I came out of this looking inept. Or dead.

Following his advice seemed like a surefire way to screw myself over. Whatever Maverick did, I'd just have to find some way of laying down the law that didn't involve murdering him. Then I'd be happier and Octavio would be unhappier, and at least it'd be a win in those two ways.

And if Mom didn't like it, she was welcome to hand over the role of second-in-command to this cabrón here and cut me loose.

Our car pulled into the chosen meetup spot first, a dusty stretch of hard-packed earth in the middle of nowhere, about halfway between Austin and Dallas. The transport truck carrying the high-end stolen cars collected by one of Mom's subsidiary gangs rumbled after us, followed by two more cars that contained my squad of backup lackeys.

Maverick wasn't the only one who needed to think about how he'd come across in front of his companions tonight. If I betrayed any weakness while Mom's underlings were watching, things could get *very* difficult back at the house.

I stepped out into the night. The fresh country air was a relief as it flooded my lungs, but I didn't dare step more than a few feet beyond the hood of the car. Even with supposed allies, you had to be cautious.

Our headlights caught on a few cars parked a couple hundred feet away. A cluster of figures peeled themselves out of the shadows around those vehicles and sauntered over to meet us.

I hadn't seen Maverick in three years, but it was easy to recognize the prick right there in the middle of the pack. He held himself like a tubby, redneck Napoleon surrounded by his shittily tattooed army. Arrogance radiated from his stance like a bad stench.

As they approached, I drew my frustratingly short frame up a little taller and held my ground.

He aimed a sneering grin at us with a glint of his

crooked teeth. "Cordova sent her little girl, huh? Maybe I should take that as a gift."

I rolled my eyes. "The less time I have to spend anywhere near you, the better. You can see we brought the cars. Where's our money?"

He clucked his tongue at me. "Now, now. Don't get your panties in a twist. You shouldn't have come out here if you were on the rag."

His fellow goons snickered. Frustration prickled through my veins, but I kept my tone totally bored. "Do you have the cash or not?"

Maverick motioned at one of the guys behind him. The sunburned thug swung a duffel bag for Maverick to grab.

The asshole took a couple of steps toward me but then stopped rather than continuing forward to offer up the bag. Instead, he set it on the ground in front of him and unzipped it.

Normally it'd be my people doing the counting to make sure the Hellborn were giving us what we were owed. I would have said as much, except Maverick didn't just paw through the bag's contents. He immediately started pulling out wads of bills and tossing them in a growing heap beside him.

"What the hell are you doing?" I demanded.

He glanced up at me, a gleam lighting in his eyes that was both sadistic and a little crazy. "You're not the real woman in charge, now are you? I figure you're worth barely half my respect. So you get half the payment. Seems fairer that way, don't you think?"

Another chorus of guffaws, these ones both shocked and awed, carried from his crew.

My teeth set on edge. "Actually, I don't think so. I

didn't drive all the way out here to be insulted, and I carry the full authority of the Cordova family. Deliver the agreed upon payment *now*, or you're going to regret it."

"Big words from a little pipsqueak of a girl." Maverick shook his head. "Nah, I like my way better." He took another handful of cash out of the bag.

Fury seared up through my chest. Fury that this idiot was mocking me. Fury that because of who he was and who I was, I was going to need to betray every shred of morality I had in me to set this right.

But his gang was watching, and so was mine. I couldn't let his blatant disrespect go unpunished, not if I wanted my deal with Mom—and the safety of the men I loved—to stay intact.

I had to act—and fast, while the element of surprise could offset the size difference between me and my opponent.

I could have gone for the gun tucked into the back of my ripped jeans. I could have blasted the prick away where he squatted. But that would be playing into Octavio's plans, not mine.

Instead, my hand dug into the pocket of my hoodie and closed around the handle of my knife. Without any warning, I launched myself at Maverick.

He might have had nearly a hundred pounds on me, but I'd trained against bigger guys my entire life. Helpfully, he was already crouched on the ground.

I slammed into him and knocked him onto his back before he'd even registered he had a fight on his hands. He grunted and swung a fist, which froze in midair as I pressed the blade of the knife to his exposed throat.

"That's right," I said in a tight, dark voice, my knee

digging into his gut. "Stay right there, or this goes straight through your jugular."

I held out my free hand toward the Deadly Rose underlings. "Another blade, please? I think Maverick here needs a more constant reminder of who has the real power."

One of the men darted forward and pressed a switchblade into my waiting fingers. I flicked it open and stared down at my victim.

I wasn't going to kill him, but I did need to make a statement. Well, I had always appreciated a nice visual.

Ignoring the queasiness winding through my gut, I brought the second knife to Maverick's forehead. At the first prick of the blade, he swore and thrashed in an attempt to buck me off him.

I pressed my weight down and dug the first blade into his throat deep enough that blood welled up along its edge. With a choked sputter, Maverick went still again.

"Better," I said. "You questioned the Cordovas' authority, so now I'm leaving our mark on you."

With several flicks of the switchblade, I carved an image into his forehead—the three-petaled rose with a spike of a stem that served as the symbol of both the Cordovas and the Deadly Rose, to those who knew enough to be aware of our empire's real name.

Blood seeped from the cuts over Maverick's forehead. He spat curse after curse at me that I ignored, my knife at his throat keeping him otherwise still.

He'd heal from that soon enough—but my etching would leave a lovely little scar for an awfully long time.

As I finished the last line of the pointed stem, a momentary hesitation gripped me. This was reasonable punishment for the insult to my family, but what about the personal humiliation he'd tried to subject me to?

I couldn't leave any doubt that Luciana Cordova, even on her own, was no one to be messed with.

An idea so perfect it made me a little sick swam up through my mind. Mom had taught me well in all sorts of ways I couldn't feel the least bit happy about.

But until I could get away from her, I had to play by the rules of this world.

I snapped my fingers toward my watching associates. "Two of you—pin down his arms."

"What?" Maverick sputtered. "You bitch! Get your hands off—"

I dug the knife into his neck again, and he cut himself off with a tremor that ran the length of his body. Maverick was a hotshot, all right, but he wanted to live.

Two of the Deadly Rose lackeys yanked at his arms and rammed their feet down to hold them in place. Keeping one hand at Maverick's throat, I adjusted my position to kneel beside him and yank up his sweat-stained tee.

"I feel like it's my duty to make sure *every* woman who considers getting up close and personal with you is aware of how you treat a lady," I said tartly, and tipped the switchblade into the flesh just below his belly button.

When Maverick squealed and thrashed, my knife drew another shallow line across his throat—and my lackeys stomped on his fingers hard enough to crack a few bones. As his protests dwindled into raging whimpers, I dragged my second blade through his skin to write out my brief but incisive message.

I AM A DIPSHIT.

When I'd finished the T, I shoved myself off the guy

and took a couple of steps back, restraining a flinch at the sight of my gory artwork. I couldn't let any of Mom's people, especially Octavio, catch a hint that I had any regrets about how I'd handled the situation.

"Grab the money, and let's go." My words were hollow—I hardly recognized my voice as my own. "I don't want to have to look at this pig and the rest of his swine for another minute."

"You got it, *boss*." Octavio slid me a snake-like glance and strode forward to stuff the money Maverick had removed back into the bag. From the sharpness of his voice and his movements, he was pissed off at how the situation had turned out. Because I hadn't killed Maverick like he'd suggested?

But when I turned toward the rest of my crew, a few dipped their heads to me, unmistakably impressed. One guy even gave me a full salute.

I'd lived up to my mother's name. Hurray for me.

As Octavio hefted the bag, I marched back to the car without looking back. My men closed in around me to bar any thought of retribution from the rest of the Hellborn goons, although they hadn't risked making a move since I'd tackled Maverick.

My driver was still waiting at the wheel—I couldn't afford to so much as tremble as I slid into the back seat, even though I was shaking like Jell-O on the inside. It was all I could do to hold in the urge to vomit.

I'd done what I had to do. At least the blood on my hands wasn't an entire life I'd ended. My conscience was that clear.

It seemed to take forever before the trunk squeaked open and the duffel thumped inside. The driver gunned the engine, and Octavio sank onto the seat beside me.

As the car pulled onto the road, he glanced over at me, barely holding back a glower. "You good, chica? I told you to put that asshole *in* the ground, not just on it. Lost your nerve?"

I stared right back at him, letting my anger at being jerked around burn away my nausea. "Put him in the ground, and we leave the Hellborn rioting. Send him back to them with a message about what they get for defiance carved right into his skin, and no one fucking forgets. I think my mom will approve, whether you do or not."

His mouth twitched, but he didn't call out my implication that the order hadn't actually come from Mom. Even if he realized I thought he might have attempted to betray me, he was smart enough not to force my hand by pushing the issue.

As we settled into a tense silence, my burner phone buzzed in my back pocket. I yanked it out before another alert could go off.

Several texts came through in quick succession from a number I'd labeled as BH from my brief exchange of texts with the Blood Hunter after the Storm had filled her in on my concerns. Remembering the strength that the slim, dark-haired woman had emanated when I'd met her in the coffee shop, I couldn't help thinking she could be the key to holding Mom at bay, but she'd been noncommittal in our initial conversation.

She had a lot more to say tonight.

I think I might have some evidence for you to build your case. This was one of my front businesses.

That opening statement was followed by a link that took me to an article on a news website. The headline had my eyes widening. *Sports Club Littered With Bodies After 21 Die of Food Poisoning,* the title read.

My eyes widened. Twenty-one people all dead in one go—from food poisoning, of all things?

The article went on to report that the twenty-one people in question had all been employees or long-time regulars of the club. They'd stayed late into the evening for some kind of event, and the bodies had been found the next morning. Tests indicated they'd been the victims of severe food poisoning from a source that hadn't yet been definitively identified.

But one line in particular jumped out at me. *The Riverside Sports Club has been a long-time fixture in this suburban neighborhood, with sprawling grounds on the edge of the Rosewood River.*

A chill wrapped around my lungs. The Rosewood—Mom had said something about that in one of her calls. That they'd put "something in the water" but "not right in the Rosewood."

Something that would look like death by food poisoning? But why?

The Blood Hunter's following texts held the answer. *All of the dead were important employees of mine not far from my main base of operations. This feels like an attack, not an accident. And it can't be to simply take over territory. No one has made a move to claim the club or anything in the surrounding areas. I get the impression that for now they're just aiming to weaken my manpower.*

I'm increasing security and prodding the Deadly Rose in my own way to see if she'll reveal more, but I have no direct proof she was responsible. If you can do more with this information than I can, feel free. I'm not liking the direction this situation appears to be heading in.

My heart thumped for several halting beats before I typed out a hasty *Thank you* in response. After a moment,

I added, *I'm sure my mom was involved, but I don't know if it was her people or a co-conspirator.*

The Blood Hunter deserved to know that much. There was no doubt in my mind that the "they" who'd set out to weaken the Blood Hunter was Mom and her allies.

Now I could prove that one part of a conversation I'd recorded was definitely Mom plotting to attack a fellow Devil's Dozen member. I hadn't gotten anything so concrete before. I couldn't say it was enough to upend her plans, but it felt like a major step forward.

A smile tugged at my lips. But as I tucked the phone away, I caught Octavio eyeing me suspiciously before he tugged his gaze away. His expression stayed dark as he stared out the window instead.

My smile faded. Had I really made the right call by ignoring his instructions? Now he knew that I definitely didn't trust him... which meant he'd be working even harder to displace me before I earned any more of Mom's trust.

I was balanced way too precariously already without throwing more problems into the mix.

I folded my arms over my chest, just shy of hugging myself, and held my posture straight. But my fears and misery in the life Mom had dragged me back into closed in around me with the whir of the car's engine, on the verge of suffocating me.

NINETEEN

Luciana

AS JASPER LOWERED me from the final lift, a twinge ran through my ribs. With our last few moves, it deepened into an ache. I hit our ending post with a hitch in my breath.

Jasper's gray-green eyes darkened with concern. "Are you okay?"

"Yeah." I rubbed my side instinctively, and his mouth tightened. He'd been there, rushing to my aid, when Sheeran's men back in Boston had battered my side with a flurry of kicks. "Maybe I just need a short break—and some water."

"Always good to stay hydrated," Niko piped up from where he was watching near the boards.

Jasper slid his arm around my shoulders in a quick but tender embrace and kissed my forehead. "We've been at this a while. Take all the break you need, Punk."

I had been pushing myself hard today, but getting to skate with my guys had helped me distance myself from the worst memories from a couple of nights ago. All yesterday, every time I'd glanced down at myself, I'd flashed back to the splatters of Maverick's blood dabbling my hands.

I'd still been a little shell-shocked when I'd shown up this morning, and my boyfriends had caught on immediately. But when Niko had asked if I wanted to talk about it, my throat had constricted until I felt like I was choking.

"It's all right," Jasper had told me. "You don't need to get into the details with us. We know whatever you needed to do, it's what you had to do to survive. It doesn't mean anything about who you really are."

Then I'd choked up for a completely different reason, tears of relief pricking at the backs of my eyes. But the burden of my unwanted duty had lifted as I'd skated, until I really did feel like myself again.

At some point, I might tell Rafael about what exactly had gone down with Maverick. He'd understand the violence I'd needed to turn to in a way the skater guys couldn't totally. But having permission not to lay out the gory details of my role as Mom's heir was the best gift anyone could have given me.

At least Mom had seemed satisfied enough. She'd even let out a sharp chuckle of amusement when I'd told her how I'd dealt with the asshole's mocking rebellion. Then she'd patted me on the shoulder and complimented my "creativity."

No mention of any expectation that I'd have killed the man. I was more sure than ever that Octavio's instructions had come only from himself.

When I skated over to the stands now, Niko had already grabbed our water bottles for us. I tipped mine to my mouth. As I took a few slow gulps, my gaze veered across the rink toward the other, lonely figure working on his routine alongside us.

Quentin whirled through a spin, the overhead lights flashing off his pale hair. His leg rose to the perfect angle with his body, his arms unfurling before he pulled in on himself again.

His form was incredible. I'd been able to see that even back when I'd wanted to punch him in the face every time he talked to us. But as he pushed off into a step sequence, I couldn't help thinking, like I had many times before, that there was something missing to all those strictly precise movements.

He came to a stop about ten feet away, and I set down my water bottle. We didn't normally talk a whole lot during our training periods, but the observation hit me hard enough that the words tumbled out.

"You know, you can pull off some really impressive moves. No one could ever say you're not a great skater. But there's something about your style that always looks too analytical to me. Kind of rigid."

Quentin raised an eyebrow and glided a little closer. "Did I just hear you call me a 'great skater'? And 'impressive' too? Go ahead and keep that praise coming."

He grinned, the faded slash of his scar lifting with the curve of his lips—a warmer expression than his usual smirk, but still a little wicked. And I couldn't deny that my heart skipped a beat watching his handsome face light up.

I arched my eyebrows right back at him. "I did also mention that you seem too stiff."

His grin widened. "And now you're offering tips. Trying to get into coaching too, Upstart?"

The nickname he'd apparently just come up with made me roll my eyes. "Just making an observation. If you don't want to hear—"

"No, no, it's fine." Quentin cocked his head. "It just sounds like you figure I need someone to teach me how to loosen up. Maybe you should take me on as a pet project, since you're so concerned."

There was no mistaking the teasing glint in his bright blue eyes—or the challenge in his voice. He *wanted* me to say yes, probably so he'd have an excuse to win me over however he imagined he was going to do that.

The truth was that he'd already been doing that, bit by bit, without trying directly. Possibly *because* he hadn't been laying it on thick.

He'd just been a more open, considerate version of the jerk he'd been before... and I'd been finding I kind of liked his presence in my life. The snark and the arrogance hadn't vanished, but balanced out like this, they'd become an acquired taste, like the bitterness in a good cup of coffee or the acidic tang of a grapefruit.

I wasn't sure I wanted him knowing how much progress he'd made toward his goal, though. And it wasn't just me he needed to prove himself to.

I tipped my head toward my partner, who'd leaned against the boards to watch the conversation. "You could learn a thing or two from me, sure, but Jasper's the expert at putting emotion into a performance."

Quentin folded his arms in front of him in a pose that initially looked defensive, but the raise of his chin was more determined than defiant. After a brief pause, his voice came out even. "Let's see what both of you could show me, then."

Jasper's stance tensed for a second, and I braced myself for an argument. But he eased over, giving Quentin a wary but not unwelcoming look. "You really want to do this?"

Quentin shrugged. "Why not? I won't be an idiot and say there's nothing I could learn from the great Saint Jasper."

There was a hint of wryness in his use of Jasper's fan-given title, but otherwise he sounded genuine. Enough that Jasper's mouth twitched with the start of a smile. "All right. Then let's get you moving."

Niko had headed to our portable speaker system. "It's easier to loosen up if you can relax into the music." He flicked through one of his many playlists and selected a lilting track that I knew would slowly swell with dramatic emotion.

I grasped Quentin's forearm and tugged him across the rink. Jasper skated next to us, his hand resting on the small of my back. He drew me away from the other guy and spun us around in a loose spiral before settling into a simple glide across the ice.

Quentin followed, his back straight, his arms by his sides. Jasper shook his head. "You look like a toy soldier, Wolfe. Can't you feel the melody? Let it work its way into your muscles and move with it."

Quentin frowned. "I've never skated to this song before."

"It shouldn't matter," I said lightly. "If you're *really* great, you can stop worrying about getting everything 'right' for a few minutes and let out what comes naturally."

The frown deepened into a grimace, but Quentin dragged in a deep breath. A mask of concentration came over his face.

He looked so stern I couldn't help laughing. "Stop thinking so hard. You're supposed to be *feeling*."

A hint of a slump came into Quentin's posture. He glanced away. "What if... I don't really know how that works?"

The hint of vulnerability brought a lump into my throat. A flicker of surprise passed through Jasper's eyes, and then he surprised *me* by nudging me toward the other guy. "Maybe you need the right inspiration."

I glided over to Quentin, and he lifted his hand automatically to catch mine. Even through our training gloves, the warmth of his skin seeped through. When our eyes met, a tingle raced up my arm.

"You think you can match my footwork?" I asked.

Something had softened in his expression. "I'll give it my best shot."

I shifted my feet into a series of basic steps, letting the rise and fall of the melody guide me. Quentin followed intently, but I caught a slight sway in his body and the motions of his free arm as he sank more fully into the music.

I swiveled toward him. "Want to try a sit spin?"

His gaze held mine, the smolder behind it heating me more than his touch. "I can manage that."

We pivoted together, his arms coming around my waist and mine lifting into the air. My knee brushed his thigh. He held me carefully, but I could already see his stance had loosened from when we'd started this impromptu joint coaching session.

His face, not so much.

"Come on, Wolfe," Jasper called from a few feet away, his tone playful in its heckling. "You've got a gorgeous girl in your arms. Try to look like you're happy about it."

Quentin let out a grunt, but then a smile crossed his lips—smaller but also gentler than any I'd seen from him before. Another tingle ran through my nerves as we gazed back at each other in the few seconds longer before we eased apart.

To my surprise, Quentin sent me gliding back toward Jasper. "You're already good with her. All that extra practice. Maybe I need you as a role model, old-timer."

Jasper only chuckled at the tongue-in-cheek insult and pulled me into his arms. "*Now* I get some respect. Let's see if I can get you to cough up a little more."

He picked up the pace a bit and lowered me into a dip as we swept across the ice with a crescendo in the song. Then Jasper handed me off to Quentin, watching expectantly. I gave myself over to the other guy's support, arcing back as he echoed Jasper's movements.

"Good," Jasper said. "Now a person would think you actually like her."

Quentin shot a glance over his shoulder at his rival. "Gotta learn from the best, huh?"

There was a new companionableness to their banter, as if they actually liked each other too. As if they might even be able to see each other as something like friends—if not right now, then in the not-so-distant future. Recognizing the shift warmed me as much as the feel of Quentin's arms around me.

"What've you got for me next?" Quentin asked, passing me over again.

I glided back and forth between them through several more simple moves, through one song and another. Niko shouted encouragement from his spot by the boards and after the first few exchanges hollered up through the stands. "You should come down and see this properly, Rafael. Cooperation in beautiful action."

My bodyguard emerged from his usual post by the main doors and came most of the way down the steps to take in our unusual training exercise. I sped from Jasper to Quentin and then back again with a breathless laugh. Both of the guys were grinning freely now, and there was a fluid grace to Quentin's strokes across the ice that I'd never seen before.

My heart swelled alongside the music. Somehow, we'd headed farther down the path of becoming a united group than I'd realized was possible with Quentin in the mix. Was there a chance he could fit in with the rest of us more permanently after all?

"You know," Quentin said as he caught me again. "This is almost… fun."

Jasper snorted. "You make that sound like a bad word. I think I see part of your problem."

"Hey, I'm working on it, aren't—"

The boom of the door slamming open cut off his retort.

As we jerked around with a hiss of our skates, a throng of men stormed into the room with a thunder of stomping feet and a few warning shots from their guns. I snapped into a defensive stance instinctively, groping at my hip, but of course I didn't have any weapons on me while we were training.

The torrent of attackers had already hit Rafael, a bunch of the men attempting to pin him to the ground while he thrashed against their hold. Niko scrambled backward, but a couple of the guys caught him too, one jamming a gun to his forehead. He froze.

The rest, a dozen or so of them, barged out into the rink. And right at the front of the pack stood Octavio, a wild light wavering in his eyes and his mouth twisted into a sneer.

"What the fuck are you doing?" I spat out, rage and terror colliding inside me. I wanted to bash open his ugly mug, but I didn't have anything to do it with—or any way to protect the men on either side of me who weren't armed or trained in fighting.

Octavio's lips drew back to bare his teeth. "You don't get to take off to play these stupid games and then prance home acting like you run the show. *I* put in the time, *I've* paid with sweat and blood, and I'm taking back the respect Mireya owes me, which you never deserved anyway."

Then he sprang at me, the rest of the men lunging forward at the same time.

"Get the fuck away from her!" Jasper bellowed, and Quentin let out a wordless snarl. They leapt to my defense as the onslaught of mutinous gangsters surged forward.

We had a slight advantage in that we were more at home on the ice. As a few of our attackers' feet skidded on the slippery terrain, Jasper managed to land a powerful punch on one jerk's skull. Quentin rammed his elbow into another goon's side while the guy was in mid-trip.

One of the other thugs grabbed at me, and I whipped him around in a ghoulish version of one of our spins before kneeing him hard enough to send blood spurting from his nose. As it smeared across the frozen surface beneath our feet, two more men closed in around me.

Inspiration struck. I didn't have any weapons I could hold in my hands... but I did have blades on my feet.

I swung around with a couple of swift kicks. The bottom of my skate slashed across one goon's cheek, slitting it open all the way to the bone. As he stumbled backward with a groan of agony, I jabbed right through the fabric of the other guy's shirt, sending blood spurting from a belly wound.

Grunts and thuds carried from either side of me, but I couldn't spare a moment to check on my skating partners. More thugs loomed on me.

I threw my fists and elbows, aimed another cutting kick, and yanked up a knee that caught one asshole in the gut. My feet rasped over the ice, veering this way and that.

The goons slipped and collided with each other almost as much as they did with us, but there were too many of them. Someone punched my shoulder just as I swung my skate again, and I wobbled for balance.

A hand snatched at my ponytail and wrenched me backward, pulling my hair at the roots viciously enough to leave my entire scalp throbbing. Octavio's face, ruddy with fury, appeared in my peripheral vision.

I lashed out at him with all I could, clocking him in the jaw and slashing at his calf with my skate blade. But then he slammed his fist into my side, right where my healing ribs were tender.

Pain exploded through my torso. I bent over, trying to shield myself, but he punched me again in the same spot, so hard that a spittle-filled gasp burst from my lips.

I doubled over, dizzy with agony, and Octavio kicked my legs out from under me. My ass hit the ice, sending another jolt of pain up my spine.

Octavio jerked on my hair to snap my head to the

side. "I'm going to tell Mireya that the Hellborn tracked you down for revenge. She'll believe me, and then you won't matter at all."

He shoved me toward the ice with enough force that my temple glanced off the frigid surface. An ache splintered through my skull; my ribs were still on fire.

I manage to heave myself around in time to see Octavio raising his gun, aiming it at my head while his teeth flashed in an unnerving grin. "Good-bye for good, pequeña rosa."

His finger closed around the trigger. My sight swam as I screamed inwardly at my body to move.

A figure flung itself into view from the edge of my sight just as the bang of the gunshot tore through the air.

No new pain blazed through my existing aches. No bullet blasted through my skull.

Because Octavio was down. It was Quentin I'd seen charging at him—Quentin grappling with him on the ice before my hazy eyes.

Gritting my teeth, I shoved myself toward them, scrambling partway onto my feet. The two men twisted on the frozen turf, fists and knees jabbing at each other.

Just as I reached them, Quentin smacked Octavio's arm into the ice at an unnatural angle, and Octavio's fingers flinched open around the gun. I dove down to snatch at it, still fighting my dizziness.

My hand closed around the metal grip. I whipped it up, fit my finger around the trigger the way I'd practiced so many times, and rammed the muzzle against Octavio's forehead.

No final snarky remarks. I fired without giving him an instant to recover.

Octavio's head snapped backward. Blood gushed from

the hole just above his brow. His body sagged onto the rink, his eyes rolling upward as if looking at the wound that had ended his life.

Dead. He was dead, and I was still alive.

I didn't have time to revel in the miracle that fact felt like. Instead, in defiance of the pain lancing through my side, I hefted myself as straight as I could and aimed the gun at his closest followers.

Most of the other men looked worse for wear by now, sporting scrapes and gashes, even more unsteady than before on the ice. They stared back at me—the daughter of their boss, the woman who'd just killed the man who'd convinced them to take up this rebellion.

"Listen up, assholes," I said, my voice crackling through the arena. "You bet on the wrong guy. Get the hell out of here now before I decide to blast the rest of you away too, and maybe the next time I see you, I'll give you a second chance."

Whatever Octavio had said to them to get them on board, it clearly wasn't enough to outlive his demise. The men on the ice scrambled toward the boards without a backward glance.

Rafael was just tossing his last attacker off him. He drew his own gun and shot the prick in the face. That was plenty of motivation to get the last few goons hurtling for the doors as fast as their feet could carry them. The two who'd been restraining Niko fled for the stands after their departing colleagues.

My gun-hand dropped to my side. I found myself staring down at Octavio's corpse, at the blood pooling under his head, defiling the ice.

The image of Coach Balakin's murdered body flashed behind my eyes. A clammy sensation filled my lungs and crept over my skin. I hardly dared to lift my gaze and find out how my skater men were looking at me now—now that they'd seen just what violence *I* was capable of.

"Fucking bastards," Rafael said in a ragged voice. "I know someone who can get this cleaned up, Lou. Don't worry for one more second about that pinche cabrón."

Skates hissed closer to me. I raised my head, knowing I had to face the real music—and a jolt of shock raced through my veins.

"Quentin!"

He'd pushed himself away from Octavio and onto his feet while I'd threatened our other attackers, but I hadn't noticed—hadn't realized—

A blotch of red was spreading swiftly down his pale green thermal tee from a wound on his left shoulder.

I pushed toward him, my thoughts spinning, my pulse kicking up to a frantic pace. "You were shot! When—"

It hit me before I could even finish the question. My eyes darted up to meet Quentin's gaze. "You took the bullet he meant for me."

Quentin's face had gone sallow, his lips pinched with obvious pain, but he managed to lift his uninjured shoulder in a not particularly convincing shrug. "It's not that bad. Better my shoulder than your head, right?"

The rasp in his voice told me I couldn't believe his spoken assessment of the injury at all. I tore off my fleece and balled it against the wound in an attempt to stop the bleeding. "That was a fucking idiotic thing to do," I said, but my voice shook with panic rather than anger.

Quentin let out a thin chuckle. "Had to show those assholes that figure skaters can handle themselves in a fight too."

"Rafael!" I hollered toward the stands. "Get the first aid stuff—do you know a doctor we could go to?"

"On it!" he shouted back.

Jasper and Niko had come up around us, Jasper pressing his hand against a shallow cut on his jaw and Niko's forehead reddening where he'd have a bruise by morning, but neither of them showing any injuries beyond that.

Jasper's eyes were wide. His voice came out in a croak. "That… that was pretty goddamned amazing, Quentin. I couldn't have gotten there in time."

Niko set a careful hand on Quentin's shoulder, his face glowing with relief. "I was so scared for her. You were there for Lou when we couldn't be."

Quentin stared at both of them, apparently more shellshocked by their gratitude than by the injury he'd taken to earn it. It occurred to me that I should probably express a little more of my own.

I grabbed his hand in mine and squeezed it. "You saved my life, Quentin. Thank you. He could have killed *you*. I never would have asked—"

Quentin yanked his attention back to me. His eyes had gone a bit hazy with the pain, but their usual intensity returned as he held my gaze.

"No fucking way was I letting that prick hurt you if I could help it. I'm in this now—whenever you need me, however you need me. You never need to ask."

Rafael hurried over to us with a handful of sterile pads and a roll of gauze from my equipment bag. "I made a couple of calls. We'll get him fixed up."

Quentin dipped his head. "Thanks."

He said that, and he kept up his brave face, but he had to recognize that he hadn't totally won here. He'd been lucky enough to make it out of the fight alive, yes… but with a wound like that, he could forget about training properly for at least a few weeks.

One more in the long line of sacrifices he'd made to be here for me, and this one might have screwed up his own dreams completely.

TWENTY

Luciana

THE LIGHT from the broad but dingy windows of the guys' loft apartment streaked across Quentin's face where he was sprawled in a boxy armchair. His eyes were closed, his face still even paler than usual, but a little of the tightness from the pain had eased from his features.

The doctor Rafael had summoned had arrived just a few minutes after we'd gotten in, cleaned and stitched up the gunshot wound with brisk efficiency, and dispensed painkillers to both Quentin and me. She'd tested my ribs first and judged that they weren't broken.

From what I could tell, they weren't even fully bruised like they had been in Boston. Octavio's two punches had knocked me down in the moment, but they were nothing compared to the rampage of kicks I'd gotten during that previous fight.

That didn't mean they felt *good*, though.

The door clicked shut as she left the space as discreetly as she'd arrived. My gaze drifted over the rest of the apartment from my vantage point where I was propped up on the modern sofa's cushions.

Calling the place Rafael had found for himself and the guys an "apartment" was really a bit of a stretch. The sprawling open-concept room with its exposed concrete walls was obviously meant to be a commercial loft, not a living space.

It did have a sink and fridge setup at one end, and makeshift bedrooms had been cordoned off with office-style room dividers. The landlord had done his best to give it a homey feel with the furnishings despite the grungy industrial atmosphere, but it'd clearly been a losing battle.

Rafael prowled along the line of windows, peering over the street below into the stark mid-afternoon sunlight. He probably liked how open the layout was—easy to get the other men out if they needed to make a hasty escape, every part of the space accessible without real doors in the way.

Jasper leaned against the wall between two of the windows, and Niko sank onto the arm of the sofa near my feet. They'd both spent the last half hour bustling around, bringing water and rags as the doctor had asked for them, pitching in every way they could.

Jasper's mouth was drawn down in a worried scowl. His gaze caught mine. "Did you have any idea those guys would attack you like that?"

My stomach knotted. In our hurry to get back here and have Quentin looked after, we hadn't really talked about the fight… or what I'd needed to do during it.

I shook my head. "I had a feeling Octavio was trying to undermine me. He obviously wasn't happy about me being back or Mom priming me as her heir. But to come at me openly… He must have been totally sure he could win and cover up his involvement. Mom would have hunted him down to the ends of the earth if she knew."

Rafael had stopped his pacing. "You spared him the tortures she'd have dealt out," he said in his low voice. "Gave him a cleaner end than he deserved."

He knew how the guilt would be eating at me—how much I hated the violent side of this life. The other guys…

Niko simply cocked his head, moving on to the next concern. "What'll happen to the rest of them—the ones who ran away? Do we need to worry about them coming after you again?"

"Nah." I pushed myself a little higher on the couch, relaxing as the painkillers took most of the edge off the lingering ache. "It was Octavio who had the big ideas. They were just following him—they won't want to show their faces anywhere near me or my mother after that mess. He must have told them he'd promote them once he was in charge. He figured he'd be next in line for leadership of the empire with me out of the way."

Jasper let out a light snort. "Jeez. And I thought Quentin had ambition."

In the armchair, Quentin's eyes popped open at that remark. He still looked more fragile than I liked, his normally neatly slicked-back hair rumpled across his forehead, but a healthy color was seeping back into his cheeks.

He flicked his gaze toward his rival with a flash of amused rancor. "Very funny, St. Pierre." As he shifted his attention to me, his tone softened. "How are you holding up?"

I blinked at him and half-sputtered my answer. "Me? You're the one who took a bullet."

Quentin lifted his good shoulder in one of his new partial shrugs. "Now I'm all patched up, good as new. Your ribs were already bothering you."

I touched my side, testing the sore spots. "I think he only set my healing back a little. They were almost back to normal."

Niko hummed and stood up. "I think you could both use some jasmine tea. It'll help you unwind and speed up the healing process."

As our coach headed for the kitchen area, Jasper raised his eyebrows. "Should we start calling you Dr. Okabe now?"

Niko shot a teasing glance over his shoulder. "Only if it turns you on."

Jasper flushed but laughed, and I couldn't suppress a giggle of my own. But my mind jarred against the weird sense of normalcy.

I'd just killed a man in front of these guys. Somehow, none of them seemed remotely bothered by it. The casual banter and the concerned affection in their gazes when they looked at me was all totally familiar.

They really had come a long way into understanding and accepting who I'd been before—who I was having to be again, while I was under Mom's thumb. They recognized as much as Rafael did that I'd only acted to save my life and protect them.

And miraculously, I'd managed to do both of those things. All four of them had made it out of the fight in one piece, if a little battered.

I just had to make sure they never faced anything worse.

Of course, I might have already lost that battle with one of them. The one who really couldn't have imagined anything worse than the fate his association with me had resulted in.

I studied Quentin's sharp-edged features. "It's going to be hard for you to compete with that injury." And Nationals were just weeks away now.

Quentin made a dismissive sound. "Getting anywhere at Nationals was already a long shot after switching to pairs and back again. No big deal. I'll be back in the game next year."

He didn't let any regret show in his tone, but I caught a flicker of disappointment crossing his face. He had the same fire inside of him for skating that Niko, Jasper, and I did. To have to call it quits on Nationals must be killing him, even if the bullet hadn't.

A lump rose in my throat. "I'm sorry I wasn't better prepared—that I didn't manage to finish the fight sooner."

"You said yourself that you had no idea that asshole would go that far. You don't have to apologize. I've got lots of time to skate. It's a hell of a lot more important to me that you're still in this world." His mouth formed a typical smirk. "Who else is going to kick my ass when I need it?"

Despite his nonchalant words, the intensity I was getting used to shone in his eyes as he held my gaze. He'd thrown himself in front of a bullet for me. He couldn't pretend it didn't mean a hell of a lot more than keeping up some friendly competition.

I opened my mouth, but the right response didn't come to me. While I was groping for it, Jasper pushed himself off the wall.

He peered down at Quentin and let out an impatient huff. "Why don't you just admit how much Lou matters to you without making it into a joke? It'll be easier for all of us if we're clear on where we stand—including you. The rest of us aren't going to run you off. It's not like you could make it any more obvious how committed you are."

Jasper lifted his gaze toward Rafael, who nodded, and then toward Niko by the kitchenette, who ambled back over, leaving the tea to steep.

"You risked your life for her," Niko said. "None of us could doubt how much you care about her."

Quentin stared at them for several seconds, looking lost for words. He wet his lips, and a hint of a smile touched his lips.

His gaze slid back to me. "I appreciate the vote of approval, but it's Lou's opinion that really matters. I don't — You said to give you time. I'm trying not to get pushy about—"

A rush of emotion swept over me, casting any hope of figuring out what to say out of reach. So much giddy warmth—for Quentin and the lengths he'd proven he'd go to for my safety and happiness, for my other men and the welcome they'd just offered him.

This one thing didn't have to be hard after all.

Since I had no words, I rose from the sofa instead. It was only a couple of steps to Quentin's chair. Only a thump of my pulse to lean over him, graze my knuckles across his cheek, and bring my lips to his.

Quentin must have seen my intent. He met my kiss without a second's hesitation, his mouth searing against mine. As the hunger of his enthusiasm reverberated into me, my hand rose to wind through his tussled hair.

This was so much better than our only kiss before, when he'd caught me by surprise and I'd still seen him as a total jerk. Quentin slipped his arm around me, his mouth coaxing mine open with a tenderness I'd never have expected from him back then—a little unexpected even now.

Then he eased back a few inches with a cocky smile that was much more typical of him. "Let's make sure you don't strain your ribs…"

With a heft of his good arm, he drew me onto his lap. As I straddled him, a laugh bubbled from my throat.

I gave his pale blond locks a teasing tug. "Always gotta try for more than you already have, huh?"

Quentin's eyes gleamed as he kept grinning up at me. "Hey, I didn't deny that I'm ambitious."

A snort from our audience brought both of our attention to the watching men. Rafael looked mildly amused, Niko was beaming, and even Jasper's mouth had pulled into a crooked smile, but I felt Quentin's body tense beneath mine.

I didn't mind them seeing this, but did he think they'd object? Or was he less comfortable with the idea of sharing me than he'd claimed back when we'd started down this road?

Niko cleared his throat, still looking delighted enough to burst. "Maybe the three of us should do a patrol around the building… for a nice long time. Just to be safe. I think these two need the chance to figure out how they're going to handle each other."

The corner of Rafael's mouth quirked upward. "You know I'll never say no to extra vigilance. Give me a call if you need us."

As I rolled my eyes at him, Jasper let out a rough chuckle. "I guess you do deserve a chance to sort things out without us breathing down your necks." He arched an eyebrow at Quentin that looked more friendly than his laugh had sounded. "Don't do anything I wouldn't do."

At Quentin's guffaw, the men I loved headed for the loft's door. A quiver of resistance ran down the middle of my chest, and my lips parted before I'd really thought the impulse through.

"You're not all going to leave without giving me a kiss goodbye, are you?"

If Quentin couldn't handle the fact that I was completely enmeshed with all three of these men too, then it was better we found out now rather than after I'd fallen for him more than I already had.

He didn't make a sound, just watching me with wary curiosity and running his thumb over my thigh. The other three guys made their way back over, understanding shining in their eyes.

Rafael reached me first. He tangled his strong fingers in my hair and pulled my head back to meet his demanding kiss as if I weren't currently perched on another man, as if I existed for him alone. And in the moment while our mouths melded together, that might as well have been true.

He eased back, leaving my lips tingling, and Jasper was there an instant later. My partner gave me one of his small but warm smiles as he leaned in to claim my mouth for himself.

Jasper kissed me deeply, thoroughly, as if to ensure I'd remember him after he walked out the door. Like there was any chance I'd forget his gruffly passionate presence. As he pulled back, Niko slid a hand up his arm to his shoulder in both a caress and a nudge out of the way.

Our coach tucked his fingers under my chin and offered a gentle kiss that was both short and sweet. He winked at me as he stepped away. "Have fun. The tea's there when you're ready for it. We'll make sure there are no unwanted interruptions."

My gaze dropped to Quentin's face. His eyes flicked from Niko back to me, and the heat I saw burning there set off an ache between my thighs. A faint flush had colored his cheeks, and when he wet his lips again, I saw nothing but desire in the gesture.

"Had to make a point, did you?" he murmured as the door clicked shut behind the other guys.

I gave him my version of his usual smirk. "I thought you liked it when I kicked your ass?"

He sputtered a laugh and reached for me, but his hand simply lingered against my face, his fingertips tracing my hairline down to my cheek. His bright blue eyes seemed to be drinking me in, like brilliant pools I could drown in.

I studied him in turn, grazing my fingers along the line of his jaw, stroking my thumb over the scar that notched his lower lip. There was no need to hurry. In a lot of ways, we were just getting to know each other.

But I already knew the most important things about him. That beneath the prickly, arrogant exterior lay a guy who craved affection and acceptance. That the man beneath me possessed a selfless streak deep enough that he'd put his life on the line for me without a second thought.

I hadn't been sure I could feel this way about him when I'd first seen him here in Austin. It'd taken time for those walls to come down, for him to show the vulnerabilities he'd been covering up and let the asshole front drop. Now, knowing I'd almost lost him, I couldn't imagine letting him go.

"I told you I'd convince you to give me a chance eventually," he said with a hint of a growl in his voice.

I laughed lightly and bowed my head over his so my breath would brush over his face. "And you only had to almost die to manage it."

Quentin made a soft scoffing sound. "Worth it."

Then he was pulling my mouth back to his.

Our early kisses were slow and lingering, tasting each other and testing what felt best while our hands explored each other's bodies, careful of our respective injuries. But with each meeting of our lips, the passion between us sparked hotter. Quentin's chest hitched, and he kissed me more fervently, dipping his hand right beneath my shirt.

I tilted my position to allow him easier access, and my pussy ground against the bulge at the crotch of his training pants. We both groaned, the sound reverberating between our lungs, and dove in for another kiss.

Quentin massaged my breasts through my bra and then slipped his hand behind me to unsnap the garment. As it drooped loose beneath my shirt, his slim fingers delved beneath the fabric to caress me skin to skin.

His thumb flicked over my pebbling nipple, sending a bolt of pleasure through my chest. I gasped and ground against him more insistently.

Quentin let out a full growl, devouring my mouth as he worked over my breasts. His hips rocked upward to press his erection against my throbbing cunt. I whimpered, a tremor of need passing through me, and he eased back with a shaky exhalation and a renewed smirk.

"I love how you tremble for me. Like you can't wait for me to touch you everywhere."

"So why are you taking so long to get on with it?" I grumbled playfully.

His answering laugh was lost in another kiss. But he answered my impatience by tugging my shirt off of me, and naturally I had to strip off his in turn, lifting it carefully around his bandaged shoulder. Then I raked my fingers down the compact but solid muscles of his slender chest and earned a tremble of my own.

Quentin ran his hands over every inch of me except the mottled patch where my skin was bruising over my ribs. Gripping my waist, he urged me forward. With a dip of his head, he closed his mouth around one of my sensitized nipples.

I moaned, rocking faster with the wave of bliss his lips and tongue sparked from my breast. The ache of need low in my belly expanded until I could barely think through the haze of lust.

He shifted his head to my other breast and tested my nipple between his teeth. My fingernails dug into his good shoulder as I arched into his hold. His pleased chuckle vibrated over my skin to delicious effect, but the straining of his cock against his pants told me he was at least as desperate for release as I was.

I wrenched at his pants, and he wriggled out of them with my help. Then his fingers hooked around the waist of my leggings. I lifted myself up so he could strip them and my panties off me, managing to wrap my hand around his erection and give it a few experimental strokes in the meantime.

"Fuck," he muttered through clenched teeth, jerking into my grasp.

"Working on it," I teased as if I wasn't equally

breathless, and snatched at the purse I'd left on the floor by the sofa.

My fingers snagged on the condom packet I'd been searching for. Quentin snatched it from my hand and tore it open, his gaze never leaving my face. I felt him prep himself beneath me and swallowed a whimper as the head of his cock rubbed over my pussy, which was drenched with longing.

As he pushed upward, I sank down. Our moans entwined as our bodies joined, his shaft filling me at just the right angle. The heady burn I'd been craving raced through my nerves.

"God," Quentin mumbled. "I love seeing you on the ice, but this is my new favorite Lou."

I conveyed my own enthusiasm with the roll of my hips over his. He sucked in a breath and thrust up to meet me, penetrating me even more fully. With every little grunt and growl, he showed how much I turned him on—and fanned the flames of my own desire hotter.

He gripped my thigh and bucked up into me even harder. I threw my head back, my vision blurring as my pleasure started to sweep me away. Plenty of sounds were spilling from my own lips—gasps and a keening I couldn't hold in.

Quentin captured the tip of my breast in his mouth once more with a scrape of his teeth that had me whimpering. Then he lifted me high enough that he slid free from me.

His voice came out full of strained yearning. "Turn around. I want to take you as deep as I can go."

I couldn't resist the promise in his demand. I swiveled over him, and he yanked me back down, spearing me so abruptly and perfectly that stars swam in my vision.

Quentin raised his hand to cup my breast from behind. As I pushed back into his thrusts, he fondled it thoroughly, pinching and pulling at my nipple between his thumb and forefinger.

My body shuddered with the rush of bliss blazing through me. "Yes, fuck, just like that!"

He leaned forward to nip at my shoulder blade, pounding into me all the while. The jolts of pain transformed into something blissful in combination with the giddy friction he was creating from within.

He was taking me, making me his, leaving his mark on me. He hissed against my skin, the pace of his hips quickening.

"You like how I fuck you?"

"Yes—hell, yes."

He was panting now, but he managed to rasp out one more demand. "Say it. Let me hear how much you want this."

My mind was so scrambled with pleasure it took a moment to form a complete sentence. "I love how you're fucking me. Oh my God, keep going—"

My orgasm hit me like a tidal wave, crashing through me and leaving me washed out with ecstasy. My body shook over Quentin's, every nerve tingling with the force of my release, and he let out a choked sound as he followed me over the edge. His cock pulsed inside me.

We sagged together in a jumble of sweaty limbs. As our breaths started to even out, Quentin rested his head against my shoulder and then grasped my waist again. "I want to see you."

I turned in his arms and tipped my head so our foreheads met. Quentin touched my cheek, gazing up at me with so much emotion in those normally cool eyes that my pulse wobbled.

He didn't speak, only searched my expression for several thumps of my heart before gathering me against his lean chest. As his arms wrapped around me, I relaxed into his embrace, drinking in his tart, musky scent.

"I'm not sure I ever really believed I'd get this," he admitted after a few minutes in a voice so quiet it was almost a whisper. "The more I see you, the more I find out about what you've survived, the more incredible I realize you are."

I swallowed thickly and nuzzled the side of his neck. "You just talk a good game with all that cockiness, huh?"

"Fake it 'til you make it, right?" He gave a short laugh, and then a thread of tension wound through his muscles. "So… are we really doing this? Not just a 'thank you for saving my life' hookup—the whole relationship thing?"

He'd tried to keep his tone casual, but the fraught anticipation with which he waited for my answer told the real story. He wasn't sure even now.

I tilted my head to look at him. "If that's what *you* want, I'm up for it."

His voice thickened with emotion. "I don't think there's anything I've ever wanted more."

A pang of affection and compassion reverberated through me at those words. Quentin had survived an awful lot too, and I didn't know if he'd ever been able to admit it to anyone before now.

I adjusted myself against him so I could tuck my arm behind his back, returning his embrace. "Then we'll give it our best and see how it goes."

The gradual relaxing of his posture beneath me felt like

a reward in itself. When he pressed a gentle kiss to the top of my head, my heart sang.

How lucky had I gotten to find not one, not three, but four extraordinary men who wanted to share their lives with me? I wouldn't have traded their devotion for any empire in the world.

So I'd damn well make sure I didn't lose them to the woman who believed I should.

TWENTY-ONE

Luciana

THE DEADLY ROSE mansion had rarely felt homey to me, even when I was a kid. But it'd never given me such ominous vibes as when I returned in the evening after Octavio's attack.

I pushed into the foyer, my gaze sweeping over the lackeys standing guard or simply hanging around near the grand staircase. I kept my stance straight and confident to hide my jangling nerves.

How many of these men had known what Octavio was planning? How many of them were going to be disappointed to see he'd failed? Could I hope that most would be glad that I'd come out on top?

Some of them nodded to me in the brisk gestures of respect that the daughter of their boss was owed. I thought I caught a flicker of surprise cross a couple of faces before they stiffened into emotionless masks. There might have been a twitch of a smirk here, a hint of a frown over there.

Nothing definitive. Nothing I could have pointed a finger at in accusation. Nevertheless, the certainty prickled over me that at least a few of these men knew what had gone down earlier today.

The goons who'd actually joined Octavio in his attack were unlikely to return, but he'd have picked low-level grunts without much direct connection to this household —the men most likely to be hungering for a step up in status. The men least likely to feel enough loyalty to Mom to warn her of an impending ambush on her daughter.

That didn't mean they had no connections at all to the men who worked out of the mansion, though. As they went into hiding, they'd have passed on news and warnings of possible retribution to come to whatever friends they had, even if those men hadn't known about the plot before.

Who could say exactly what they'd claimed about how it'd gone down? What kind of a picture they'd painted of me?

The one thing no one would have been able to deny was that I'd won. So I strode through the foyer and up the stairs with my head high and my expression stern, letting all of the watching lackeys see the cool, unshakeable mafia princess who'd stamped out a mutiny with blood and bullets.

It didn't matter that the memory of the fight still made me queasy. That my gut tangled up on itself even considering that I might face opposition like that from within my own empire again.

These men were never going to see the real Luciana Cordova. But they didn't deserve her. They couldn't understand me and my passion for skating or the love I'd found with four men, most of whom wouldn't have fit in here at all.

I was carved from totally different stuff than my mother and her horde. *That* was something to be proud of.

I'd meant to head straight to my bedroom, but another lackey moved to intercept me in the upstairs hall.

"Miss Luciana," he said, running a nervous hand through his greasy hair. "Your mother wanted you to meet her in her office as soon as you got back."

Of course Mom would send a human being to deliver her message instead of texting me like a normal person. She probably enjoyed reminding me of how much sway she held over her underlings—and reminding them of it too.

This goon's apparent uneasiness suggested she hadn't made the request in the friendliest way either. I judged his expression. "She was pretty impatient about it, huh?"

He managed an awkward grin. "I'd say you'd better get going."

At my signature knock, Mom whipped open her office door. She motioned me in with a sharp wave of her hand, the only outward indication of the tension I could tell she was holding in. She strode to the chair behind her desk and sank into it with her lips pursed.

When I'd settled into the chair across from her, willing down my own anxiety, she folded her hands on the top of the desk and narrowed her eyes.

"One of my top men is missing. Someone informed me that I should ask *you* what happened to him."

Oh, shit. I'd known Mom couldn't exactly fail to notice that a key underling had vanished, but I hadn't expected word to travel all the way up the ladder quite this quickly. I'd kind of been hoping no one would mention my involvement and she'd just assume Octavio had vanished.

At the bite in her voice, a chilling thought that hadn't occurred to me before prickled through my head. Had Mom known what Octavio was planning before he'd actually done it?

Was it possible she'd even nudged him down his traitorous path?

I could far too easily imagine her manipulating him into his attempted mutiny. She might have done it to test his loyalties, to see if he'd stay strong in the face of temptation. She might have wanted to evaluate how well I'd handle myself under attack from within her own forces.

She might even have seen it as due punishment for my own insurrection. I knew she didn't want me *dead*, but it wouldn't surprise me if she'd liked the idea of shaking me up, maybe seeing me injured beyond what that pendejo had managed.

Or she might have had no idea until an hour or two ago. The suspicions swimming through my mind were only speculation.

I gathered myself, watching her expression and pose closely. If she *was* at all disappointed that I'd returned relatively unharmed, I'd like to know just how wary I should be of her going forward.

At least I didn't have to worry that she'd be upset about what I'd done to Octavio. She expected her heir to handle insubordination with brutal efficiency.

If I hadn't killed him, she would have had to. It wouldn't have even been a question.

"I can tell you what happened to him," I said, keeping my voice cool and steady. "Because he and a bunch of goons he'd gotten to join him barged into the skating arena while I was training and tried to murder me."

Mom blinked. Her head tilted to the side as she took in my account, but I couldn't tell whether she was genuinely startled or only putting on a small show of shock.

Her mouth tightened. "Well, that is somewhat unexpected. Did he give any reason for his hostility?"

I grimaced at her. "He wasn't super talkative while he and his idiot friends were trying to bash me and my men around, but he's been grumbling about me coming back as heir from the start. He said he was going to tell you that the Hellborn had taken me out, and he obviously figured he'd be your clear choice as an alternate successor."

Mom exhaled in a rush, her eyes flashing. She was certainly putting on a good act if this was all news to her, but she was completely capable of faking it.

"I had noticed his ambitions seemed to be getting a little overblown," she said tightly. "You know what men are like—you give them a little authority, they think they're the next king of the roost." Her hands closed into fists. "But this—this is beyond the pale. If he thinks he'll get away with even attempting—"

"He didn't get away with it," I broke in. "I put a bullet in his skull. The rest of them scattered once he was finished. And now they know how deadly I can be if anyone thinks about messing with me again."

Mom's hands relaxed, a slight smile curving her lips. "You fit your role more with every new challenge, mija. I like seeing you blossom." Her gaze hardened again. "If you catch any of those traitors skulking around our territory again, you know how to deal with them. None of them should walk away from such a huge offense against the Deadly Rose."

I forced a grim smile in return. "My men and I delivered a decent beating in the moment. I'll do what I have to do if I see any of them again."

What I figured I had to do might not be what Mom assumed, but I didn't need to spell that out. I'd rather keep the corpses on my conscience to a minimum.

Mom exhaled slowly and seemed to gather herself. She'd definitely been angry—but because she was disappointed in how her gambit had played out or because anything had happened at all, I still couldn't tell.

She looked me over with an analytical air, and I drew myself a little taller instinctively.

"You're all right to continue with our usual business?" she asked.

My stomach sank, wondering what she had in store for me next, but I nodded anyway. "He didn't do any major damage."

"Good." She brushed her hands across the desk. "I have a few more meetings for you to participate in over the next week. Nothing too strenuous, but I expect you be ready to go and to represent me well."

At least I could be relieved that she wasn't sending me straight into another fight.

I stared right back at her. "I always do. I'm holding up my end of our deal."

Her smile turned a little sharp. "Yes, you are. So far. You may go."

So far. She might be proud of how I'd defended myself today, but we were still at odds, holding metaphorical knives to each other's throats.

I bobbed my head and headed out, a renewed sense of dread looming over me.

I hadn't conquered all the danger amid the Deadly Rose's ranks. The worst threat was sitting there right behind me.

TWENTY-TWO

Rafael

"IS your weapons dealer seriously named *Dolores*?" Lou asked with one eyebrow raised.

I glanced over at her as we headed down the alley to the back entrance of the building said weapons dealer worked out of. Her dark hair nearly blended into the evening's shadows, and I found myself feeling oddly nostalgic for the deep red shade she'd sported for a couple of months.

At least it'd meant I could always spot her in an instant.

I allowed myself a trace of a smile before I answered. "Old ladies have to make a living too, you know."

"Sure, I just wouldn't have expected that living to be in illicit arms." Lou kicked at a candy wrapper that'd drifted into our path, sending it crinkling away. "It's not like I really need another gun, you know. I've got the pistol

Mom gave me, and now I'll keep it closer at hand. If I decide I want something else, there's plenty of selection at the mansion."

I gave a dismissive grunt. "Anything you do there is watched. I think you should own one piece your Mom and her lackeys couldn't know about. It's always better to have at least one advantage your enemies won't take into account."

"Lo sé, lo sé." Lou gave a brief shudder. "I know. I just hate lugging even *one* of those things around with me. I'm trying to avoid shooting people, not to give myself more chances to."

I glowered at her. "If it's that or someone shoots you, you'd better put all the bullets you can in them."

The memory of Octavio's attack at the skating rink flashed behind my eyes, and my gut twisted. *I* hadn't been close enough—I'd been too busy dealing with the thugs who'd jumped me to even try to defend Lou directly.

If it hadn't been for Quentin, I'd have lost her.

The thought sickened me, but I had to admit that gluing myself to Lou's side wasn't an option. She wanted to be free, not locked in a cage... or chained to a bodyguard.

So I was going to chase the chill of my fears away as well as I could by making sure she had every possible means to defend herself.

I spotted the right door with its faded blue paint and motioned to Lou. "Let me go first. I'll introduce you."

I rapped on the door to announce my arrival and then pushed into the room on the other side.

Dolores sat at a small table, looking for all the world as if she was engaged in an innocent game of solitaire with no other business on her mind. The amber glow of the dim fixture shone off the thick lenses of her glasses. She glanced up at me and grinned, bringing the smile lines on her worn face into sharper relief.

As I gestured for Lou to follow me in, Dolores swiped a few stray strands of stringy white hair under her vibrant pink shawl and reached for a case hidden away in one of the drawers on a nearby dresser.

Her voice was as crisp and crackly as autumn leaves. "Good to see you, Rafael. And this must be your 'friend.'"

The slight lilt she gave that last word indicated she didn't buy that Lou and I were only friends for an instant.

Lou took the wrinkled hand the old woman offered her and shook it, the picture of politeness if a little awkward. "Nice to meet you. I'm Lou. I, er, I'm here to buy a gun."

"Just the same as everyone else who comes to visit me," Dolores replied in a dryly amused tone. "You're a pretty one, aren't you? Rafael, if I were you, I'd hurry and put a ring on this one's finger!"

Heat rushed to Lou's cheeks. "I —"

Dolores laughed. "I'm just joking, darling. But not about how pretty you are. Goodness, you've got the face of an angel. And those legs! Appreciate them while you have them. One day you'll get to be just as old as me."

My stomach sunk at Dolores's words. I'd almost lost Lou so many times—there had been so many close calls. At this rate, we both would be lucky if we made it to forty.

She would if I had anything to say about it. As soon as we could get her out of her mother's control for good, she could live a normal life. Well, as normal as any other figure skating pro.

Dolores wasted no time popping open her case and laying a selection of guns out on the table. "I gather you want something discreet. Most of the young ladies prefer it that way. All of these will pack a punch without making you look like you're packing." She shot Lou a wink.

Lou picked up the compact pistols one by one, testing their weight and feel in her hand. A few of them she liked enough to pass over to me so I could confirm I approved with my greater experience when it came to firearms. But the decision would ultimately be up to her.

What mattered most was that she chose a weapon she'd feel comfortable enough with to use it when she needed to.

"These are all good," I told her after she handed a fourth option over. "Dolores is picky about what she carries. Which one feels best to you?"

Lou went through them again and settled on a sleek little Glock. "I like this one. Solid but small. I could fit it in the pocket of some of my jackets, even—definitely in even my smaller purses without being noticeable."

I nodded. "The closer you can keep it, the better."

I forked over the cash without thinking about the price. It was worth any amount of money to see Lou safe.

Lou slid the gun into the kangaroo pocket of her pullover hoodie, and her mouth twisted into a bittersweet smile. "I could even have it on me when I'm skating."

I didn't think either of us wanted to talk about why that might be a good idea.

We said our goodbyes to Dolores, who returned them cheerfully, and set out into the night. Lou rested her hand on the bulging purse she'd brought tonight, where I knew she was keeping her other pistol. She'd handled herself just fine, but I could sense the tension in her.

"You okay?" I had to ask.

Lou shrugged. "Sure. Hell, I might not ever need to

use it. Really, you and the rest of the guys are the ones who should be concerned about protecting yourselves more than me. I've already taken down the biggest threat to my life."

My jaw clenched. "Your mom—"

Lou caught my gaze. "Is a stone-cold bitch, I know. But she doesn't want me dead. I can't say the same for you guys."

I couldn't help scoffing. "We can look after ourselves. Or I can, and I'll keep an eye on your skaters too. You worry about yourself."

I slung my arm around her shoulders at the same time to take the edge off my chiding. Lou immediately leaned into me, bringing the sweet scent of her hair to my nose. My heart stuttered at the same time as my cock twitched.

This woman had quite a hold on me, that was for sure. And if I had my way—

I jolted back into a deeper awareness of my surroundings with the thump of footsteps. In a matter of seconds, a crowd of aggressive figures had barged onto the narrow street we'd been walking along, their gazes fixed on us.

I jerked to a halt, my hand dipping to the pistol at my hip, and paused as recognition washed over me.

Salvador stood near the front of the group. A bunch of the others were men I'd known in my old neighborhood… members of the gang Edmundo and I had run with.

I'd hoped I'd make it through our time here in Austin without running into them again. It looked like they'd decided to force the issue.

Mierda!

A different guy stepped out in front of the others—no more than a couple of years older than me, with flinty eyes and an equally sharp jaw that jogged my memory. His attention was totally focused on me.

"I heard you were back in town, Rafe," he snarled. "Did you think you could skip a proper reunion?"

I swallowed hard and kept my voice calm. "I've been busy. It's good to see you, Anton. How's your cousin doing these days?"

Anton's lips curled back in a sneer. "Bruno está muerto. We lost him three years ago now. Not that you would care." His gaze flicked to Lou, who'd stiffened beside me. "Is this what you threw everything away for? Some Cordova puta?"

Lou glared back at him. "I'm no whore."

Anton ignored her, his eyes meeting mine again, smoldering with rage. "Your brother would be rolling over in his grave."

Even as I bristled at the insult he'd aimed at Lou, my innards turned to ice. Lou would have no idea what they were talking about—and I wanted to keep it that way. Forever, if I could.

These guys were clearly pissed, and there were a hell of a lot more of them than there were of us. What did they think they were going to do?

Were they just passing on a threat, or were they here to rain down judgment on me?

My voice tightened. "I've never betrayed anyone. Edmundo would be glad that—"

"Don't feed us that mierda," Salvador spat out. "You know what you were meant to do. You know who you owed."

"You have no idea what—"

Anton took another step forward. "Edmundo's not here to do it, so we're going to deliver the message he'd have wanted his traitor brother to get. And if you don't pay attention, next time we'll be sending you to your grave so you can make your excuses straight to his face in Hell."

The whole group surged toward us in a furious mass. I dove in front of Lou instinctively, my fists already flying.

My knuckles bashed in one guy's nose and clocked another in the jaw. I jabbed my knee into someone's gut before stomping an ankle hard enough that the bone cracked.

I had to take them all down—topple them all before they got close enough to hurt Lou.

I dared to reach for my gun, and maybe that was a miscalculation. In the small opening when one of my hands was out of commission, some prick hurtled into me from the side.

As I staggered backward, my fingers clenched around the pistol's grip—and the next thing I knew, something was slamming against the back of my head with a blast of pain.

A board, I registered as I grappled for balance. A few more assholes had come up behind us too—one of them had hit me with a fucking slab of *wood*.

More arms and feet lashed out at me. A bash to my forearm sent my pistol spinning away. I managed to grasp hold of two pricks' heads of hair and slam their foreheads together with a satisfying thud, but with each body that wobbled away, three more seemed to rush in to take its place.

As I swung in one direction, someone in the other rammed a kick against my shins. Multiple pairs of hands yanked and shoved.

I sprawled on my ass, sputtering curses, still hurling punches as well as I could. Then some cabrón drove his heel down on my knee with the full weight of his body behind the blow.

Agony exploded through my leg, like a thousand shards of glass digging into the joint. A groan burst from my lips.

They'd broken my goddamn knee cap. Fuck, fuck, fuck.

Anton loomed over me, clamping his hand around the short coils of my hair. He heaved my head into the pavement beneath me—once, twice, sending more white-hot pain fizzing behind my eyes. A throbbing sensation reverberated through my skull.

I blinked, but I couldn't clear the thickening haze from my eyes. The click of a safety sliding off brought my gaze jerking upward. Salvador stood over me by my broken knee, pointing his pistol at me.

I tried to thrash at him, but other goons jammed my limbs against the concrete. Salvador gave me a vicious grin, his fingers tensing—

And a shot rang out, but from beside me rather than in front of me.

Salvador crumpled, blood spurting from a wound on his chest. A short but fearsome figure shoved into view.

"Get the fuck away from him, or you're all dead!"

Lou fired another bullet into the thigh of one of the men pinning me down. He scrambled away with a string of expletives, clutching the gushing hole in his leg. She braced herself above me, the pistol she'd gotten from her mother clutched in one hand, the Glock I'd just bought for her in the other, murder in her eyes.

"If you don't get the hell out of here *now*, I'm just getting started," she snarled. In that moment, there was no doubting whose daughter she was, even if she'd only brought out the Cordova in her under duress.

Anton held up his hands, but his mouth had twisted with revulsion. "Está bien. We've already delivered our message. Oh, but one last present."

He stomped his foot down on my hand hard enough that a fresh explosion of pain radiated up my arm. I winced inwardly at the crack of bone.

I wasn't going to be holding a gun—or much else—for a good long while.

"Enjoy your goodbye present," Anton spat out, and waved to his men. Supporting the few we'd injured badly enough that they had trouble walking, the horde of them surged back into the side-street they'd emerged from.

Lou stayed poised over me, a tremor running through her body. Her arms quivered but held in place, keeping both guns aimed at the retreating men as they disappeared from view.

I groped at the gritty concrete beneath me with my uninjured hand, searching for leverage to heave myself upright. My head came up—and swam with a whirlpool of pain and dizziness.

Lou dropped down next to me, shoving one gun into her purse so she could wrap her arm around my shoulder. "Don't try to get up. You could make it worse. Dios mío, Rafael, your leg—there's blood all over the back of your head—"

I knew things were bad when she started slipping Spanish in there. The fact that when I opened my mouth, I nearly vomited was another major indication.

I swayed in her hold. My voice came out in a croak. "Sorry. I should have been… protecting you…"

"Fuck that," Lou snapped. "They practically buried

you." She pawed through her purse and yanked out her phone. "I'm calling an ambulance."

"Lou," I protested raggedly. "No hospitals. No—"

"I don't want to hear it." The panicked note beneath her words startled me silent. "I don't care what the doctors think about how you ended up like this. I'm not losing you, and no back-alley doctor is going to be able to fix all of this."

I tried to find the wherewithal to keep arguing, but bright spots were forming in my vision, pulsing in time with the throbbing of my head.

"You saved my ass there," I mumbled instead. "Not supposed to be like that."

"Well, it is like that. So live with it. As long as you *live*, I don't fucking care what you think about it."

The desperation in her tone cut right through the center of me. Even as my sight blurred completely, guilt wrenched through the worst of the pain like a wound in itself.

I'd failed her yet again. And how the hell was I going to protect her after this, with my body broken and battered?

TWENTY-THREE

Luciana

RETURNING FROM THE HOSPITAL, Rafael scowled the whole way up to the loft. It was hard to tell whether he was more frustrated with his injuries or the help he was forced to accept.

"I can still *walk*," he muttered, thumping along on his crutches. "You don't need to coddle me."

I ignored his grumbling, shooting a grateful smile at Jasper when he opened the building's front door for us, and studied my bodyguard's face for signs of concussion. A large bandage swathed the back of his head where he'd been bleeding the evening of the attack, two days ago. When I'd come to pick him up this morning, the doctor had told me that the most dangerous period had passed, but that I should still keep a careful eye on him.

That bandage was far from his only lingering impediment from the ambush. He needed the crutches because of the cast encasing his left leg from calf to thigh to stabilize his broken knee cap. Another cast covered his right hand and wrist, where the one asshole had stomped on him right before he'd left.

I should have shot that prick too.

The broken fingers made maneuvering on the crutches significantly more difficult. Rafael swayed a little as we approached the elevator, and Niko extended a hand to steady him.

Rafael's scowl deepened, but he grunted a brief "Thanks."

Quentin jabbed the button to summon the elevator, and Rafael outright glowered at him. "What are you even doing down here trying to take care of me? *You've* got a bullet hole in you, remember?"

Quentin shot him a wry grin. "I've also got two working hands and legs, which is more than you can say, old man."

He kept his tone light enough that Rafael simply rolled his eyes. Their banter smoothed the edges of my distress. If they could joke around like normal, things couldn't have gone *too* horribly wrong, could they?

Every time I looked at Rafael, I had to reassure myself all over again.

I didn't even understand why that gang had attacked him in the first place. They'd said something about his brother and accused him of betraying them. How did that make sense?

I'd asked him about it in the hospital after he was bandaged up, and he'd brushed off the question, saying they were guys from his old neighborhood who'd taken it as a personal insult when he'd gone to work for the Cordovas rather than getting in deeper with them. That they'd gotten increasingly angry the longer he'd avoided them.

The explanation didn't sit totally right with me—but this didn't seem like a good time to badger him about it.

When he was healed up, I'd insist on getting the full story.

The elevator deposited us in the hall outside the loft. Jasper hurried ahead to open the loft's door, and Niko and I flanked Rafael on his lurching journey toward it with Quentin bringing up the rear.

Inside, Rafael thumped over to the sofa and sank onto it with a faint groan of relief. "Fuck hospitals."

Niko headed over to the kitchen. "I'll make us some lunch."

Rafael's mouth pulled even tighter, and I expected him to argue about being served. Instead, he simply said, "Hold off on that for a minute. There's something I need to say."

As the guys came up around the sofa, I sat down gingerly next to Rafael and rested a supportive hand on his abdomen. He slid his fingers around mine and squeezed.

"Lou, you were right," he said gruffly. "I was so caught up in protecting *you* that I wasn't thinking about the threats the rest of us might face, and look where that got me. Now I can't defend you at all."

A pang ran through my heart, and I twined my fingers with his. "It's not your fault. I don't know how anyone would have been prepared for—"

He shook his head to cut me off. "I know you're tough. I know you can look after yourself. But you'll still need help sometimes. And since I can't provide that until I've recovered, you shouldn't be afraid to let the other guys help you. So I'm going to make sure that *they're* as prepared as they can be—to protect both you and themselves. I already made the call."

I knit my brow. "Call? What are you talking about?"

Before he needed to answer, a knock sounded on the loft door. My gaze darted to it with a hitch of my pulse, but Rafael smiled. "Someone go get that. We don't want to leave her waiting."

Her?

My confusion mostly faded when Niko opened the door and I spotted a familiar bright pink shawl in the hallway beyond.

Dolores bustled past Niko and peered around the space, blowing a strand of her faded hair away from her eyes. She had a large case dangling from each aged hand.

"Nice to see you again," she said to me with a grin. "Wish it was under better circumstances. Not a bad place. Lots of pretty views." Her gaze flicked admiringly to Niko, who chuckled in amusement.

Rafael eased himself upright carefully enough that I didn't feel the need to jump in and admonish him. "Thank you for making the house call, Dolores. These guys need firearms of their own if they're going to take care of themselves and our woman properly."

Niko's eyebrows shot up, and a flash of surprise crossed Jasper's face. Only Quentin didn't look particularly startled, though he sucked in his lower lip for a second with a hint of concern.

I spun to meet Rafael's eyes. "Are you sure this is necessary? We've been trained to use guns. They—"

"I'll train them," Rafael said. "The basics, anyway. That'll be enough. We're up against experienced criminals, Lou. You can't let them go into this without the right equipment."

As Dolores laid out a selection of pistols on the coffee table, like the guns were pieces in a Tupperware party, I clamped my mouth shut. My gut stayed twisted.

I'd wanted to keep my skating life totally separate from my criminal past. But that past had become my present, and the guys had already been exposed to more violence than anyone should be. I couldn't pretend I could keep them totally innocent in this situation.

But arming them and preparing them to potentially murder people in my defense felt like a big step farther than they'd already come. A step that made me queasy just thinking about it.

How far would I end up dragging them into the horrible parts of my existence before I finally broke free?

But if I'd been right before, then Rafael was right now. I didn't know what threats we might face next. It wouldn't be fair for me to expect the other guys to turn down any possible tool they could use to keep themselves safe just to absolve my conscience.

I'd have a hell of a weight on my conscience if any of *them* got murdered when having a gun could have saved them.

Dolores stepped back so the men could gather around the table. Rafael studied the offerings and motioned to the other guys in turn.

"Niko, this Sig should suit you well. It's light and easy to carry, good for those slim hands of yours. Nothing too complicated. See how it feels."

Niko picked up the gun Rafael had indicated and eased his fingers around it. My stomach churned, watching him position it in his hand, the weapon looking completely incongruous with his cheerful demeanor.

"Most of my knowledge is from movies," my coach

admitted with a nervous laugh. "But I'll do my best to learn. It doesn't feel *bad*."

I couldn't keep silent any longer. "You don't have to do this, you know. I mean, it's true that having a gun might come in handy. But if you're not comfortable carrying one, we're not going to force you."

Niko lifted his bright gaze to meet mine and offered his trademark sunny smile. "I can get used to it. If this is what it takes to keep all of us safe, especially you, then I'm in."

If he could smile like that while holding the pistol, then maybe this wasn't the end of the world. I dragged in a breath and nodded my acceptance.

Rafael had gestured to Jasper as he pointed out another of the guns. As he started to speak, I scanned the rest of the spread more closely.

"You might do best with this Smith & Wesson," he said. "It's a good beginner gun, not too heavy on the firepower."

I made a soft noise to cut in. "I don't know, Jasper has a pretty good grip. I should know from all those lifts. And didn't you tell me that your dad's taken you hunting before?"

Jasper paused, his shoulders stiffening. "I mean, he insisted. It's not as if I liked it. And those were rifles. But I guess I do have some experience with things like how the kick feels."

I nodded. "If we're doing this, we shouldn't skimp on power. I bet you could handle the Ruger." I pointed out the one I meant.

Jasper grasped it and held it up to get a feel for it. "Okay, that's a lot less cumbersome than a rifle. Just holding it, I think I'm okay with this one."

We both glanced at Rafael, who admittedly had a hell of a lot more firearms knowledge than I did. My bodyguard raised an eyebrow at me, but he tipped his head approvingly toward Jasper. "I'll never say a man should downplay what he can handle. I didn't realize you weren't a total newbie."

Quentin stepped closer with an impatient air. "What about me? I don't want anything wimpy."

Rafael contemplated his shoulder. "You're righthanded, aren't you? So the injury shouldn't mess with your aim."

I examined the remaining guns with a frown. "But better not to pick anything that's got too much of a kick. You've got to brace your whole body against that."

"I'll be fine," Quentin started to say.

I aimed a narrow look at him. "We're not making the injury worse."

Dolores, who'd been sitting patiently through our conversation, cleared her throat. "If I could make a suggestion… This model of Beretta has a good balance of power and subtlety."

Rafael took the pistol she'd indicated and looked it over, then passed it to me so I could check it out before Quentin finally got his hands on it.

He aimed it at the wall and then the window without putting his finger on the trigger. A smile crossed his lips. "I could get used to this."

"It feels all right?" I confirmed.

"Oh, yeah. I might not have fired a gun before, but I'm not squeamish about it. Just train me up."

The corner of Rafael's mouth ticked upward. "That's exactly what I've got on the schedule for tomorrow. I'm hauling the three of you out to a shooting range so you can get comfortable with firing those things."

After he'd handed over the cash for the three guns, Dolores cleared the others from the table and then opened her second case to reveal an assortment of knives. "Don't forget about these beauties. In close combat, a blade will often do you better than a bullet."

Niko immediately gravitated to a double-edged tactical knife. Just his initial swipe of it through the air made me think anyone stupid enough to try to take him on while he was holding that thing would quickly regret it.

Jasper went bigger, hefting a serrated hunting knife. He pricked his finger on the deadly tip and hissed before blotting beading blood from the scratch on his shirt. "Christ. This thing's pretty damn sharp."

"Of course it is. Dolores doesn't sell dull blades, young man." The old woman gave him a wink that looked suspiciously flirty.

I glanced over at Quentin, who was still eyeing the options. "Anything calling to you?"

"Maybe…" He turned a switchblade over in his hand, testing how responsive the blade was to the button. It snicked in and out. "I've always had a thing for these. You think it'd be a good choice?"

"Sure," Rafael said with a trace of amusement. "And it saves you worrying about chopping your own balls off while you're carrying it around."

Quentin guffawed. "Let's go with this one, then."

When Rafael had paid for those too, Dolores got up, beaming in her unnervingly grandmother-like way. "You're always a sweetheart, Rafael. And lately, my best customer. You send out a word if you ever need another house call."

"Will do."

As I deadbolted the door behind her, Rafael was already leaning forward to start instructing the other guys. "We'll deal with gunmanship tomorrow at the range, but I can go over the basics of knife combat right now. You might not get a whole lot of time to react, so you want to know the best places to strike to disable someone quickly and how to avoid a block."

He beckoned me over. "Lou, I'm going to need you to stand in for me here, since I can't play target very easily."

I wiggled my eyebrows. "Ooh, knife play. When did I get so lucky?"

Rafael just shook his head at me.

I did take the practice seriously once we got down to it —and the solemn expressions that had come over the skater men's faces might have been funny if I hadn't known their lives could be quite literally on the line. Rafael talked us through several scenarios, directing our positions and the tentative jabs and cuts the guys acted out, never actually doing more than grazing my clothes.

None of his three pupils made so much as a murmur of complaint. While I stepped back so that Rafael could demonstrate a grip and a twist with his good hand, my gaze traveled over all of my men, and a strange mix of trepidation and affection tangled in my chest.

I still didn't like seeing these three acting more like gang stooges than athletes… but there wasn't anything I could do about that. And when I let myself admit it, the fact that they were so committed to holding their own in the mess I'd dragged them into was something incredible.

I'd never have imagined they'd be devoted enough to get their hands this dirty for me.

A buzzing from my pocket broke through my thoughts. My burner phone.

The men looked up as I pulled the phone out and checked the screen. "It's Beckett," I told them with a leap of my pulse, and tapped through to see what the acting Storm had to say.

Would it be possible for us to meet in person in the next couple of days? There's something I'd like to discuss with you that I'd rather there wasn't any kind of concrete record of.

A quiver ran through my nerves. This could be something big if he was being so cautious about it.

I can manage that, I typed back and considered the demands Mom had made on my time this week. *Tomorrow afternoon?*

His reply was instant. *Perfect. Make sure you're not followed. I'll see you then—and fill you in on everything.*

TWENTY-FOUR

Luciana

I WOVE through the throng of shoppers that filled the thoroughfare of the huge mall complex. The constant shifting of bodies and the cacophony of voices had my unsettled nerves even more on edge, but I knew the setting was for both my and Beckett's protection.

As we blended into the mass of ordinary people that flooded the place in the late afternoon, no one was likely to notice our clandestine meeting. We wouldn't be visible from more than a few feet away.

And it meant neither of us could ambush the other with a larger force. You'd have to be insane to stage an attack with this many witnesses around, before even getting into the logistical problems of fighting amid a gazillion human obstacles.

No doubt Beckett had made the same calculations when he'd suggested this spot. Really, he had even less reason to trust me than I did him. I'd told him outright that my mother was scheming against him, and for all he knew, she might manipulate me into turning on him too.

You didn't survive long in our world without a healthy sense of caution.

Over the heads of the shoppers around me, I spotted the top of the marble fountain Beckett had mentioned. I made my way over to it and stopped by the tiled wall around the edge of the pool as if I were admiring the abstract sculpture. To my eyes, it looked like a gigantic flower an even more gigantic bird had chomped up and spit out.

Hey, there was no accounting for artistic taste.

The burbling of the water mingled with the voices carrying from all around me. I didn't hear Beckett's footsteps, only registered his lanky form and sandy hair ambling over at the edge of my vision.

He stopped a couple of feet away, gazing at the fountain like I was. Nothing about his stance indicated that he knew me or had any interest in talking to me.

"Thanks for meeting me," he said evenly, only just loud enough to be heard over the noise of the mall.

I matched both his tone and his volume. "I'm glad you reached out. What's up?"

"I'll keep this brief and to the point, because the less time we're together, the safer it is. I have reason to believe that the Deadly Rose has been trying to poach many of my top people."

I blinked, resisting the urge to peer over at him. "Poach?"

"Get them under her thumb rather than working for me. Thankfully, my employees are loyal, and several of them tipped me off that they'd gotten sudden, huge financial opportunities offered to them… on the condition that they cut ties with me first. Which naturally made them suspicious."

Mom hadn't mentioned anything about this to me— but then, she'd been cagey about her exact strategies from before she'd even realized I was collecting evidence against her.

"What kind of opportunities?" I asked.

"High level jobs with extensive benefits at a bunch of different companies, supposedly independent of each other. But obviously having them all come in short succession can't be a coincidence. I had my tech experts trace the businesses' operations, and ultimately they all led back to a couple of shell companies. We found significant but not undeniable proof that those shells are part of your mother's portfolio."

I made a face. "I don't need undeniable proof. What you said is enough—I'm sure it's her. Shit. I'm sorry. I had no idea she was planning anything like that, or I'd have warned you."

It was awfully similar to what she'd done to the Blood Hunter, only less fatal. Maybe there hadn't been a good setting to off a bunch of the Storm's key people all at once, so this had seemed like a reasonable alternative. Or maybe she figured the Storm would be a trickier opponent, and she'd been hoping his people would offer up inside intel once she had them under her sway.

Whatever the case, her ultimate motive was clear. She wanted to weaken the Devil's Dozen members she planned to move against so that it'd be easier to crush them later on. How many others of her colleagues was she messing with?

Beckett's lips curled in a slight smile. "You don't have

to apologize. I wouldn't be here if I thought there was any chance you're on board with her plans. But you're in the best position out of anyone to do something about the overall situation."

"Aren't you going to take her to task when she went after your people like that?"

"Oh, I'll create some trouble for her to show the attempt didn't go unnoticed. But simply trying to win over someone else's top people would be seen more like reasonable strategy to my colleagues than a violation of our codes."

He darted the briefest of glances toward me. "You have the key pieces—and coming from one of her own, it'd be clear any accusations weren't a gambit of our own. If you get an opportunity to take her to task, I want you to have every bit of information available to make that as easy as possible."

I exhaled raggedly. "Right. Thank you." It all came down to me—I was the one living with the woman, seeing her every day.

I was the one she'd punish the harshest if I lost my grasp on the leverage I was using against her.

Beckett started to turn away. "I'll send you the proof we do have of the financial connections we dug up and a report of my employee's stories. Is the same phone number still good for that? I don't want to get you in trouble."

"Yeah, she doesn't know about that phone. I'll save the files to a separate server and delete the texts right away too."

"Good. You stay safe. I know it can't be fun finding yourself in the middle of this conflict. If there's any way I can help, let me know."

With those parting words, he vanished into the crowd.

I lingered by the fountain for a minute longer before drifting toward the exit. As I crossed the parking lot to my car, a heavy weight settled in my stomach.

More evidence meant more leverage. That was all great. But what would it take for me to be able to leave this life completely?

I had trouble even imagining having enough for that.

Just as I came up on the car, the sharp ringtone I'd assigned to Mom's number pealed from my purse. I groped for my regular phone and yanked it to my ear, knowing the conversation would be less uncomfortable if we didn't start it off with her complaining about a slow response.

"Hi, Mom," I said tentatively, bracing myself as I opened the driver's side door.

Her voice crackled through the line in an even more domineering tone than usual. "Luciana? Where are you? I need to go over a few things with you, in person. Immediately."

Oh, great. What plans did she have for *me* now?

My gaze slid to the nearby freeway. The mall was about an hour outside of Austin, but I'd rather give myself a little breathing room. "I'm not in the city. I can get there in a couple of hours."

I'd been checking my car over for tracking devices every time I took it out of the garage and hadn't found any since the first one Mom had admitted to. She shouldn't be able to tell exactly where I was.

"A couple of hours? What on earth are you doing? I need you to be ready when I have work for you."

I willed the irritation out of my tone. "The deal was that I get to have my own life too. If you want me for something important, you need to give me more than five minutes' notice. I'll get there as fast as I can."

"The deal was that you fulfill your duties as a Cordova. If you're not going to hold up your end—"

"I can't just magically teleport myself there in an instant," I snapped, and then reined in my temper before I could go too far. "I told you, I'm coming. We already had that meeting this morning. I had no idea there was anything else you'd urgently need me for."

"Well, now you know. If you expect me to believe you have any loyalty left at all, I expect to see you in my office by seven o'clock sharp."

She hung up without giving me a chance to respond. I gunned the engine, my blood boiling. After everything, she still saw me as a puppet whose strings she should be able to pull however she liked, whenever she liked.

As I merged onto the freeway, my heart pounded with a mix of anger and fear. Mom had no right to expect me to appear the second she beckoned, but that didn't mean she wouldn't punish me for failing to predict her demands. Part of me wanted to take my time driving back, to show up at seven and not a moment earlier so she'd know she hadn't frightened me. The part of me that *was* frightened wanted to flat-pedal it so I could diffuse her rage.

It took several minutes for the initial upheaval from the conversation to wear off… and a more subtle anxiety to creep in.

Why *was* Mom so desperate to get me back to the house? She didn't usually pull out the threats and show real anger unless it was absolutely necessary—she'd rather appear coolly in control.

She'd been awfully vague about what she wanted me there for. To go over a few things with me? If it was so urgent, why couldn't she have talked to me about it on the phone right away?

No, what she'd really been insistent about was getting me back to the mansion. Why? Because she had something bigger in store for me there?

Or maybe because she wanted to be sure I *wasn't* someplace else?

Once the idea had taken hold, I couldn't shake it. A chill prickled through my veins. Finally, I wiggled my burner phone out of my pocket and set it in the cupholder.

"Speakerphone on," I said in voice command. "Call Rafael."

Rafael picked up after two rings, his deep baritone a balm on my nerves. "Everything all right, Lou?"

"Yeah. I was just about to ask you that. Nothing strange has gone down at the loft?"

I could almost hear his frown in his pause. "Business as usual around here. We got back from the shooting range a couple of hours ago—your skaters didn't embarrass me too much. Why, what's going on?"

"Oh, maybe I'm just being paranoid. My mom—"

A sudden screech of a siren blared through the speaker, making me flinch. "What the hell is that?"

Rafael raised his voice to talk over the pulsing wail, sounding annoyed. "I think that's the building's fire alarm. They didn't warn us about a drill. Someone must have done something stupid in the halls."

A deeper chill pierced through my gut. I couldn't have said exactly what the problem was, but I had a bad feeling about all of this. "You should get out of the building just in case. And... be careful. I'm heading straight over—I'll get there soon."

The second the call ended, I pressed my foot to the gas pedal. Weaving through the other cars, I roared along the freeway as fast as I dared.

The loft was on the edge of the city, closer than the Deadly Rose mansion. I'd already covered a lot of the distance back to Austin. If all went well, I could cut the rest of the journey down to no more than fifteen minutes.

I just had to hope that didn't make me fifteen minutes too late.

I tore down the exit ramp and through the streets to the loft, only slowing when the building came into view up ahead. A small throng of residents milled on the sidewalk outside and across the road.

With a frantic flick of my eyes, I spotted all four of my men in a cluster near the parking lot. I pulled over to the curb, sprang out, and dashed over to them.

No smoke seeped from the building's windows. No flames danced behind the glass. My suspicions deepened with every thud of my heart.

Niko saw me first and welcomed me into their group with a sling of his arm around my waist.

Rafael swiveled on his crutches to face me. "What's going on, Lou? I didn't think you were coming over today."

I grimaced, my stomach churning with apprehension. "I don't think the fire alarm was a random coincidence. My mom's up to something. We need to check the loft."

He started to straighten up as much as he could with his leg in the cast, but I grasped his arm. "No. You've got to stay down here with the crowd. You know you won't be able to move fast—but you can keep an eye out and give us a heads up if anything changes down here."

And he'd be safer. I didn't want Rafael getting even

more hurt than he already was. But if I said *that*, I'd wound his pride, and who knew what idiotic things he'd do.

My bodyguard's stance tensed, but he nodded in acceptance. I tugged the other guys around to the building's back entrance.

When I pushed open the door, the air inside smelled stale but not the slightest bit smoky. My certainty that this was some kind of a trick only grew.

"What do you think we're dealing with?" Quentin asked as we clambered up the stairs.

I let out my breath in a nervous rush. "I'm not sure. But be prepared for a fight."

They all accepted that order without hesitation or surprise. It'd have pained me more to see them adjusting to the craziness of my life so easily if it hadn't seemed so vital to their survival.

I slipped my hand into my jacket pocket and curled my fingers around the Glock that Rafael had insisted I buy from Dolores. If I had my way, I'd handle most of whatever fight we encountered.

We burst from the stairwell near the loft's door. The guys stuck close to me as we hurried down the hall.

Jasper hissed through his teeth. "The door's open."

It was—just an inch ajar. So slight we could almost have thought the guys must have simply failed to secure it properly in their rush to evacuate, but I knew Rafael would never have been that careless.

My whole body tensed. I took the lead, striding up to the door, girding myself, and then shoving inside with my gun held in front of me.

In the main room, three men in dark sweatsuits spun around. One held a knife that he'd been digging into the sofa cushions. Another looked like he'd been ransacking the kitchen cabinets, with cereal, dry pasta, and crackers strewn across the counters from their opened boxes. The third had been prying at a floorboard.

I recognized two of those faces. I'd seen them around the Deadly Rose mansion.

These were Mom's men. She'd sent them to search the loft... for evidence I might have stashed here, presumably, or a clue about how to get access to all the digital proof I'd stored in the cloud.

One of the men gave a shout. Another's hand twitched toward his hip where I could see the bulge of a pistol.

I jerked my gun toward him. "Don't even think about it unless you want to lose that hand."

Two more men came barging out from behind the dividers that separated the makeshift bedrooms. One of them lunged toward us with a growl, but then all three of my guys whipped out the guns they'd been practicing with earlier this afternoon.

"Just try me," Quentin gritted out, his pale eyes flashing with fury. He held his pistol perfectly steady. At my other side, Niko's and Jasper's stances were a little more awkward, but determination was etched in their expressions.

They'd blow these goons away before they gave them an opening to hurt me.

And the goons could obviously recognize that too. Four to five, with the four of us already prepared to shoot, it wasn't any contest.

The one who'd lunged and the one with the knife lifted their hands in a gesture of surrender. I motioned with my pistol at the one who'd reached for his gun, and he echoed the pose, scowling.

I glowered right back at them. "I can see what you were doing here. Get the fuck out of this building and tell my mother I won't be home until tomorrow. Maybe she'll be ready to treat me and my associates with all due respect by then."

Flickers of nervousness passed across a few of their faces. "The boss isn't going to be happy about that," one muttered.

"I don't give a shit what makes her happy. She should have thought about that before she went behind my back. Now get going!"

At the wave of my gun, the five thugs hustled over. We stepped to the side so they could file out the door, keeping our gazes and our weapons trained on them the entire time.

The thud of their feet resounded down the hall outside, and then they were gone.

My shoulders slumped as the tension released from them. Jasper's arm dropped, a strained chuckle tumbling from his lips. "Holy hell. I can't believe we just did that."

Niko set his gun down on a side table as if he didn't want to tuck it completely away just yet. He glanced at me. "Those were your mother's people—what were they looking for?"

I sighed. "They probably hoped they'd be able to get at and destroy the evidence I'm using as leverage against her. I should have realized she'd figure out where you're living and try to undermine me that way."

"It's not your fault that you don't think like that vicious bitch does," Quentin said firmly, scanning the loft. "Is there any chance they *did* get at your stuff?"

I shook my head. "Everything's online, and I know better than to write down passwords. It's totally secure." I paused, giving myself a moment to try to think like the Deadly Rose would. "But we need to search the place for surveillance bugs. They might have planted some during their search so she can listen in."

Niko rubbed his hands together as if the search sounded like a wonderful game. "What exactly do we look for?"

I pulled out my phone. "I'll show you some pictures… Can one of you go down to help Rafael get back up here? He'll be wondering what the hell's gone down."

Jasper reached for the door. "I'll fill him in."

I took in the mess Mom's men had left behind and restrained a shudder. We were going to be doing a lot of cleaning as well as bug-hunting.

But what would even be the point of relocating? Mom owned this city—I had no doubt that she'd figure out where the guys had holed up no matter where I set them up in town. And they'd made it amply clear that they had no intention of leaving Austin without me.

"All right," I said, putting on my best unfazable tone. "Let's start in the kitchen."

But as we crunched through the rummaged food that'd spilled onto the floor, my spirits were sinking.

Mom was getting awfully restless in our arrangement. How far would she go in her attempts to regain the upper hand?

TWENTY-FIVE

Luciana

THE ONLY UPSIDE that came with the shitty day was that it gave me an excuse to stay overnight with my guys. Once the confusion around the fire alarm had died down, we ordered in Thai—which had enough options that even Quentin was satisfied with the spread—and settled into the living room together, watching a cheesy old movie playing on one of the cable stations and shouting at the characters' wacky decisions.

It was so comfortable and cozy that I could almost forget the trauma we'd endured since arriving in this city.

Refusing the guys' emphatic offers to give up their beds, I took the sofa, pointing out that I was the smallest by far of the bunch of us and so fit it best. The loft had only come with twin beds, so it wasn't as if I could snuggle in next to any of them all that easily.

And so, in the middle of the night after the light beyond the thin curtains had dimmed and the only sound was the rasp of sleeping breaths from the makeshift bedrooms, I found myself sprawled on the sofa, staring at the ceiling.

The niggling thoughts I'd been managing to dismiss over the last few days crept in more insistently. Rafael was doing okay—but he still hadn't revealed anything further about the guys who'd jumped him. What had their warning even been about? What did they expect him to do now to avoid the threat of additional retaliation?

I understood where my mom was coming from, but what if they came after him again too?

And how did his brother fit into all this? I hadn't even known he *had* a brother. He'd never really talked about his family.

I should have pushed more. Asked more questions. Privacy was a precious thing in our line of work, but our lives were totally entangled now.

A soft grunt reached my ears from the direction of the farthest bedroom on the left, the one I knew belonged to my bodyguard. It was followed by the rustle of blankets as he must have turned over, and then a restrained sigh.

I hesitated for a second and then shrugged off my own blanket and pushed to my feet. If neither of us was sleeping, it couldn't hurt anything for me to go talk to him now. I didn't think he'd want to have this conversation in front of the other guys anyway.

I padded through the dimness to the dividers that framed Rafael's "room" and eased open the one that served as a door, just long enough for me to slip past it. As I pulled it closed again, Rafael was already raising his head to peer at me.

"What are you up to, brat?" he murmured with drowsy fondness.

Despite my worries, a smile tugged at my lips. I climbed onto the bed and tucked myself close against his brawny frame under the covers—both out of a craving for his warmth and out of necessity, given the size of the bed. Hooking one leg over his uninjured one, I rested my head on his shoulder and tipped my face toward his ear so I could speak quietly and not risk waking the others.

"I couldn't sleep. Too many thoughts spinning in my head. It sounded like maybe you were having a similar problem."

"And you figured misery loves company?"

I teased my fingers up his chest, rumpling the thin fabric of his undershirt. "Are you miserable that I'm here?"

Rafael let out a light chuckle. "Never, Lou."

I could have taken the moment in a very different, much more enjoyable direction right then, but the questions I'd been grappling with gripped me too tightly. "Rafael… the guys who attacked you talked about your brother. Would you tell me how he fits into all this?"

There was a long stretch of silence. Rafael's muscles had tensed against my body, but he reached over to stroke my hair with his good hand as if to show he was still with me, just figuring out what he wanted to say.

"It's a long story," he said finally.

"That's okay. I mean, you don't *have* to talk about him. But it'd make me feel better having a clearer understanding about what happened that night and why."

His fingers grazed over my hair in another gentle caress. When he spoke again, his voice was still low but rougher.

"Edmundo was my older brother—five years older. It's

because of him that I got into this kind of life. My parents would never have expected it. They were totally law-abiding, just regular people. They ran a gardening and flower shop together, if you can believe that."

I pictured a tiny version of Rafael wandering between shelves of potted flowers and grinned. "You know, I think I can."

"It was their dream," he went on. "They worked their asses off getting the business off the ground, every bit of that a labor of love, and by the time I was in elementary school, it was just starting to take off. We weren't getting rich or anything, but they could buy take-out for dinner once a week, and we got a big TV to replace the old crappy one we'd bought at a garage sale. Stuff like that."

"That's great."

He nodded. "Yeah. But a successful business can attract the wrong kind of interest. There was a gang in the neighborhood that started hitting my parents up for protection money like they did other places in the area. Just a little at first, but then the demands grew. My dad got frustrated and made some snarky remark one time when they came around, and they took it as an insult to their authority."

My body stiffened. "Oh, no."

I felt more than saw Rafael's grimace. "Yeah. They broke into the shop one night and smashed up the place—the windows, the furniture, the merchandise. Most of it wasn't salvageable. It put my parents even deeper in the hole than when they'd first started out, and all they could do was struggle to get the store off the ground again. In most of my memories from after that, they were always stressed and overworked."

A lump rose in my throat. "I'm so sorry."

Rafael gave a brief shrug. "It is what it is. But Edmundo—he was twelve when it happened—it really got to him. Maybe because he'd been more aware of how hard they'd worked in the first place to build the business up, when I'd been too young to really pay attention."

"He must have been furious." I was plenty pissed off myself, even hearing about it decades later.

"Furious and determined. He decided he was going to get tougher than the gang—and make tougher friends—so they couldn't intimidate our family ever again. He ended up getting involved with another gang through some friends he met in high school. And when I was old enough that they could find some use for me, he brought me on board too."

The pieces clicked together in my head. "The guys who beat you up—they were part of that gang?"

Rafael exhaled raggedly. "Yeah. I don't know a lot of them anymore. It's been a long time since I ran with that bunch. But a few of them know me from back then."

I knit my brow. "But why were they so angry with you? Why did they think your brother would be?"

He paused, tipping his head back into the pillow. "They see me moving on to a bigger organization like your mom's as a betrayal. Like I was saying they weren't good enough. And—Edmundo was killed a while back, not that long before I came on board with the Deadly Rose, and they expected me to take his place. They were pissed that I jumped at a different opportunity."

Rafael turned his head toward me and kissed my forehead. "Not that I've ever once regretted the decision myself."

The affection in his voice sent a tingle of heat through me, but something about his story was still gnawing at me. "It seems like an awfully long time for them to hold a grudge. That all must have happened, like, ten years ago!"

"I guess they haven't had anything else offend them to take their minds off it," Rafael said dryly.

Before I could ask anything else, his tone dipped lower with a pained edge. "But I never meant to let it affect my ability to look after you. I was *useless* today because of the injuries those assholes gave me. I couldn't do anything to protect you or the other guys."

I bristled. "You've got nothing to apologize for. The assholes are the ones who screwed us over—they're the only ones I'm angry at. We all protect each other. It doesn't just go one way."

Rafael grunted. "I'm the one who knows this city. I'm the one who's seen what your mom is like. You need me to be at my best while we're here, and I—"

"Hey." I tipped closer to him and set my fingers on his lips to quiet him. His self-recriminations over his supposed weakness sent an ache through my gut.

Did he really think I saw him as less of a protector just because he'd been temporarily laid up? That I believed he'd let me down somehow?

Maybe it'd help if I proved to him just how much of a man I still saw him as—how much the strength I knew he still possessed turned me on.

"You're everything I've ever wanted you to be," I murmured, letting my hand trail down his neck and over his chest. "You always will be. And when you get knocked down for a bit, that just means I've got to work a little harder to show how true that is."

I rolled right onto him, careful of the cast around his

leg, and leaned down to seek out his mouth. Rafael's lips parted beneath mine, his tongue sweeping in to claim my own, refusing to totally give up his usual role as the aggressor.

He tasted so damn good and felt even better under my body. His good hand rose to twine through my hair with the firm grip that could make me swoon. He might not have been all that mobile at the moment, but that didn't stop him from shifting his hips to press his erection against my pussy through our clothes.

I smothered a moan against his mouth. If we were doing what I hoped we were going to do, we'd have to stay quiet. No need to disturb the others' sleep while we got our rocks off.

Rafael wrenched my head back and branded my neck with another searing kiss. I swayed against him, grinding into his erection until both our breaths stuttered. When he briefly loosened his grip, I bowed my head over his again.

"You don't have to prove anything to me. I already know just how much of a man you are."

Rafael gave a muted growl. "Oh, I can show you that even more. I'm not too bashed up to satisfy you."

I swallowed a gasp as he rubbed his rigid cock against my pussy again. My panties were already soaked, and there was no ignoring how badly he wanted me too.

I'd always wanted him. Every single day from the moment I'd been old enough to know what this kind of wanting was.

With a slide of my hand, I palmed him through the boxers he'd worn to bed. He mumbled a curse as his cock twitched against my palm.

It only took a slight raise of my hips and some deft

maneuvering to free him from the fabric without displacing myself. I pumped my hand up and down his thick shaft, humming in appreciation.

Rafael's eyes flashed in the darkness. He pulled me down over him, capturing my mouth as I claimed his cock.

"I hope you're not going to stop at just teasing me, brat," he muttered against my lips.

A breathy giggle tumbled out of me. If he'd had any idea how much I was aching for him, he couldn't have suggested that.

Deciding I could make a little show of it, I lifted myself up over him until I was standing and then shimmied slowly out of my plaid leggings. Rafael's gaze traced my curves, avid enough that I felt its heat coursing over my skin.

I wriggled out of my panties too and then hesitated. But he could guess my concern.

"Top drawer," he rasped, pointing at the crate-like nightstand. "I figured I should have a few on hand… just in case."

I snatched out a foil wrapper. Before I could open it, Rafael grabbed it from my fingers and tore it with his teeth. He managed to roll the condom over his cock at lightning speed even one-handed.

"Very impressive," I murmured, lowering myself over him. "I think you should get an immediate reward…"

I lined up and sank down, taking his entire cock into my slick cunt in one fluid movement.

Rafael muffled another groan and grasped my hair again. "I'll never get over how good you feel, Lou."

I rocked up and down over him, my vision already

fizzing with the pleasure as he stretched me. "Right back at you."

We bucked against each other with as much furor as Rafael was capable of with his broken knee. His breath gushed hot against my neck and then my breasts as he shoved himself up to nip his way across my chest. His hand dropped as well, and I had to choke back a moan as he squeezed one nipple between his fingers.

"Shh," he said. "You don't want to wake everyone up, do you, brat?"

Instead of answering, I just rolled my hips faster, fucking him harder. He matched my pace, thrusting up into me with a power that took my breath away. His fingers moved to my ass and dug into the flesh there, sending jolts of pain and bliss through my nerves.

"Oh, fuck," I mumbled as the waves of pleasure rolled through me, sending me spiraling higher and higher. I bit my lip, squeezing my eyes shut as if closing my eyelids would help contain any sounds I'd make.

"Next time we'll let them hear you," Rafael said, his voice sizzling with dark promise. "Let them know how good I treat this pussy."

Oh, he was working me over good, all right. My breath came in short, hot bursts, my eyes unfocusing. I was dangerously close to losing hold of what little control I did have.

Rafael must have sensed my weakness. His voice took on a huskier note. "That's right. Come for me, Lou."

I did exactly as I was told.

My orgasm exploded through me in a whirlwind. I shuddered over Rafael, my bliss spiking higher at the feel of his cock pulsing inside me. A cry I couldn't totally hold back burst from my throat.

Rafael yanked me back down to him and buried his face between my neck and shoulder. I muffled the rest of my ecstatic whimpers in the short twists of his hair while he groaned against my skin.

The world slowly fixed the tilt of its axis as I floated back down to Earth. My vision was still sparking bursts of color from the intensity of my release. Remembering the sound that'd escaped me, I listened carefully as I relaxed against Rafael's broad body. Maybe it hadn't been *too* loud.

At first I thought we'd succeeded in our attempt at discretion. No noise reached my ears from the rooms next to ours.

Then Quentin's voice, a little tired but with typical cockiness, carried from a couple of dividers over. "Next time you decide to have some fun in the middle of the night, I expect to be invited too."

A snicker followed that I was pretty sure was Niko's. Okay, so much for keeping our hook-up on the downlow.

Rafael chuckled under me. I let out a giggle of my own and offered up a rueful, "Sorry for disturbing your sleep!"

"You'd better get some now too, Punk," Jasper piped up from the nearest bed.

I couldn't deny that he was right. I considered slipping back to the sofa, but it was hard to peel myself away from Rafael's solid warmth.

He didn't show any signs of minding me simply sprawling over him like he was a human mattress. He tugged the blanket back up over the two of us and slung his arm over my waist. "You stay right here."

My eyelids slid shut. Sleep finally crept up on me, the pleasure having washed away the worst of my worries.

But in the last few moments before I drifted off

completely, I couldn't stop one last question from prickling through my mind.

I'd told Rafael that I meant to protect him just as much as he protected me. Could I really defend the four men in this room from everything my mother had in store for us next?

TWENTY-SIX

Luciana

AS I PULLED through the gate outside the Cordova mansion, the music from my and Jasper's free skate kept playing on a loop in my head. I went through the motions of easing the car into the garage and parking, but behind my eyes I was playing out every move—every spin, jump, and lift.

Not even the ominous atmosphere that hung over my family home could dampen my spirits. It was less than a week before Nationals. Tomorrow we were all going to head up north to Portland, where the competition was being held, to get used to the rink ahead of time.

I'd warned Mom that I'd be gone for several days, and she'd accepted the news with cold silence. After her men had failed to destroy any of my leverage and I'd sent them running in an embarrassing fashion, there'd been a tense peace between the two of us. To try to ensure that she wouldn't sabotage the upcoming championships, I'd been as obedient as I could bear to be, following her orders efficiently and with forced enthusiasm.

I'd given her nothing to complain about. She'd survived without me for months before—she could give me a week now.

A bounce came into my step as I walked over to the front door, still hearing our song in my mind. If the few underlings hanging around keeping watch thought I looked dorky, I really didn't give a shit at this point.

I stepped into the foyer, switching to picturing the leftover Polish takeout I'd like to dive into to replenish some of the burned-off calories, but the clack of heels on the hardwood floor broke through my imaginings.

"I hope you're not thinking of heading off to your room."

My head jerked around. My mother emerged from the shadows at the top of the staircase like a grim reaper in Gucci. Her dark brown eyes narrowed dangerously. Both red-nailed hands were curled into fists on each hip.

She looked ready to deal out a wave of death. My stomach knotted. What had gotten her in a mood like that?

"I wasn't," I said carefully. "Not if you need me."

She smirked at me, and I hated myself. "Good answer. As a matter of fact, I do need you. Come down to the basement, and I'll fill you in."

My gaze flicked to the doorway off to the side of the foyer—the one that led to a narrow staircase and the maze of halls and rooms that stretched out below the mansion. Some of those rooms were just for storage, but I doubted Mom just wanted me to haul supplies.

The other rooms… Nothing good happened down there.

As Mom descended the stairs with brisk steps, I swallowed thickly. "The basement? You didn't mention anything about… work we'd need to do down there."

There was something oddly twitchy about Mom's movements as her head turned toward me. I got the impression that she was on edge, holding herself back from revealing even more coiled tension.

That didn't bode well for this afternoon's activities either.

Her gaze sharpened into a glare. "I'm mentioning it now. You'll come along if you know what's good for you— or do you need a reminder of who you're talking to?"

I held up my hands, even more uneasy than before. "All right. No problem. I was just asking."

With dread winding through my gut, I followed her down the stairs into the cooler air of the basement.

We passed several closed doors, making our way to the far end of the basement where most of the rooms were secured behind heavy locks. Where things went on that even most of the lackeys weren't privy to.

Mom stopped in front of a plain but solid door that I knew led to one of her "interrogation rooms." Heavily soundproofed so that no hint of what went on in there would seep through to the outside world.

She motioned to me. "Open it."

My throat constricted, but I didn't even know what was going on here to argue against it. Squaring my shoulders, I twisted the doorknob and pushed it ahead of me as I stepped into the room.

The second I'd moved past the door enough to see the far corner of the room, my feet stalled in their tracks.

A thin figure was standing in the corner, his hands raised over his head, restrained there by a chain that dangled from the ceiling. He'd been stripped to a wifebeater undershirt and his boxers, both soiled with sweat and in the case of the boxers, maybe worse. His skin looked sickly sallow, but he stared at me with a clenched jaw and a sullen expression.

Mom brushed past me and rested her hand against the prisoner's cheek. When he tried to move away from her touch, she slapped him with a rake of her fingernails.

Stark red lines formed across his face where she'd scratched the pale skin. He hissed and thrashed against the chain, but Mom stepped away, turning back to me.

"This young man works for one of my Devil's Dozen colleagues," she informed me in a cool voice. "We caught the snake trying to sniff around some of our operations. So now he gets to spill everything he knows about his boss's work. It seems he needs a little more incentive to start talking, though. Your job is to get all of it out of him."

My heart lurched. "*Me?*"

I wouldn't have dared let so much shock show if I hadn't been so very startled. Mom had forced me to watch a few of her interrogations in the past, but she'd never had me so much as pitch in with the actual torture, let alone direct it myself.

She was throwing me right into the deep end. And this was a pool I had zero interest in swimming in.

Her lips drew back, and a hint of a snarl came into her voice. "You. Everything's laid out. Get to work."

A metal stand stood next to the wall beyond the reach of the guy's feet. It held rows of vicious instruments, ranging from knives to clamps to a propane lighter and thumb tacks. Bile rose in my throat, but I willed it down, not wanting Mom to see my nausea.

I dragged my feet over to the stand and stared down at the tools. My fingers curled toward my palms, resisting the idea of so much as picking any of those objects up.

Mom tsked her tongue behind me. "Let's get on with it, Luciana. It's better that this pendejo gets a beat down than your beloved boyfriends, isn't it? Of course, if you'd rather see one of *them* tortured, I can certainly—"

"No," I snapped, fighting to keep my voice steady through the wave of horror her suggestion had provoked. I inhaled deeply, cringing inwardly at the dank smell of the room. "I'm just deciding on my approach."

I could do this. Prod him for answers, show that I meant business—maybe I wouldn't have to go too far to get him to open up.

If he was working for one of the other Devil's Dozen members and digging into Mom's business, he had to know the risks. He'd signed up for this. He wasn't some innocent.

Even more queasy at the thought of drawing blood, I settled on a steel baton. My palm started to sweat against the cool metal as I hefted it and turned to face the guy.

I tapped the weapon against my other hand. "We could cut straight to the chase. Tell us why your boss sent you to spy on the Deadly Rose."

A flicker of panic crossed the guy's face. "I have no idea what you're talking about. What's the deadly rose?"

So he was going to insist on making this difficult. I gritted my teeth and thought back to the lessons I'd learned from watching Mom in scenarios like this over the years and from my combat training.

I slammed the baton against the guy's side just below

his rib cage, hard enough to send pain spiking through his organs but not to actually damage them. I'd rather I never had to get to that point.

The guy jerked and cried out. Tears started to leak from his eyes even as his body went rigid with resistance. "Please, I swear—I have no idea what any of this is about. Can't you—"

Another sharp whack on the opposite side of his torso. A jab right to his belly. A forceful smack across his knuckles, nearly cracking them.

With each spasm of his limbs and gasp that jolted from his lips, my nausea gripped me tighter. The only thing spilling from his mouth were frantic pleas of ignorance. It was all I could do to stop my own hand from shaking.

Lowering the baton, I clamped my free hand around his throat—not to strangle, just to warn and to lift his trembling face so his eyes would meet mine.

A sickly smell rose off of him—if he hadn't pissed himself before, he had just now. But the stink wasn't what made my stomach flip over as I stared him down.

He wasn't just a "young man." I hadn't seen it before with his head low, his hair hanging forward to partly obscure it, and the defiant act he'd initially been putting on, but this guy was a *kid*.

The face before me couldn't have belonged to a boy older than sixteen. That was grit smudging his jaw, not a five o'clock shadow. There was even a bit of baby fat still rounding his not-quite-mature features.

It took all my willpower not to blatantly recoil in horror. What the fuck was Mom playing at here? She really thought this *child* held some crucial secret?

What if he wasn't lying about having no clue what was

going on? That possibility seemed increasingly likely with every second longer I gazed at his tear-streaked, agonized features.

My mind darted back to my conversation with Rafael the other night—to the young teen version of himself who'd been roped into a much smaller gang to appease his brother's hunger for vengeance—and my nerves rebelled even more than before.

"What kind of work does your boss have you doing?" I said, firm but quiet. "In general, I mean."

"I—I don't do all that much," the kid stammered. "Just hang around the house following whatever orders he gives me. Bring him coffee, clean his car, that kind of thing."

"Did he tell you to go someplace else and take notes about what you saw, or anything like that?"

The boy shook his head frantically. "No. I was just walking home and these guys grabbed me and brought me here. The boss doesn't let me in on anything interesting yet. He always closes the door if he's going to talk business, shuts me out so I won't overhear the important stuff. I don't even know his *name*—we just call him 'Boss.'"

Nothing about his demeanor or the tremors that were shivering through his body suggested he was lying. I *had* broken him already, and he simply didn't have anything else to say.

I'd tortured a teenager a few years younger even than me. A high school kid.

I had to clamp my lips tight against the urge to vomit. Stepping back, I dropped the baton with the other torture instruments and spun toward Mom.

"I'm done here. I'm not going to keep tormenting

some kid, especially one who seems like he doesn't know anything and hasn't done anything to hurt us."

Fury flared in Mom's gaze. She caught my arm and yanked me toward the doorway.

Only once we were in the hall with the door shut behind us did she start speaking, her voice taut with a vicious edge. "You never undermine me in front of a prisoner. Aren't you already clear enough on the consequences of disobedience?"

I narrowed my eyes at her, my muscles rigid to stop myself from trembling but a surge of my own rage fueling my confidence. "You knew he wasn't anyone important to the Devil's Dozen, didn't you? You kidnapped some lackey from the lowest level specifically to prove that you could make me beat up a kid who didn't deserve it. Do you have any idea how sick that is?"

Mom's hand lashed out, too fast for me to dodge. Her palm connected with my cheek in a flash of pain.

I jerked backward, my face stinging, my hands drawing up into fists.

"I make the rules here, mija," Mom said, spittle flying with the words. "If you won't do as I say, I'm happy to bring all of the men you've been whoring around with here to offer them similar treatment."

With every word, my spine grew stiffer. I let my anger color my voice. "I wouldn't do that if I were you. You know how easily I can blow up all of your plans. Do you really want to push me that far?"

Mom scoffed and motioned to my hands. "You wouldn't want to blow up your own life either. You're complicit now—you've aided in the kidnapping of one of my rival's underlings. You're tangled up in my plans. Do you really think our enemies would spare your lives or your lovers'? Or that you'll get very far after you've flushed your inheritance down the drain?"

"I think *your* enemies will see that I've gone my own way, especially because I'm giving up that inheritance," I shot back. "And whatever they think, I'd rather take my chances with them than live under your roof if you're going to act like a total psychopath."

"I'm warning you, Luciana—"

"No, I'm warning you. When I say no, I mean no. And if I catch the slightest hint that you've sent anyone to mess with my men, all the evidence I've gathered is going to end up in the laps of the last people you'd want it to. And believe me, I've got even more than I did before."

Mom fell silent, her eyes blazing. We eyed each other for what felt like an eternity.

Finally, she broke the standoff. "I don't think you want to ruin your family that badly."

I raised my chin. "Feel free to call my bluff. I'm leaving town tomorrow for a week, like I already told you. If you can stick to your end of the deal, I'll stick to mine, and we'll see where we're at when I get back."

I swiveled away from the interrogation room and marched down the hall to the stairs. Mom didn't follow. My breaths shook as they spilled from my lungs. I couldn't believe I'd said all of that to her.

But I'd had to. There were some lines I wasn't going to cross.

More nausea unfurled through my stomach at the thought of the boy I was leaving behind. I wanted to barge in there and unlock his chains—but Mom had the key. And if Mom knew saving his life mattered that much to me, she'd gut him on the spot just to spite me.

His only chance of survival was if I didn't make a single gesture toward ensuring it.

I sent up a silent prayer as I hurried upstairs to my room. There, I grabbed my laptop and logged into the cloud server where I'd stashed all the evidence.

I'd set up the automated email with Beckett's help, CCing all of the Devil's Dozen members he had email addresses for. Every day, I scheduled it to send the following day if I didn't pop in to bump the time forward again.

If I ever disappeared for more than twenty-four hours, Mom would be totally exposed.

And I intended that exposure to be as total as I could manage. I dragged the latest files that Beckett and the Blood Hunter had sent me over to the folder that was linked in the email and then sat back on my bed with a ragged sigh.

I *didn't* want to have to burn down my entire family legacy, whether I wanted to claim that legacy or not. But if Mom pushed me any farther, she was going to find out that I hadn't been kidding around.

And after what I'd just seen, I couldn't deny that some part of me almost hoped that she forced my hand.

TWENTY-SEVEN

Quentin

AS I GAZED around the massive Portland arena under the brilliant overhead lights, I couldn't restrain a smile. Now *this* was what I'd been missing back in Austin. This was where skaters of our caliber ought to be performing.

Of course, I wouldn't be skating on that rink today. The gunshot wound had been healing well, but my shoulder still ached if I stretched the muscle there much. I hadn't been able to properly practice my routines since the injury.

Oh well. My chances of earning top marks after all my time off from singles would have been slim anyway.

This sophisticated setting would make a perfect backdrop for Jasper and Lou's routines, though. They were due up for their first chance to wow the judges, their short program performance, in just a half hour.

Seeing the glow that came into Lou's face when she

glanced around her at the packed stands, it was hard for me to regret how the last couple of months had played out.

At least, she *had* been glowing a minute ago. When I glanced over at her now, tipping her head toward Rafael to make some comment to him, a shadow had darkened her expression. She clasped her hands together in her lap, her fingers twisting with tension. Not even the vibrant colors of the skating costume Jasper had sewn for her, which I had to admit was incredible, could disguise her uneasiness.

Rafael's frown suggested that he'd noticed the evidence of her nerves too, although on the other hand most of the expressions I'd seen the guy make involved frowning. I suspected he'd rather have been standing at the top of the aisle, watching over the whole arena for threats, but with his leg still locked in a cast, he couldn't have stood guard the usual way. He'd settled for taking a spot with us near the front of the stands.

Niko had vacated the spot at Lou's other side to go chat with a couple other skaters he knew. I sidled closer and nudged her with my elbow. "You okay there, Upstart?"

Lou's gaze twitched to me, the stiffness in her posture telling me the answer before she tried to cover it up. "Yeah, sure. You know, it's just a little nerve-wracking heading onto the national stage for the first time."

Her smile was unconvincingly tight, and her eyes darted away from me to flick over the stands in a wary circuit. My stomach sank.

She was worried about her mom—of course she was. It might actually be a surprise if that menace *didn't* try to interfere with Lou's big day somehow.

But she couldn't keep worrying about that. The rest of

us were here to protect her. All I wanted her to be thinking about was taking her audience's breaths away.

I tucked my fingers around her arm and gave her a gentle tug. "You've still got some time. You know what always helps me shed the jitters? Getting moving rather than sitting like a statue. Let's take a walk up and down the hall."

Lou's gaze turned skeptical, but she stood without argument. I led her up the stairs, carefully avoiding a news team who looked like they were searching for people to interview, and ushered her down one of the quieter halls outside.

Lou gave her limbs a little shake as if trying to propel the tension right off her, but she kept scanning her surroundings at the same time. Always on the alert.

"Hey," I said, drawing her to a stop when I was sure we were out of anyone else's hearing. "You've got this. You know that, right? I can't wait to see you blow the rest of those idiots out of the water."

Lou arched an eyebrow. "I think it's a little early to assume we'll be that far ahead. We're up against the best of the best—and we only placed second at Finals."

I waved her protest off. "I've watched all of them before. And I've spent the last two months watching *you* as up close and personal as it gets. If anything, I feel a little sorry for them. They don't even know how badly they're about to get massacred."

That comment earned me a brief but genuine laugh. God, I could listen to that sound all day.

But then Lou's expression softened in the way that stole my heart even more. "Are you sure you're feeling okay—about not getting out there yourself?"

I shrugged, willing away the twinge of disappointment

that was so small in comparison to all the things I was happy about today. "I've had a chance in the spotlight before, and I'll get it plenty of times again. This weekend is about you. You kicking a whole lot of figure-skating butt."

Lou lowered her eyelids to peer at me through her lashes. She touched the middle of my chest and walked her fingers slowly up to the collar of my fleece pullover, sending tingles racing through me with every brush of their tips.

"Who would have thought a few months ago that you'd be here with me at Nationals pumping up my spirits?" she said in a wry tone that was still sultry enough to make my cock rise to half-mast. "After all the insults you threw at me and Jasper—"

I held a playful finger to her lips, waggling it when she tried to give it a nip. "We don't have to talk about the distant past. Anyway, I might have been an asshole, but you have to admit it was great motivation to get you and St. Pierre pushing yourselves to do better."

Lou rolled her eyes. "Hmm. So suddenly your jerkishness is a heroic act. How convenient."

She offset the sarcastic remark by stepping close enough to offer up a kiss—brief but so sweet it had me wanting to drag her into the nearest room and see just how many times I could get her off before she was due on the ice.

I reined in my hormones. I hadn't brought her out here for a quickie.

I hooked one of her hands in mine and teased my thumb over the knuckles. The words stuck in my throat for a moment before I forced them out.

"It might not help all that much, but you know, I've

been where you are, in a way. I know what it's like to have a mom who can make your heart plummet and your gut bottom out with a single word, where you never know how or when the next hit will come."

Lou's fingers tightened around mine. She hadn't been there when I'd opened up to Niko and Jasper, but I could recognize the dawning comprehension in her eyes. "I'm sorry. I've overheard you on the phone before—and I remember some of the news stories from a while back… I wish you hadn't had to go through all that."

"You shouldn't be feeling bad for me," I said firmly. "It isn't anywhere near the level of shit that you've experienced. But being with you, seeing how you stand up to your mom every way you can despite how dangerous she is—it's given me the strength to hold my ground with mine. I blocked her number the other day. Never have to hear her tearing me down again."

The smile that curved Lou's lips now was sadder than I liked. "That's good. You deserve to live a life where you're not being berated all the time."

I nodded. "And so do you. So I want to see you block your mom right out of your head so she doesn't get the chance to dim your shine out there, not by one tiny fraction. Do you think you can handle that?"

Lou inhaled deeply and drew her posture up straighter. Her eyes met mine with the determined glint I loved so much. "Yeah. We both got here by our own efforts, right? We're standing on our own two feet, and no one's going to hold us back."

I found myself grinning. "That's the spirit. Now let's get back to the rink before Jasper has a nervous breakdown thinking I've kidnapped you."

We made it back to the others just as the pair before

Lou and Jasper took to the ice. Jasper caught Lou's hand, and they moved to the spot by the boards that they'd enter the rink from when called. I sank down onto the bench next to Niko, who was perched on the edge of his seat as if his skaters had already set off.

After the current couple finished up their short program, which I found boring as hell, the announcer summoned "Jasper St. Pierre and Luna Garcia." Lou was still competing under the assumed name she'd given to hide from her mother, since she'd been registered under that.

The two of them glided into the middle of the rink to assume their starting position. I found myself holding my breath as the music warbled through the arena.

And then they moved.

Synchronized spins leading into a triple axel, followed by some brisk footwork before they launched into their first lift. They hit every beat, their limbs flowing with the melody in a way I'd come to not just expect but admire.

Watching them without my pride getting in the way, I couldn't deny that Jasper was still better than I was. Maybe not by much, and maybe I could nail a few of the specific poses with slightly more accuracy… but he had a power and artistry that I couldn't quite match yet, no matter how much I'd heckled him before.

That was okay. It gave me a goal post to aim for. Someday, with enough practice and honing my skills, I'd get to the point where I could at least match the guy.

And the funny thing was, I could believe he'd now cheer me on when I did.

Beside me, Niko was beaming. "They're really something, aren't they?"

"Yeah," I said without a shred of resentment. "They really are."

I tore my attention away to steal a quick glance at the crowd. To my satisfaction, everyone's eyes were glued to Lou and Jasper with expressions of dazed amazement.

Well, everyone except for a few burly guys who looked unusually grim for an event like this. My gaze caught on them near the top of the aisle that led down to the opening where Lou and Jasper would come off the ice. One of them made a furtive gesture to the others, and they tramped down the steps toward that spot.

The hairs on the back of my neck stood on end. These guys definitely weren't typical figure-skating fans—they moved with an aggressive air that set off all my alarm bells. And the one with the heavy forehead and squinty eyes looked unnervingly familiar... Was he one of the thugs we'd caught searching our loft back in Austin?

Shit, shit, shit. Lou's mom really had decided to fuck this up for her daughter. What had she ordered those pricks to do?

My hands clenched at my sides. My first impulse was to dash over there and confront the assholes, getting right in their faces. Defend Lou like I'd promised her I would, like I had before.

But even as I tensed on the bench, an image played out in my head of how that confrontation would probably go—with just me, my injured shoulder, and a gun I'd never fired at a human being before against those three goons.

I'd already been more of a champion than she'd ever expected—and I had two guys beside me who were just as eager to protect her. It was a hell of a lot more important that we made sure Lou wasn't in any danger than that I got to take all the credit.

I cleared my throat. "Niko, Rafael, I think a few of the Deadly Rose's thugs have just joined the party."

When Rafael's gaze jerked to me, I tipped my head toward the men I'd noticed. His expression hardened with a flex of his jaw.

"Motherfuckers," he muttered.

Niko rested his hand against the side of his hooded sweatshirt. "I have my knife, if we need it."

Rafael inclined his head, fury blazing in his dark eyes. "We don't want to make a scene and distract from the performance. We go over there quietly and take care of things, fast and firmly."

It was kind of a relief letting the actual bodyguard among us take the lead. Gripping the one crutch he was making do with now, he eased past the two of us. We followed, hunching low so as not to block people's view on the higher rows.

We stepped out into the aisle as the thugs came to a stop just a few steps above us. Rafael moved toward them without hesitation, moving with his crutch as if it were an extra limb, so Niko and I flanked him.

When we reached them, he drew his gun in the space between us where no one else would be able to see it, keeping it low but clearly in view of the goons. He'd only gotten the cast on his dominant hand off days ago, but he held the weapon steadily enough. Taking my cue from him, I lifted the hem of my shirt to reveal the concealed holster at my hip.

"It's time for you three to take off," Rafael growled, low but forceful.

The guy in the lead eyed the weapons but adjusted his

stance with a hint of a swagger. "Who the fuck do you think you are to order us around, you cripple?"

Rafael's lips drew back to bare his teeth. "I think I could outshoot you in my sleep with my hands tied behind my back. Last time I checked, I don't need my leg to pull a trigger."

One of the other guys snorted. "Are we supposed to be scared by that?"

Rafael did the most terrifying thing he could have—he pushed his mouth into the fiercest grin I'd ever seen. "Yes. Because I'd happily see you six feet under just for whatever you're *thinking* of doing to my woman. If you try to actually do it, the only thrilling news from the arena today will be about three strange goons who were gunned down because they didn't know what was good for them."

I was practically pissing myself, and I was on his side. The thugs exchanged a glance, and I hooked my fingers around the grip of my own gun.

With a sputter of frustration, they turned and marched back up the stairs. We watched them vanish through the doors. Rafael had tucked his gun away, but we didn't budge from our current position, guarding the woman we were crazy about while she flew on across the ice.

I turned to watch just as she and Jasper whirled through their final sequence. They struck their ending pose, and the crowd erupted into applause and cheers. A smile crossed my face, hard but genuine.

They were getting everything they deserved. And I'd put my life on the line as many times as it took to make sure that continued to be true.

TWENTY-EIGHT

Luciana

THE PAIR before us whipped into motion with the start of their free skate song, launching immediately into a sequence of swift and intricate footwork that took my breath away. And I didn't have a whole lot to spare.

Beside me by the boards, Jasper bumped his arm lightly against mine. "Those two know how to make a dramatic start, huh?"

"No kidding."

I swallowed thickly, willing down my nerves and trying to shoo the worries from my mind. We were third after yesterday's short program, a fact that should have overjoyed me, considering our free skate was where we normally shone the most.

It *had* made me rejoice yesterday. But after we'd arrived at the arena this morning, my stomach had gotten more and more twisted up with uncertainty.

My doubts hadn't been provoked only by the competition, although that was definitely tight. We were up against the best skaters in the country, some of whom had been competing for over a decade when this was only my first year. Only three pairs would be selected to compete for the United States on an international level, and while Nationals played a large part in that decision, it wasn't the only factor taken into consideration.

A bronze medal here wouldn't be a guarantee. If we could nab the silver or even the gold, then we'd be pretty much set. But that depended on us nailing every single move in the routine and nuance in our performance.

We'd done it before. I knew we could do it again. That definitely wasn't the only problem.

The pair on the ice pulled off a spectacular twist lift. Jasper gave my ponytail a light tug, careful not to shift the sparkly barrettes and carefully coiled ribbons that matched our costumes and kept all the strands neatly in place. "Are you ready to kill it, Punk?"

I shot him a grin, hoping he couldn't tell how tight it was. "You know it."

But with my head turned, my gaze slid past him over the massive audience around us. My eyes caught on trim blazers over collared shirts, elegant jackets over silky blouses.

These were the kinds of people who bought tickets to watch the National Championships. Sure, there were folks in sweats or chunky down vests in the crowd, but to afford the tickets, chances were they'd picked those outfits for comfort, not because it was all they owned.

I was surrounded by so many polished yuppies who could never have imagined the kind of life I'd led. Who had no concept that empires like my mother's even existed.

How had I convinced myself that I belonged here?

How would all those awed faces fall if they found out I'd killed people? How would they look at me if they'd known I had a gun in my equipment bag right now? That I'd shot a man right on a skating rink just weeks ago?

No matter what costume I wore or what makeup I painted my face with, I was tarnished underneath that mask. I wasn't the kind of skater they wanted to support. I'd just tricked them into thinking I was.

My ribs seemed to constrict around my lungs. When I tried to drink in a deep breath of the cool arena air, my chest ached.

The warble of the announcer's voice stirred me out of my uneasy reverie, but I didn't catch what he actually said.

Niko had come up next to us. He set his hand on my shoulder. "You two can beat that score—you have before."

Had we? I hadn't even heard what it was. But then, it wasn't how anyone else did that really mattered. It came down to our own performance.

The voice boomed from the speakers again, announcing our names. Jasper tipped his head toward the ice. "Let's show them what we can do."

What we could do. The thought spiraled out through my mind as I followed him to the center of the rink on autopilot.

I could shoot an attacker before they shot me. I could carve open a man's skin to leave my mark.

I could bruise up a literal kid trying to torture him into coughing up answers he didn't have.

The memory of the teen cringing and whimpering flashed through my mind, bringing a surge of queasiness with it. My lungs clenched even more—and my jaw tightened with a jolt of the same defiance I'd felt when faced with that scene in reality.

I hadn't wanted to hurt the kid. Mom had demanded it, threatening to do worse to the people I cared about most if I refused.

And when I'd realized just how innocent he was, I'd defied her anyway. I'd played the only card I had, been prepared to blow up my family's empire right then to avoid doing any more harm.

I was still prepared. I didn't stand with her or for the horrible acts she carried out. I might be the only person who could really stand against her—and I'd already taken huge steps toward interrupting her vilest plans.

My resolve broke through the vise of tension that'd been suffocating me. I raised my chin and looked up at Jasper, so striking in his sea-green and gold costume that coordinated perfectly with mine. As he looked back at me, his eyes gleamed, shining with affection and confidence.

He was nothing but eager to show the world what we were capable of.

I spared a quick glance toward the stands. It wasn't just my skating partner who believed in me and supported my dreams despite the hell that was my heritage. There was no missing Niko's buoyant enthusiasm where he stood by the boards. The quirk of Quentin's lips where he stood next to my coach brought back an echo of yesterday's pep talk when he'd reminded me of how much we could survive.

And right by the aisle, watching over me protectively as always, Rafael's stern gaze spoke of his own determined conviction.

My answering conviction steadied me. I could be more

than a criminal heir apparent; I had to be, for both myself and the men I'd fallen for.

I *was* more than that already. Yes, I had blood on my hands, but I couldn't let that be all this audience saw. I could create sweetness and joy. I could make people feel things while watching my art, ease their pain, if only for a few moments. Even that—*just* that—was more light than my mom had ever tried to bring into the world in her entire life.

Maybe, just maybe, if Mom happened to watch this performance to see exactly what I was getting up to beyond her grasp, I could prove even to her just how much skating mattered to me. Why this was where I was meant to be.

I smiled at Jasper, and he smiled back, with all the faith he had in me. A rush of exhilaration propelled words I hadn't meant to say right now from my throat. "I love you."

His eyelids stuttered in surprise, but it took only an instant for his smile to widen, warming me from the inside out. "I love you too."

And then the opening notes of our song pealed out into the air.

My heart pounded in time with the melody. My body had never felt so light. It was as if I'd shed a hundred pounds of anguished weight that left me free to be no one but the woman I was underneath.

We swept through each move, leaping and twirling and soaring, every motion in sync with each other and the music flowing through me. I was the song and it was me, playing out through movements as small as the flick of my hand and as big as our most epic lift with its following throw. I landed the boosted triple Axel as if I'd been born on the ice and glided straight into the next sequence.

I *was* the routine—the ice and the art—and my body was just the instrument. Here there was no bloodshed, no fear or pain. There was only beauty and creation.

And love.

Jasper met my eyes as we landed our last jump. His fervor glinted within his gray-green irises. Our big finish was looming on the horizon—we either nailed it, or this was all for nothing.

I pushed off with my skates, gaining speed and momentum as I sailed across the ice like the angel Niko always referred to me as. Jasper's hands found their places against my limbs to boost me upward. We spun like one being, balanced precariously but melded together.

This was who I really was, and I was proving it to *every* person watching me, whether here in the arena with me or from a TV screen.

A collective gasp from the audience mingled with the music. Jasper lowered me to the ice, and we hit the last few beats before striking our ending pose.

The moment my body was still, a wave of exhaustion washed over me. I'd wrung every drop of emotion out of me into our routine—but wow, did it feel fantastic to have put it all out there.

Applause thundered through the arena. Jasper dropped our hands and grabbed me in a quick but emphatic kiss, and I'd swear the cheers got even louder. Grinning like a maniac, I skated with him to the stands.

When we reached the bench, Quentin was grinning too. "Hell, yeah! You two wiped the floor with the rest of these dopes. That was fucking amazing."

Niko laughed, his own face bright with joy. "He's not

lying. Best performance yet, hands down. I didn't know you could top Finals, but I'd say you just did."

"Really?" My mind was reeling with giddiness and fatigue.

Before either of them could answer, the announcer's voice echoed through the arena. My spine stiffened as I waited for the judges' verdict.

"For Jasper St. Pierre and Luna Garcia, a score of one hundred and forty-five point five seven."

As a fresh wave of applause flooded the arena, my jaw dropped. That was a whole nine points higher than our previous high score. And—

Next to me, Jasper crowed with unexpected abandon. "Holy shit. Lou, that shoots us right to the top spot."

"And by a large margin," Niko said, beaming. "Knowing who's still to go, I've got no doubt those gold medals are yours."

A whoop spilled out of me. I caught Niko in a hug, and then Jasper and Quentin, and finally Rafael who'd come over to join the celebration. My bodyguard tucked his head over mine and squeezed me hard. "That was really something."

Niko clapped his hands, radiating excitement. "Ten weeks, and then World Championships, here we come!"

TWENTY-NINE

Luciana

I GOT no real welcome on my return to the Cordova mansion. A few of the underlings hanging around dipped their heads to me in acknowledgment, but it was hard to tell if they even realized I'd been gone for a week.

Better if they couldn't tell. Better if my absence had proven just how little my presence was needed in the running of the Deadly Rose empire.

I'd thought that Mom might be eager to drag me straight back into her schemes, but my phone had remained silent even though I'd texted her this morning to let her know I was on my way home. As I stepped into the foyer, I braced myself to meet her piercing gaze or hear her cutting voice carrying from the top of the staircase.

Nada. *Her* absence was so jarring that I hesitated for a moment at the foot of the stairs, feeling like I was an actress in a play who'd just realized she'd missed memorizing a few pages of the script. Now what?

I gathered the determination that'd carried me since our victory at the National Championships around me, as bright as the shine on my skating costume. I was wearing my gold medal, tucked under the collar of my long-sleeved band tee. The high of our performance still quivered through my veins.

I knew where I belonged, beyond any possible doubt. It was time to stop pretending and stride forward into that future.

And maybe, after all of this, Mom would finally understand that running the Deadly Rose empire wasn't the life I was meant for. She might be stubborn, but she wasn't stupid. It would be way better for her to have an heir who actually appreciated the role too.

Keeping my posture straight and confident, I motioned to a nearby lackey. "Let my mother know that I'm home—and that I'd like to talk to her as soon as possible."

He nodded and hustled off, pulling out his phone. That didn't tell me anything about where she was or when she'd get here. I tramped up the stairs and made my way to my childhood bedroom.

Sitting down on the edge of the bed, I glanced around the expansive space. Funny how this was the largest bedroom I'd had in all my jaunts around the continent, but it felt by far the most suffocating. It was barely even mine. Mom had picked out the décor, dictated what I was allowed to hang on the walls.

What here would I even want to bring with me when I left? I'd taken all the essentials when I'd first run away.

I hadn't been able to pack much in the way of clothes,

though. There were some outfits I'd missed: my black cargo pants with the zippered pockets and buckles, my super-cozy hooded sweatshirt with the plaid sleeves, my black-and-neon-pink checkerboard leggings that I could just imagine Jasper's expression on taking them in. My studded leather jacket would have come in handy as the weather cooled off.

Well, I might as well pull everything together while I had the time. Go forward as if I expected to succeed—that was the best attitude, right?

I was just squishing a few pairs of stripy socks I'd always been fond of into a suitcase when my regular phone buzzed. A text from Mom appeared on the screen: *We can speak in my office now.*

My heart gave a little lurch, even though I'd asked for this meeting. I took a deep breath, swiped my hands over my hips to make sure they weren't sweaty, and marched down the hall to face the music.

I rapped on the door in my usual pattern and waited for her terse reply: "Come in."

I entered the room to find Mom's back to me where she was standing by the window next to her desk. She waited until I'd come to a stop in the middle of the room before turning to face me.

Her face might as well have been carved from ice, and her voice was equally frigid. "You're back from your little vacation. It's time we get down to work."

Oh, no, I wasn't letting her direct the conversation this time.

I squared my shoulders and met her gaze steadily. "It wasn't just a vacation. My partner and I placed *first* at the National Championships—that makes us the best in the whole country." My hand rose to the disc of my medal under my shirt, but I didn't pull it out, gripped by the sudden fear that Mom would wrench it away from me.

Mom offered me nothing but a derisive snort in response. "The best at spinning around on the ice in a sparkly costume. What an honor." Sarcasm dripped from her tone. "You got what you wanted. Now that the distraction is dealt with—"

"Dealt with?" I broke in, frustration crackling through my veins. "I'm not finished. Placing that high means we've earned a spot at the World Championships, to compete with the best from every other country. Only a handful of people manage that every year. I worked my ass off to get good enough to make it."

"And I'd like to see you apply the same obsessive focus to our *real* work," Mom said. "You'll have plenty of opportunities to do so now that you've had your moment in the spotlight. I have you meeting with the head of one of our Houston affiliates tomorrow afternoon, and there's a deal I expect you to supervise the following night. I want to see you training with the troops every morning this week as well."

My jaw clenched. I shook my head. "No, Mom. You're not listening. I *can't*. Worlds is in just a couple of months —we have to keep training and—"

Mom cut me off with a flash of her dark eyes. "You *have to* get your head out of the clouds and be the Cordova you're meant to be. I'm not going to tolerate any more talk of your ridiculous hobby. I think I've been more than lenient. It's time for you to give your full commitment."

My frustration erupted into full-out rage. She never listened—she never cared. She never even bothered to *see* the woman I was standing right here in front of her, too busy imagining the daughter she wanted me to be.

If anyone was obsessed around here, it was her. And it was time for that obsession to end. *I* knew who I was, and I couldn't squeeze myself into the box she wanted me to fit into any longer.

"No," I repeated, sharper this time. "If it's all or nothing now, then I'm done with everything to do with the Deadly Rose legacy. I never wanted the empire anyway. You can find someone else to inherit your throne."

Mom walked up to me, her expression still a frozen mask but so much fury seething beneath it that it wafted off her and sent goose bumps prickling up my arms. "You've entertained your stupid dream for long enough. You *will* get your act together now and play your part, or every one of the men you claim to care about will pay for it for *days* before I finally see them buried."

She meant that threat. She would torment all four of my men in every way she knew how, drive them to the limits of pain, just to shape me to her image. I recoiled inwardly, horror turning my stomach.

My hands clenched at my sides as I hardened myself against the instinctive panic. "You wouldn't dare. Not when I can expose your master plan to the only people who could make *you* pay."

Mom's eyes narrowed. "If you try to destroy me, you'll only be destroying yourself. I'll see that you and everyone you care about suffer until those men curse the day they met you and you wish you'd never been born, and then more after that. You won't get away with it."

With that last sentence, Mom sprang at me, swift as a cobra striking. She snatched at my ponytail and wrenched me against her into an embrace that was all venom. I struck out, thrashing in her hold, but Mom clamped me tight—and rammed a hard muzzle against my lips.

My mouth jolted open at the pain lancing through my face even as the rest of my body froze in recognition.

Still clutching my hair hard enough to send jabs of agony through my scalp, Mom shoved the barrel of her pistol between my teeth. I fought the urge to gag at the oily metallic flavor that seeped over my tongue.

"This is what your lovers will feel right before they eat their last bullet," she said, her voice so fraught it was almost a hiss. "Hold on to that memory. Remember it every time you think about defying one of my orders."

With that, she heaved me away from her. I stumbled and caught myself on a side table before I fell to my knees.

"Get out of my sight," Mom snapped. "The next time I send for you, you'd better be ready to play your role."

Blood trickled through my mouth from where the gun had scraped my tongue. My mind had gone blank. I groped for the doorknob and stepped into the hall on shaky legs.

She'd nearly killed me. She'd had her finger on the goddamn trigger.

She'd treated me like a minor underling—like a dog she'd put down if I didn't jump to fulfill her every command.

Like she didn't give a shit whether she had a daughter. She'd rather I was dead than happy on any path other than the one she'd chosen for me.

I made it back to my bedroom without much sense of how I'd arrived there. My head kept spinning. I wandered to the bed and gripped one of the posts for balance.

Something had broken inside me with that act of

violence. After everything Mom had done over the years, somehow I'd never been prepared for her to go that far, to treat me so callously.

I could crumple like a rag doll and give in. The fear wavering inside me liked that idea. Pretend my heart out, protect my men, appease Mom's ego.

But even as the idea presented itself, the rest of me resisted.

I'd already tried playing along, and it hadn't worked. I couldn't live like that... Frankly, *I'd* rather be dead than become nothing more than a puppet carrying out Mom's bloody ambitions.

Nothing short of transforming into a person I could never be would be enough for her. No matter what I did, sooner or later I'd disappoint her. And then she'd go after my men as punishment.

I'd have proven that my threats really were a bluff. She'd want to get rid of the distraction they presented too, as soon as possible, with the slightest excuse she could use to justify it.

None of us would ever be safe as long as Mom was fixated on carving me into the heir she expected. Our lives were on the line either way.

At least if I gave her something bigger to worry about, it'd keep her busy while we made our escape. Maybe it'd even bring down her and her empire completely.

The second I made the decision, a lump of guilt formed in my gut. In spite of everything, she was still my mother. This empire had been built by my ancestors going back generations. I could be bringing that effort all crumbling down.

But the loss was on Mom's shoulders, not mine. I'd told her where I stood, and she'd refused to listen. All she'd needed to do to avoid disaster was appoint some trusted underling as her next-in-line and let me go.

Her refusal wasn't on my conscience.

I grabbed my burner phone and tapped out a message to Rafael with trembling fingers. *I'm on my way. Get ready to leave immediately—for good.*

Then I looked at the half-packed suitcase on my bed. It'd be a little more obvious than I liked if I walked out of here carrying that.

I pawed through my closet for a backpack, shoved my laptop and as many pieces of clothing into it as I could, and hurried through the house with it slung over my shoulder. My thumb darted over my phone's screen, summoning an Uber.

When I passed through the gate and walked down the block, the car was just pulling up at the corner I'd indicated as the pick-up spot. I slid into the back and peered down at my phone as the driver hit the gas.

I could log into the scheduled email I'd set up from this device too. I opened up the message with its explanation of all the evidence that the Deadly Rose was working to upend the very foundations of the Devil's Dozen and hesitated.

With one click, I could blow up the entire foundation of my life.

But I'd never really wanted that foundation anyway. Better to bulldoze over it and build fresh from the ground up.

I dismissed the scheduled send time and tapped the button to send the email now.

The phone chimed as the email flitted off to the inboxes of the Devil's Dozen's top dogs. A breath rushed out of me, shaky with a mix of terror and exhilaration.

I'd done it. I'd really done it.

As I sagged back in the seat, tears pricked at the corners of my eyes. I swiped at them, steeped in a strange mood that was more relief than anything else.

By the time the car reached the loft building, my head had started to clear like the first bright, refreshing sunlight after a thunderstorm. At the sight of all four of my men waiting out front, suitcases beside them, my spirits lifted.

I scrambled out to meet them, hauling my backpack with me.

"What's going on?" Rafael asked immediately, his words tangling with Niko's, "Are you all right?"

I found myself grinning at all of them like this was the best day of my life. Which maybe in some ways it was.

"I'm fine," I said. "I'm free. We're getting the hell out of here and never coming back."

THIRTY

Luciana

"AH," Niko said, taking a big sip of his Calpis as we walked through the doors into the rink area of the small arena. He waved to one of the men on the arena staff who was sweeping the stands at the far end of the room. "It's good to be home."

I couldn't help laughing at him. "Are you going to say that every time you drink one of those for the whole time we're in Japan?"

He grinned back at me with a familiar twinkle in his eyes. "If it's still true, why not? I can see you've started appreciating my country's many benefits too."

He nodded to the can I had clutched in my hand, what was technically hot chocolate except… cold. I never would have thought I'd get into drinking hot chocolate out of a can, let alone hot chocolate that wasn't even hot, but I had to admit I was finding the stuff strangely addictive now that I'd tried it.

Quentin took a chug from his bottle of iced green tea and stretched out his arms toward the rink below us. "I appreciate that even the out-of-the-way rinks look all clean and pristine. Maybe I'll have to move here."

Jasper elbowed the other guy lightly. "Who would have thought all Quentin Wolfe needed to put him in a good mood was tidy stands?"

"Hey," Quentin protested. "No one wants to skate in the middle of a mess."

I shook my head at the two of them and their mock-antagonistic banter before trotting down the steps to the benches nearest the ice. We'd been in Tokyo for two weeks now, training for Worlds, which would be held in nearby Nagano. With my family's empire in an uproar, it'd seemed safest to put plenty of ocean between us and my mother, and also not to train *too* close to the city she would first think to search for me if she had time to look.

No one had thought to look for us here at all. Niko fielded phone calls from reporters several times a day, giving them a vague story about our training progress after our win at Nationals and putting me or Jasper on to do brief interviews with the ones he felt would boost our profile the most, but we'd escaped all in-person media attention so far. He'd been able to keep the rest of the US team satisfied with the scraps of information he'd given them about our whereabouts too, other than a couple of video-chat meetings since we'd arrived.

Unfortunately, laying low had meant leaving Rafael back at the apartment Niko had found for us, because he stood out too much with the cast on his leg and his crutch. But we were hoping he'd be able to get the cast removed this weekend and be back to close to his old self.

From the bits and pieces of news he'd gathered from back home, the Deadly Rose's operations had been thrown into so much turmoil it wasn't likely she'd have had the manpower to search for me in the state of Texas, let alone all over Japan.

But still, it was best to be cautious. The Devil's Dozen had their fingers everywhere. I wasn't sure which of them owned territory in Tokyo, but no doubt someone had the local criminal elements under their sway. And we couldn't be sure whether that someone would be on Mom's side or against her.

I gulped the last of my chocolate drink and pulled on my skates, eager to get moving and stretch my muscles. By the time I'd stepped onto the ice to start warming up next to Jasper, anticipation was tingling through my nerves. "So, what's the latest word on our competition?"

Niko brightened up, always happy when he had new information to advise us with, and dug into his bag on the bench beside him. "I talked with another one of my friends from Team Japan last night. Like the others, he's being cagey about the specifics of their routines, but I did get him talking about the *other* countries' practices he's caught glimpses of."

Quentin rubbed his hands together. "Inside intel. Bring it on."

He wasn't going to be competing, of course, since he wasn't on the official US team. But we'd brought him with us to keep him out of my mom's sights, and he'd fallen into the role of unofficial assistant coach when he wasn't honing his singles routines for next year. His shoulder was almost back to full functioning now.

Niko tapped on his phone to bring up our songs. "One of the Russian pairs and maybe the Chinese too are trying out something a little new—adding some extra difficulty to their jumps. If we want to make sure we stand out equally well, I think we could adjust your routine to—"

The door at the top of the stairs slammed open, and a barrage of dark-clothed figures burst into the room. My heart stopped with a terrifying sense of déjà vu, hurtling me back to the moment in Austin when Octavio had come for me. Then my gaze caught on the semi-automatic rifles the strange men were jerking toward us.

"Get down!" I cried out, and snatched at Jasper's arm to haul him flat on the ice with me.

We hadn't ventured far from the stands in our warm-up. As bullets boomed through the air overhead, we cringed in the shelter of the boards. The tempered glass shattered, pelting us with a torrent of pebbles.

A hoarse cry rang out from the other side of the arena, where the staff person had been sweeping. I hoped he'd gotten out of the way fast enough.

The guns thundered for what felt like an eternity while I hugged the ice and clutched Jasper's arm. There was a brief pause. Just as I was sure our attackers would descend all the way to the rink and pick us off, sirens wailed loud enough to hear them through the arena walls.

Someone had called the police, and they were almost here. Thank God.

One of the shooters barked out an order I couldn't make out. Footsteps thudded as the men dashed off the way they'd come.

The second the door had banged shut behind them, I scrambled to my feet. My head jerked around as I scanned the stands. There—there was Quentin, the top of his blond head visible as he eased upright from where he'd hit the floor between the benches. And Niko—

I shoved myself closer to the stands and jarred to a halt. A cry broke from my throat.

Niko lay sprawled against the bench next to his bag, his head lolling and a scarlet blotch blooming on the front of his shirt.

ABOUT THE AUTHORS

Eva Chance is a pen name for contemporary romance written by Amazon top 100 bestselling author Eva Chase. If you love gritty romance, dominant men, and fierce women who never have to choose, look no further.

Eva lives in Canada with her family. She loves stories both swoony and supernatural, and strong women and the men who appreciate them.

Connect with Eva online:
www.evachase.com
eva@evachase.com

Harlow King is a long-time fan of all things dark, edgy, and steamy. She can't wait to share her contemporary reverse harem stories.

www.ingramcontent.com/pod-product-compliance
Lightning Source LLC
Chambersburg PA
CBHW051127190726
48290CB00006B/1718